EPPING

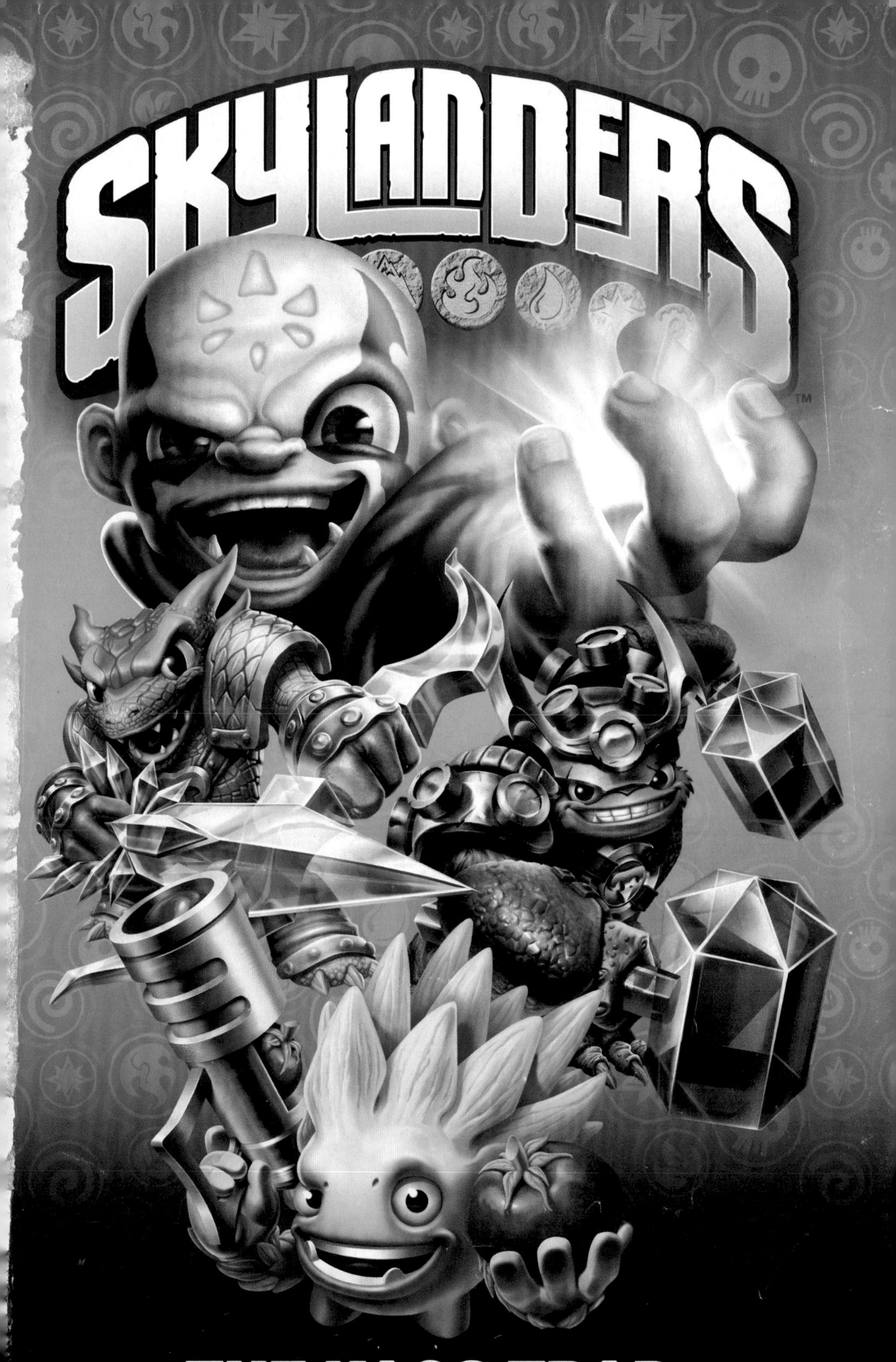
SKYLANDERS™

THE KAOS TRAP

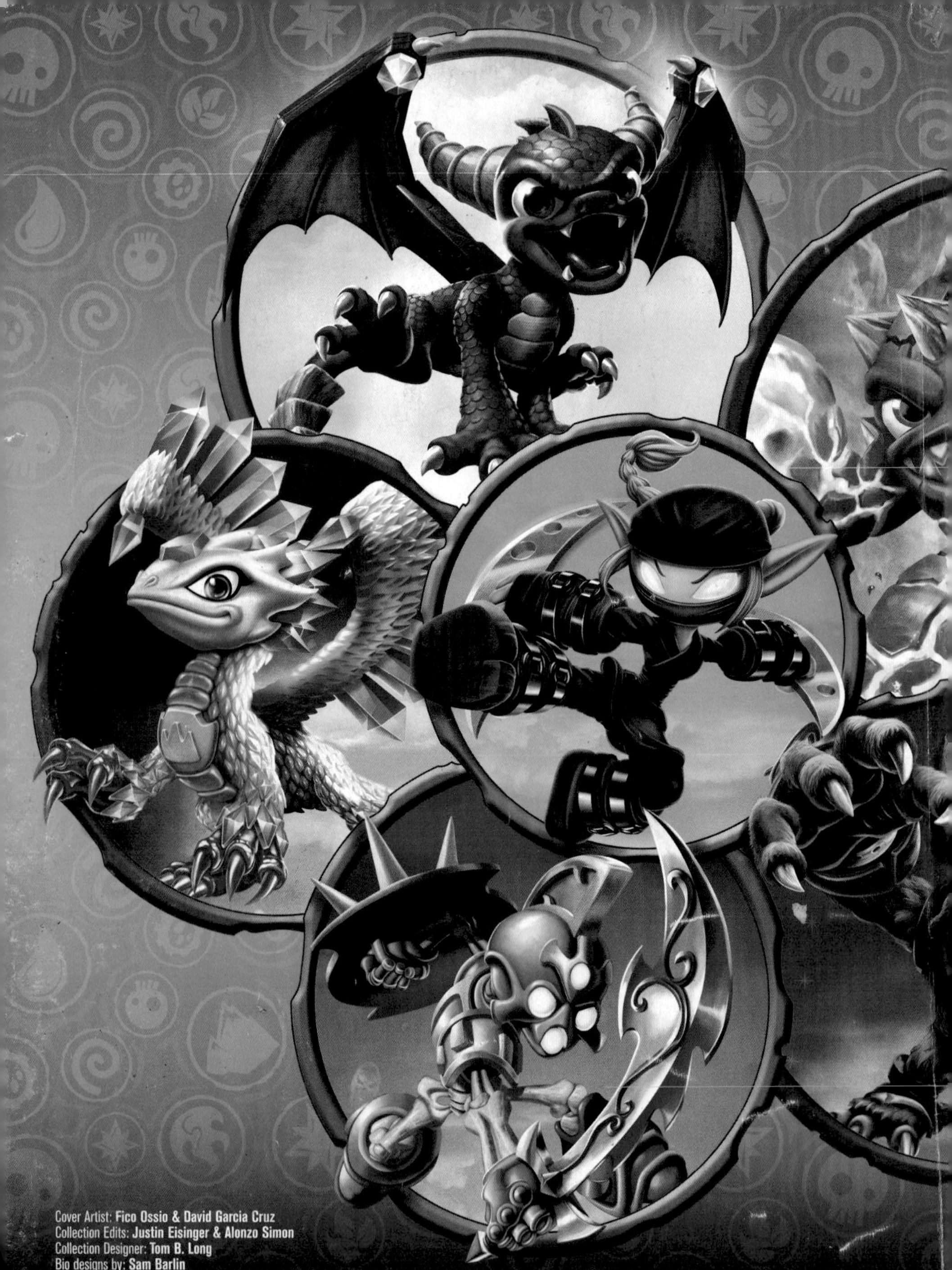

Cover Artist: **Fico Ossio & David Garcia Cruz**
Collection Edits: **Justin Eisinger & Alonzo Simon**
Collection Designer: **Tom B. Long**
Bio designs by: **Sam Barlin**

HARDCOVER ISBN: 978-1-63140-141-1 SOFTCOVER ISBN: 978-1-63140-193-0 17 16 15 14 1 2 3

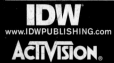

IDW
www.IDWPUBLISHING.com
ACTIVISION

Ted Adams, CEO & Publisher
Greg Goldstein, President & COO
Robbie Robbins, EVP/Sr. Graphic Artist
Chris Ryall, Chief Creative Officer/Editor-in-Chief
Matthew Ruzicka, CPA, Chief Financial Officer
Alan Payne, VP of Sales
Dirk Wood, VP of Marketing
Lorelei Bunjes, VP of Digital Services
Jeff Webber, VP of Digital Publishing & Business Development

Facebook: **facebook.com/idwpublishing**
Twitter: **@idwpublishing**
YouTube: **youtube.com/idwpublishing**
Instagram: **instagram.com/idwpublishing**
deviantART: **idwpublishing.deviantart.com**
Pinterest: **pinterest.com/idwpublishing/idw-staff-faves**

SKYLANDERS™

THE KAOS TRAP

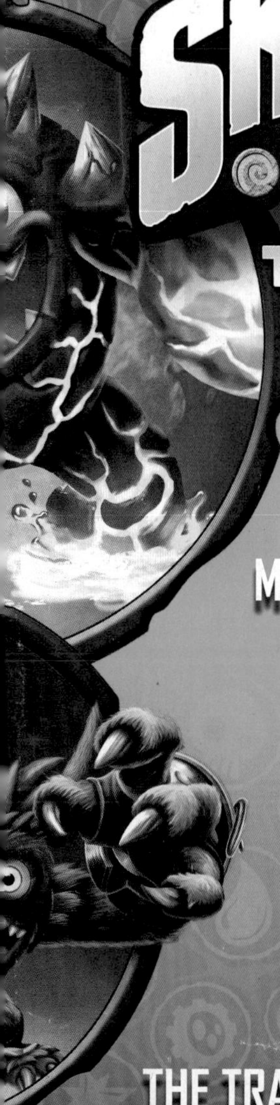

FORGETTING FLYNN

Story by:
RON MARZ and **DAVID A. RODRIGUEZ**
Art by:
MIKE BOWDEN
Colors by:
FERNANDO PENICHE

MINI BUT MIGHTY

Story by:
RON MARZ and **DAVID A. RODRIGUEZ**
Art by:
DAVID BALDEÓN
Colors by:
DAVID GARCIA CRUZ

WELCOME TO SKYLANDER ACADEMY

Story by:
RON MARZ and **DAVID A. RODRIGUEZ**
Art by:
FICO OSSIO
Colors by:
LEONARDO & ALICE ITO

THE TRAP MASTERS

Story by:
DAVID A. RODRIGUEZ, ALEX NESS and **MICHAEL GRAHAM**
Written by:
DAVID A. RODRIGUEZ
Art by:
MIKE BOWDEN
Colors by:
DAVID GARCIA CRUZ

Letters by:
DERON BENNETT & **TOM B. LONG**
Edited by:
DAVID HEDGECOCK

FORGETTING FLYNN

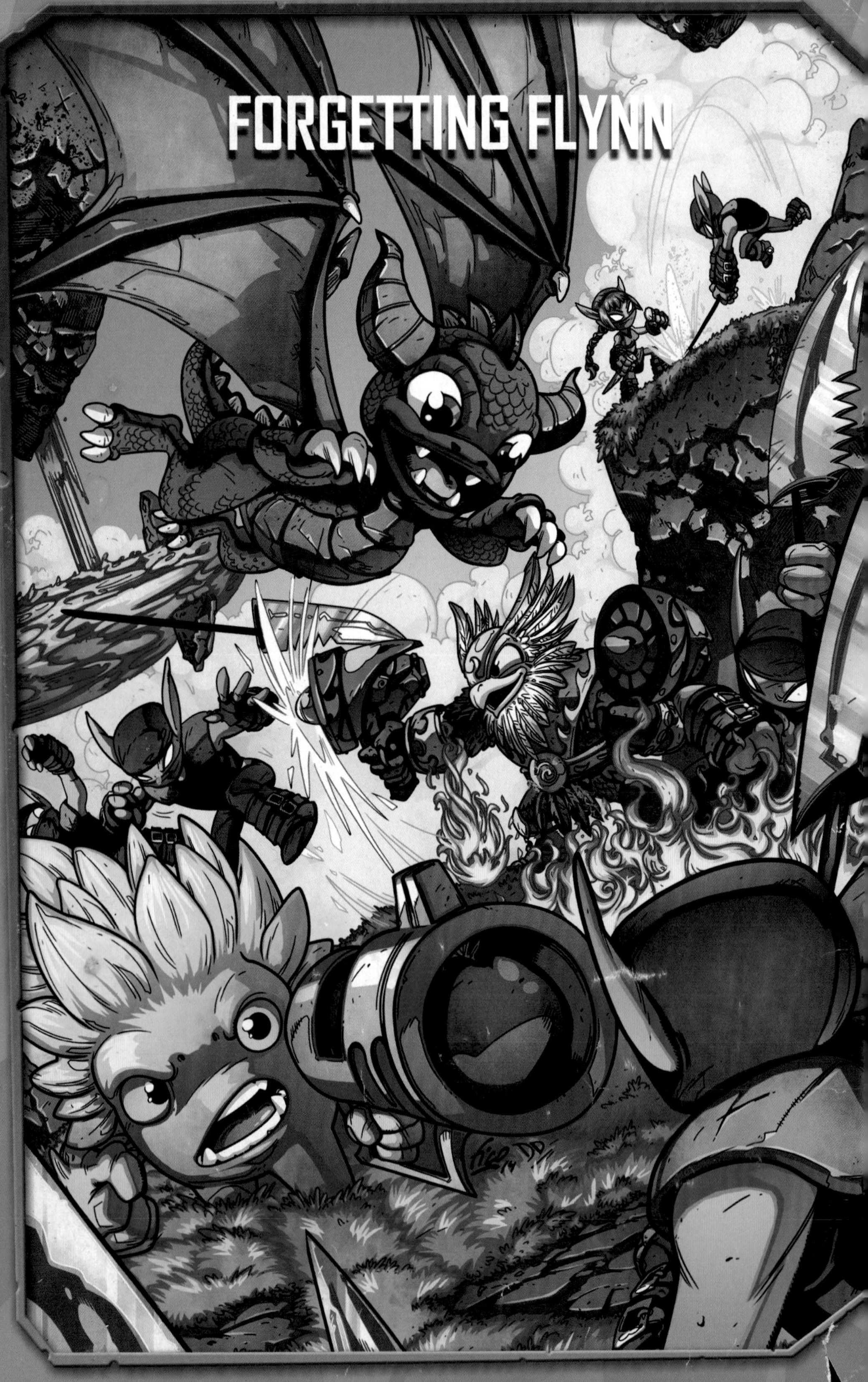

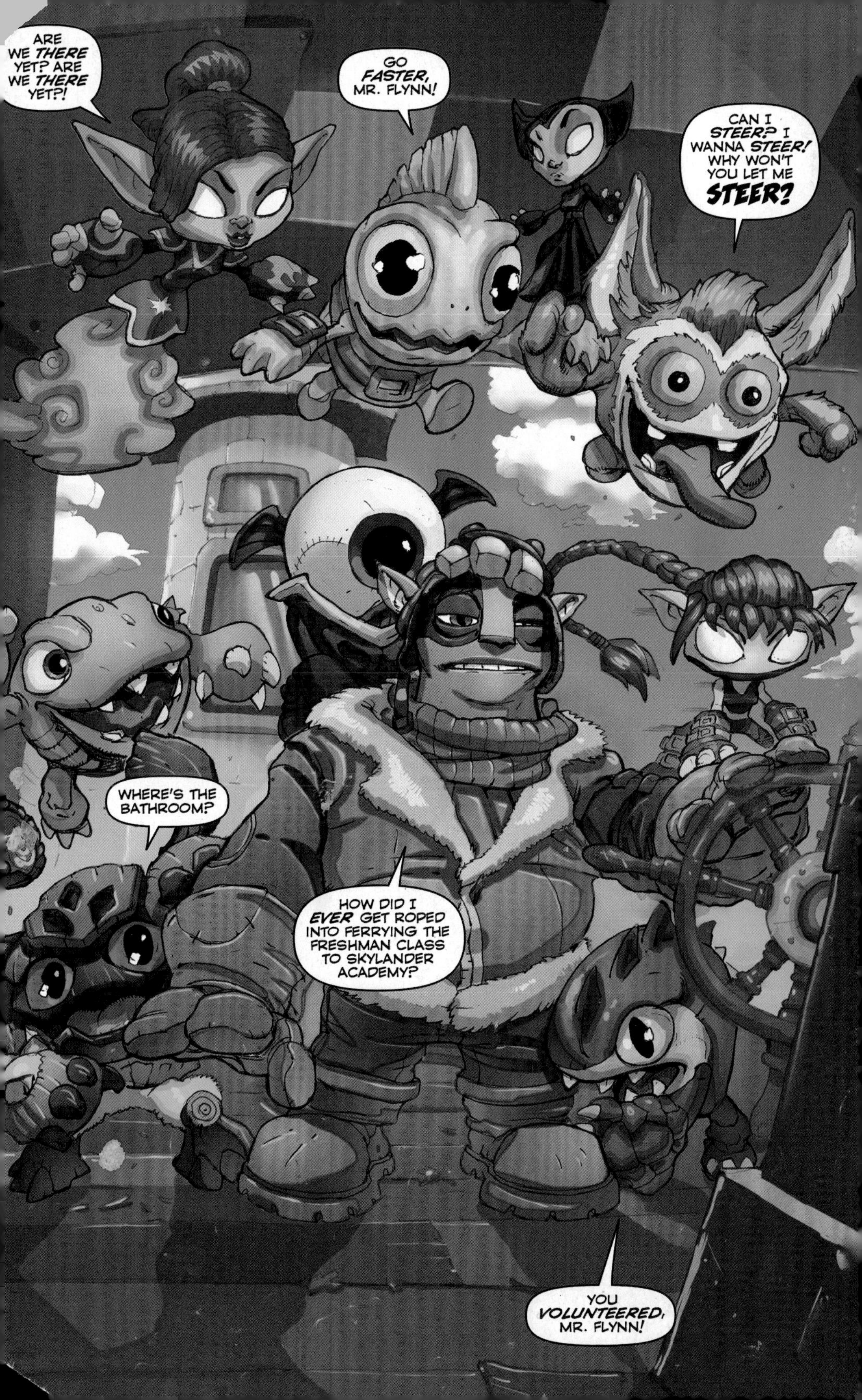
ARE WE THERE YET?! ARE WE THERE YET?!
GO FASTER, MR. FLYNN!
CAN I STEER? I WANNA STEER! WHY WON'T YOU LET ME STEER?
WHERE'S THE BATHROOM?
HOW DID I EVER GET ROPED INTO FERRYING THE FRESHMAN CLASS TO SKYLANDER ACADEMY?
YOU VOLUNTEERED, MR. FLYNN!

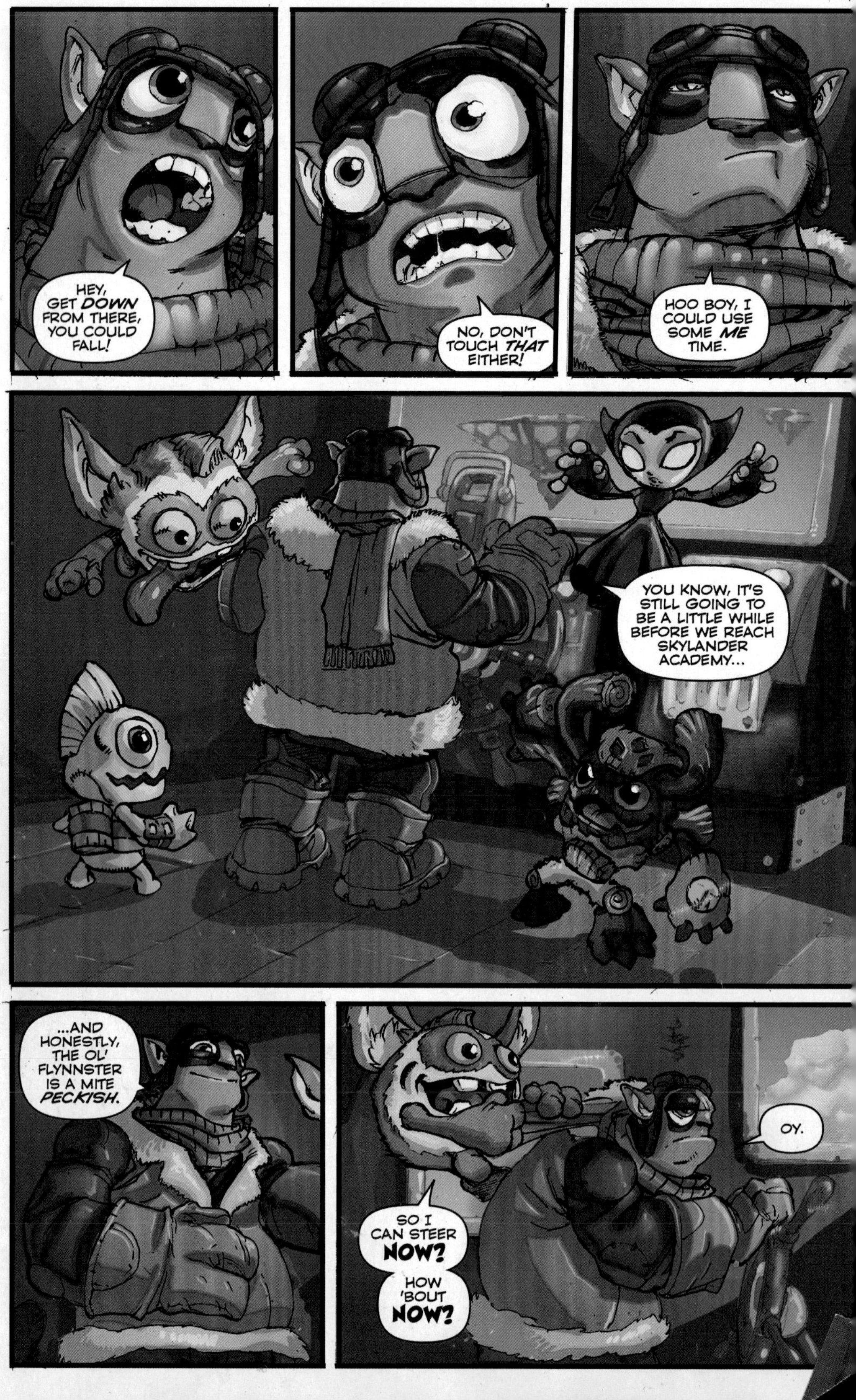
HEY, GET *DOWN* FROM THERE, YOU COULD FALL!
NO, DON'T TOUCH *THAT* EITHER!
HOO BOY, I COULD USE SOME *ME* TIME.
YOU KNOW, IT'S STILL GOING TO BE A LITTLE WHILE BEFORE WE REACH SKYLANDER ACADEMY...
...AND HONESTLY, THE OL' FLYNNSTER IS A MITE *PECKISH*.
OY.
SO I CAN STEER **NOW?**
HOW 'BOUT **NOW?**

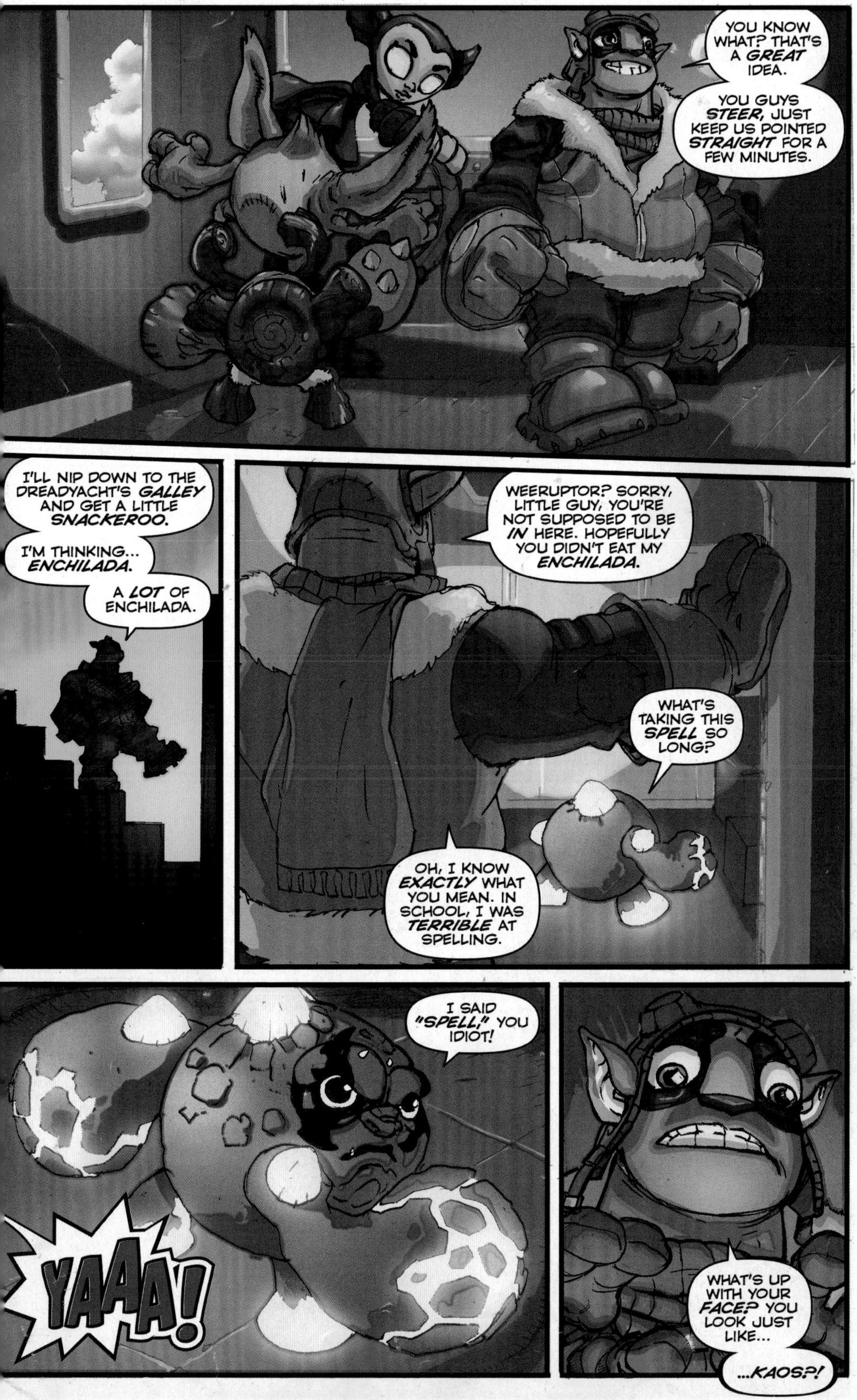
YOU KNOW WHAT? THAT'S A GREAT IDEA.
YOU GUYS STEER, JUST KEEP US POINTED STRAIGHT FOR A FEW MINUTES.
I'LL NIP DOWN TO THE DREADYACHT'S GALLEY AND GET A LITTLE SNACKEROO.
I'M THINKING... ENCHILADA.
A LOT OF ENCHILADA.
WEERUPTOR? SORRY, LITTLE GUY, YOU'RE NOT SUPPOSED TO BE IN HERE. HOPEFULLY YOU DIDN'T EAT MY ENCHILADA.
WHAT'S TAKING THIS SPELL SO LONG?
OH, I KNOW EXACTLY WHAT YOU MEAN. IN SCHOOL, I WAS TERRIBLE AT SPELLING.
I SAID "SPELL," YOU IDIOT!
YAAAA!
WHAT'S UP WITH YOUR FACE? YOU LOOK JUST LIKE...
...KAOS?!

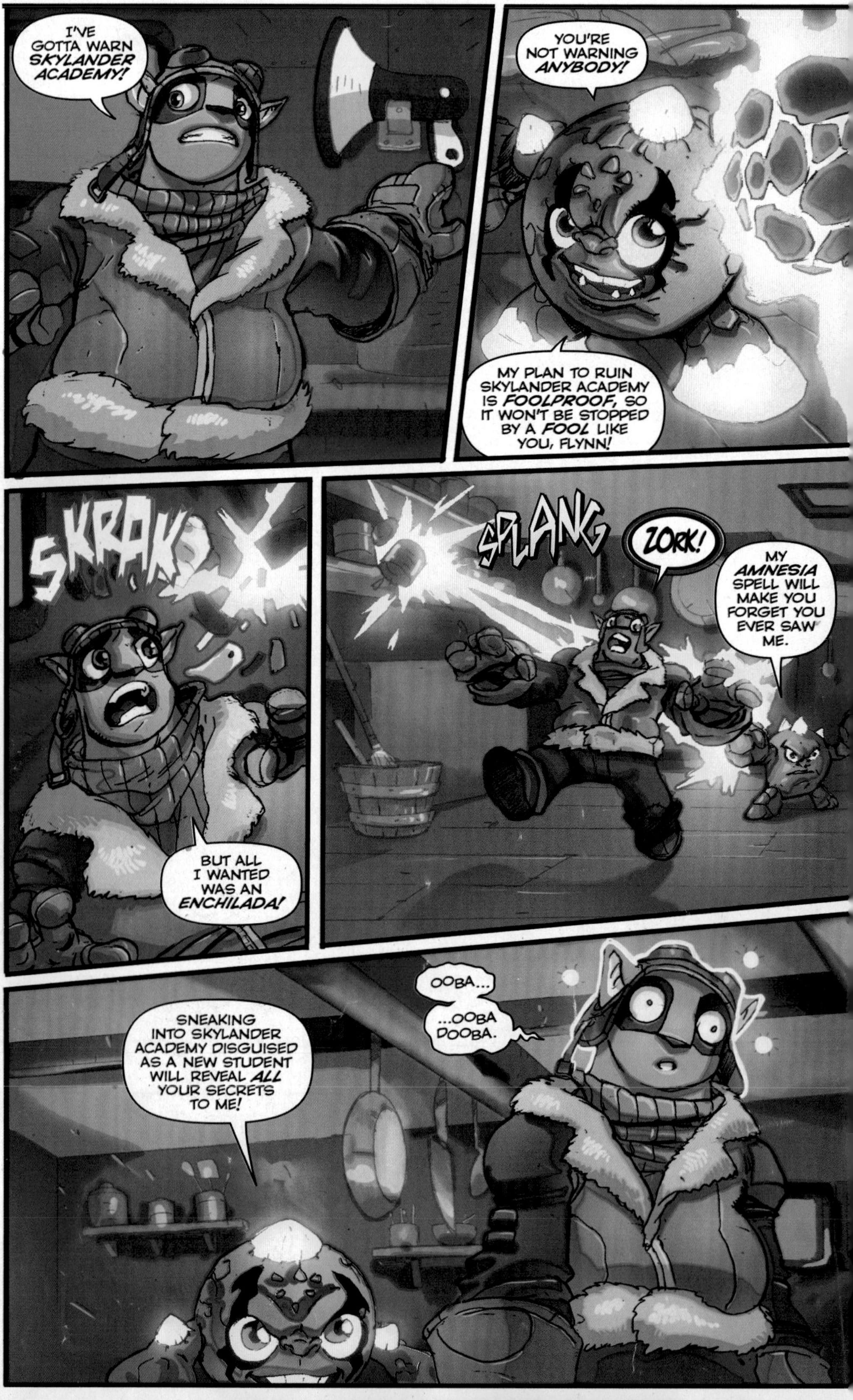
I'VE GOTTA WARN SKYLANDER ACADEMY!
YOU'RE NOT WARNING ANYBODY!
MY PLAN TO RUIN SKYLANDER ACADEMY IS FOOLPROOF, SO IT WON'T BE STOPPED BY A FOOL LIKE YOU, FLYNN!
SKRAK
BUT ALL I WANTED WAS AN ENCHILADA!
SPLANG
ZORK!
MY AMNESIA SPELL WILL MAKE YOU FORGET YOU EVER SAW ME.
SNEAKING INTO SKYLANDER ACADEMY DISGUISED AS A NEW STUDENT WILL REVEAL ALL YOUR SECRETS TO ME!
OOBA...
...OOBA DOOBA.

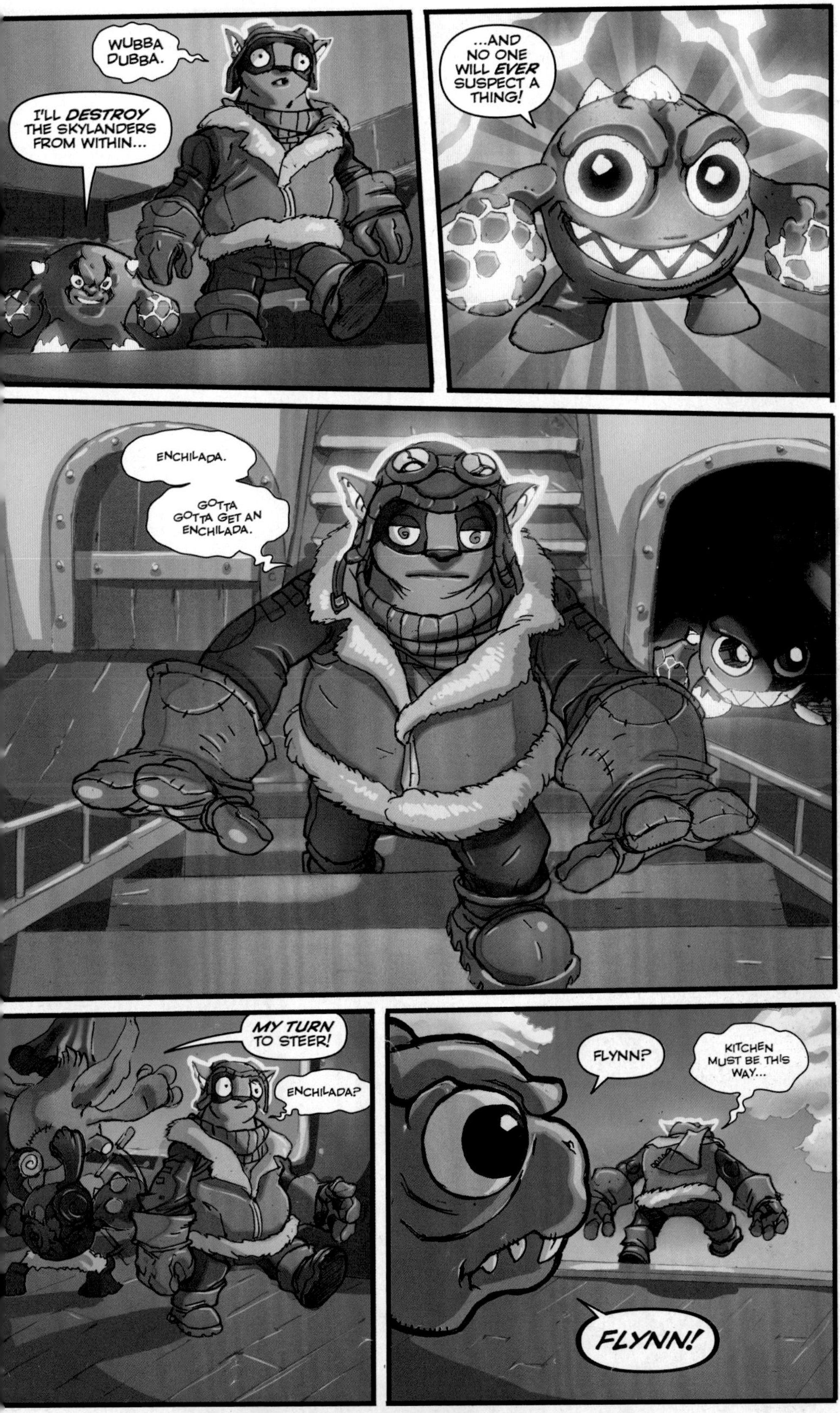
WUBBA DUBBA.
I'LL DESTROY THE SKYLANDERS FROM WITHIN...
...AND NO ONE WILL EVER SUSPECT A THING!
ENCHILADA.
GOTTA GOTTA GET AN ENCHILADA.
MY TURN TO STEER!
ENCHILADA?
FLYNN?
KITCHEN MUST BE THIS WAY...
FLYNN!

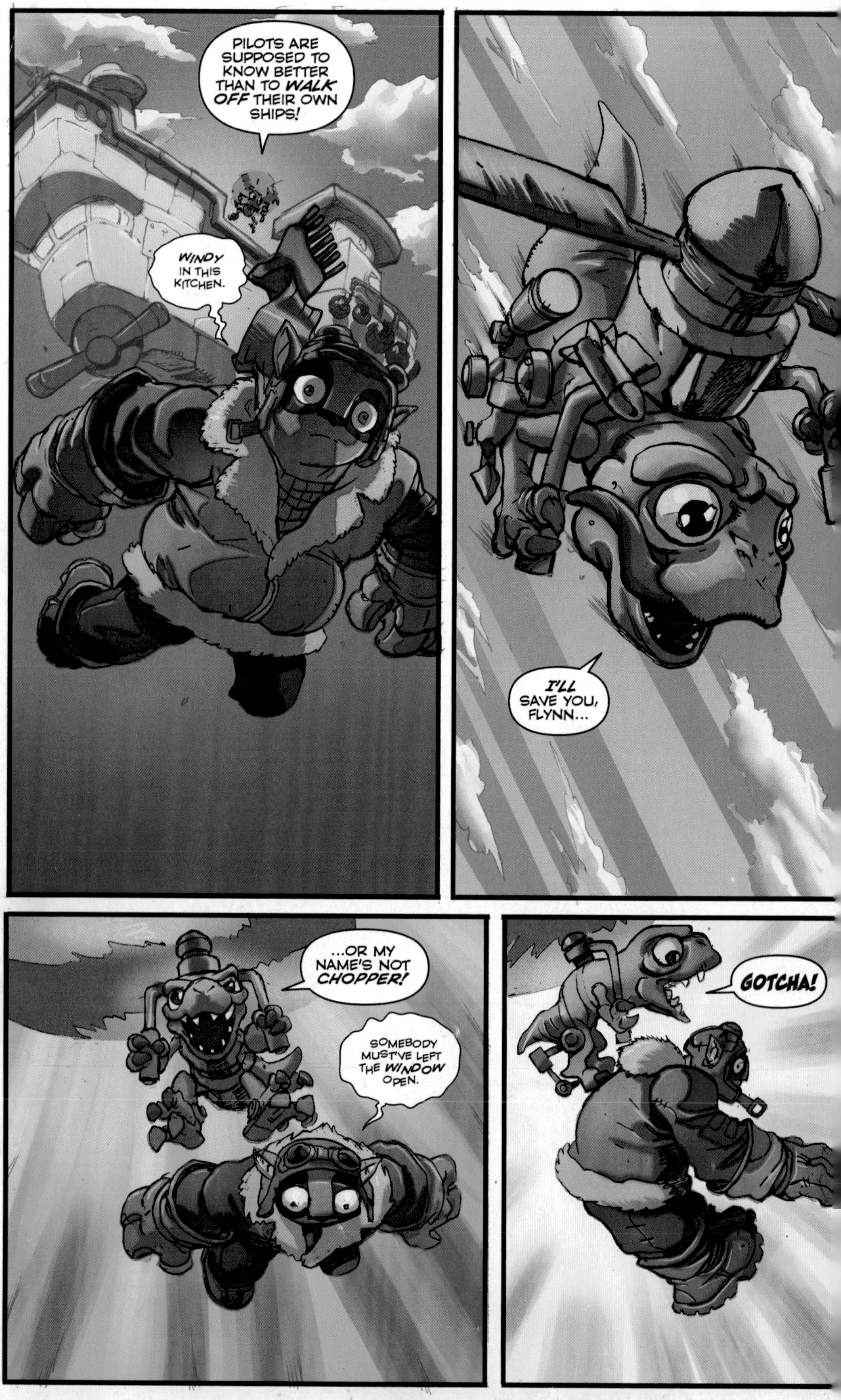
PILOTS ARE SUPPOSED TO KNOW BETTER THAN TO *WALK OFF* THEIR OWN SHIPS!
WINDY IN THIS KITCHEN.
I'LL SAVE YOU, FLYNN...
...OR MY NAME'S NOT *CHOPPER!*
SOMEBODY MUST'VE LEFT THE *WINDOW* OPEN.
GOTCHA!

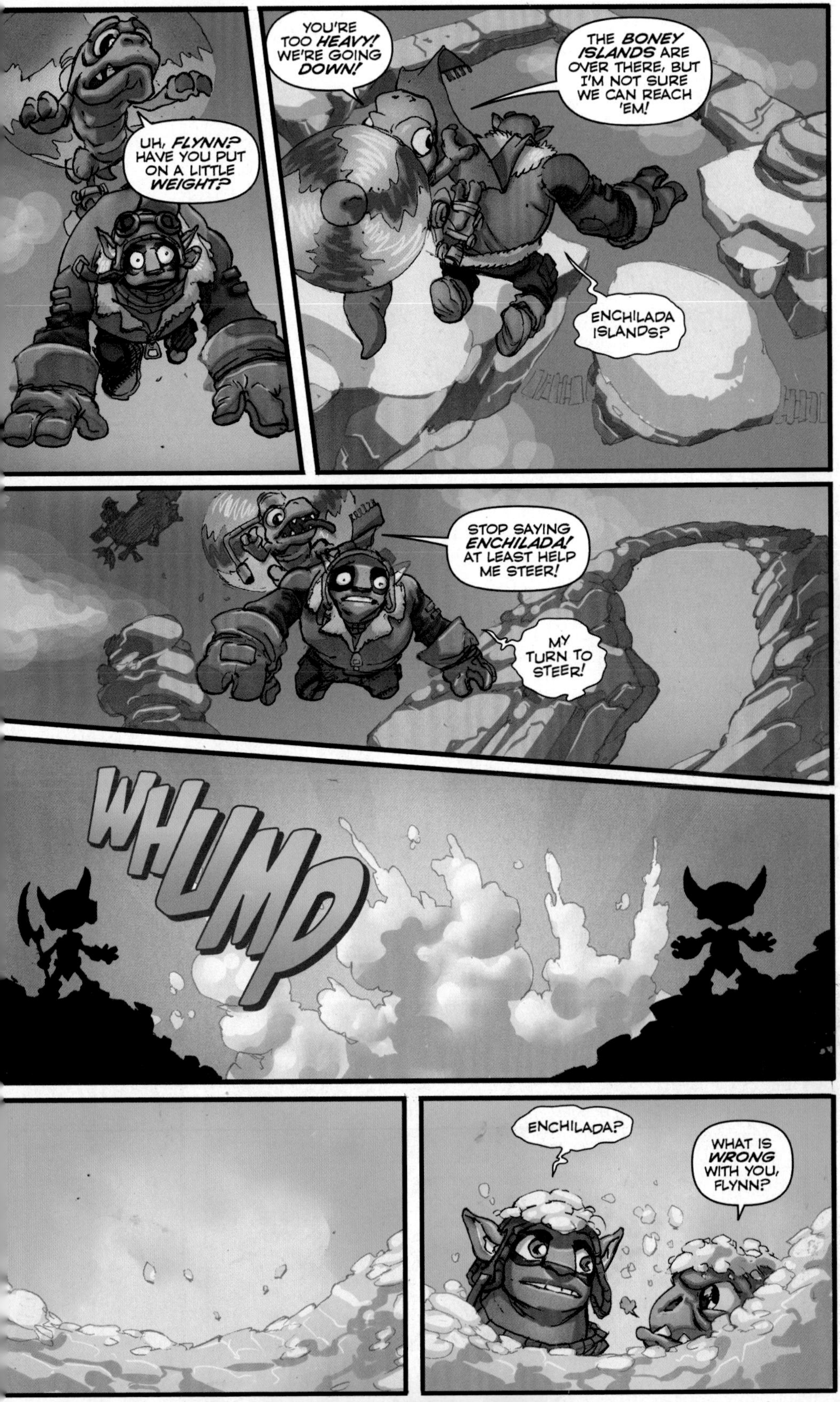
UH, *FLYNN?* HAVE YOU PUT ON A LITTLE *WEIGHT?*
YOU'RE TOO *HEAVY!* WE'RE GOING *DOWN!*
THE *BONEY ISLANDS* ARE OVER THERE, BUT I'M NOT SURE WE CAN REACH 'EM!
ENCHILADA ISLANDS?
STOP SAYING *ENCHILADA!* AT LEAST HELP ME STEER!
MY TURN TO STEER!
WHUMP
ENCHILADA?
WHAT IS *WRONG* WITH YOU, FLYNN?

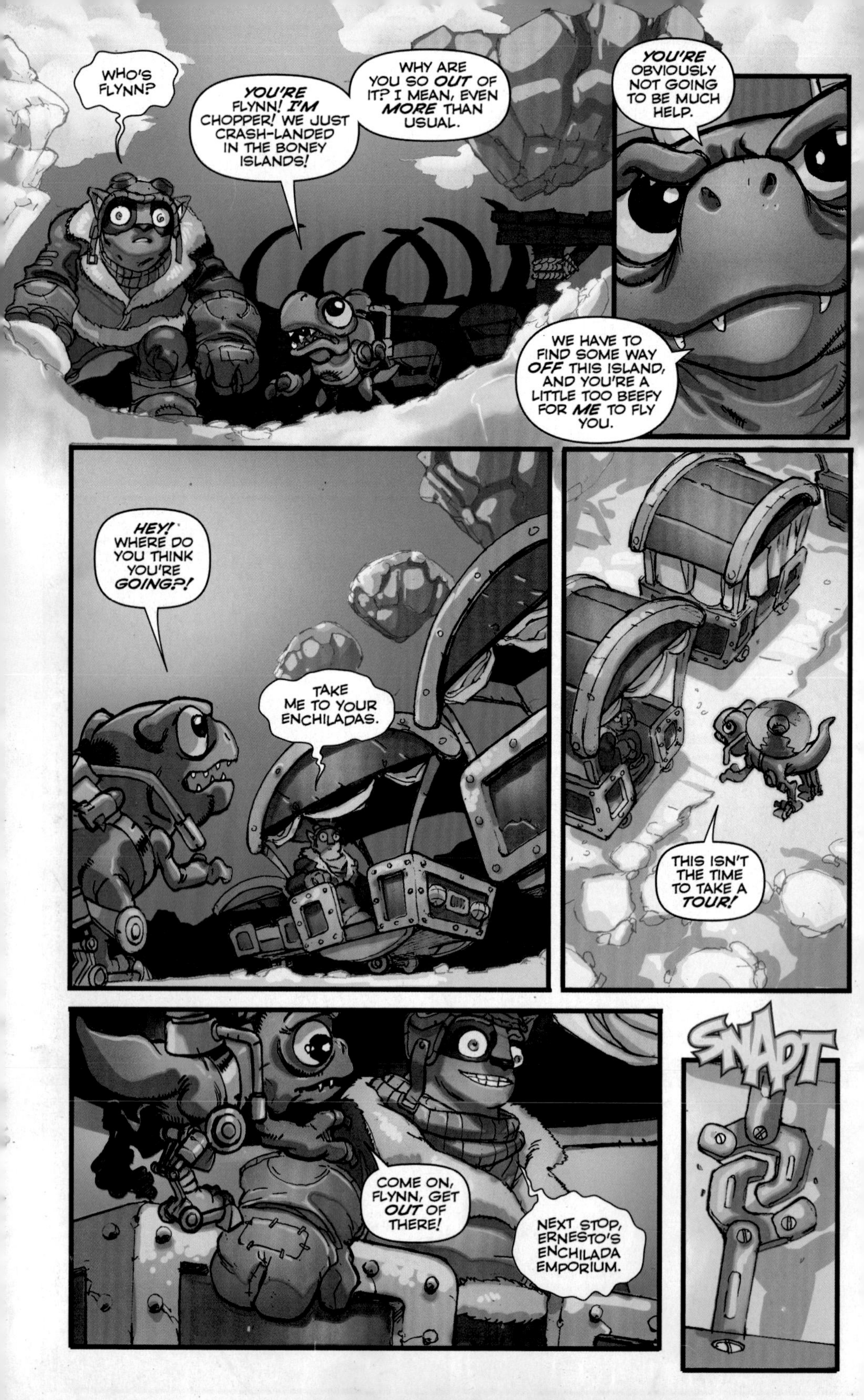
WHO'S FLYNN?
YOU'RE FLYNN! I'M CHOPPER! WE JUST CRASH-LANDED IN THE BONEY ISLANDS!
WHY ARE YOU SO OUT OF IT? I MEAN, EVEN MORE THAN USUAL.
YOU'RE OBVIOUSLY NOT GOING TO BE MUCH HELP.
WE HAVE TO FIND SOME WAY OFF THIS ISLAND, AND YOU'RE A LITTLE TOO BEEFY FOR ME TO FLY YOU.
HEY! WHERE DO YOU THINK YOU'RE GOING?!
TAKE ME TO YOUR ENCHILADAS.
THIS ISN'T THE TIME TO TAKE A TOUR!
COME ON, FLYNN, GET OUT OF THERE!
NEXT STOP, ERNESTO'S ENCHILADA EMPORIUM.
SNAPT

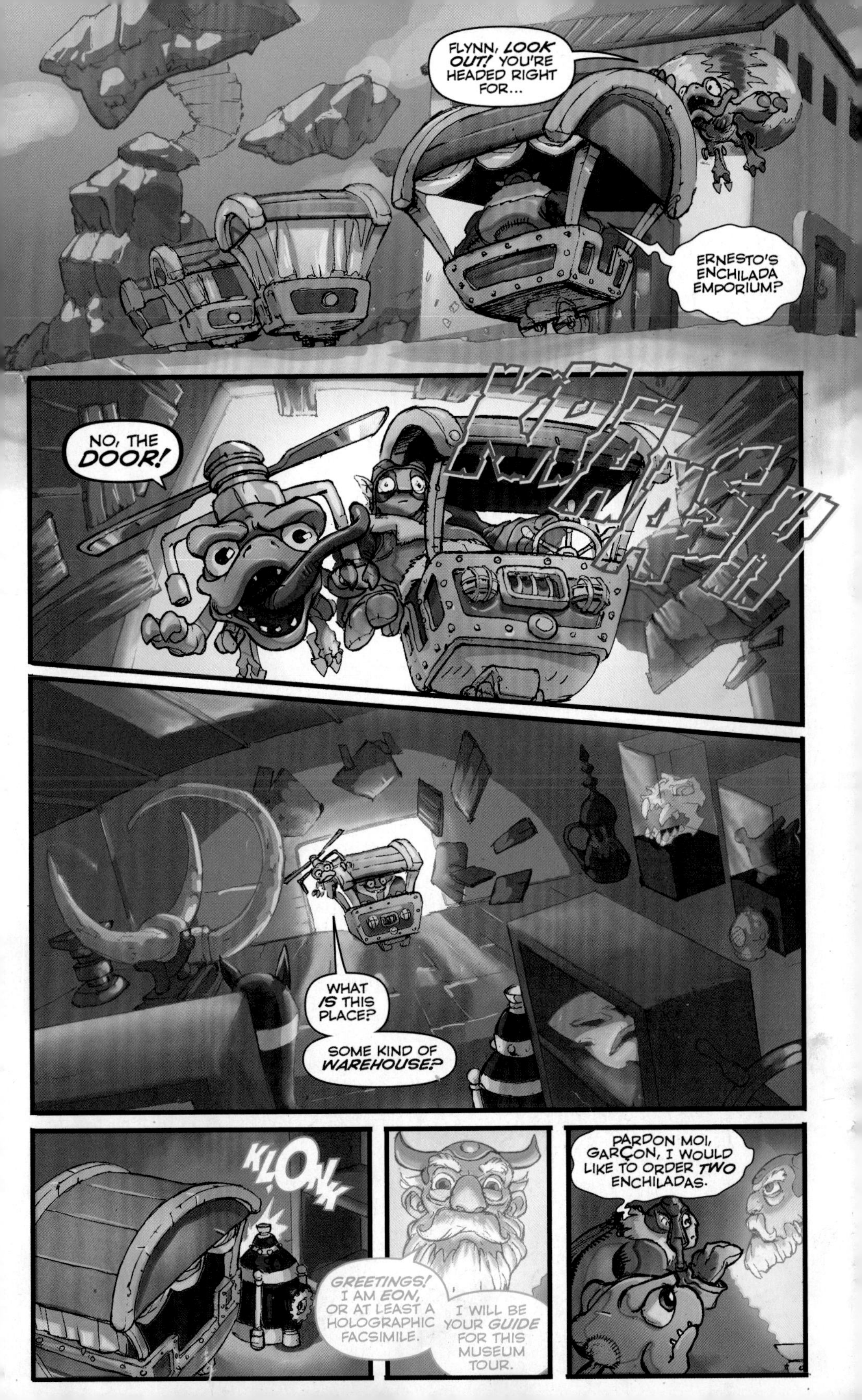
FLYNN, LOOK OUT! YOU'RE HEADED RIGHT FOR...
ERNESTO'S ENCHILADA EMPORIUM?
NO, THE DOOR!
KRAASH!!
WHAT IS THIS PLACE?
SOME KIND OF WAREHOUSE?
KLONK
GREETINGS! I AM EON, OR AT LEAST A HOLOGRAPHIC FACSIMILE.
I WILL BE YOUR GUIDE FOR THIS MUSEUM TOUR.
PARDON MOI, GARÇON, I WOULD LIKE TO ORDER TWO ENCHILADAS.

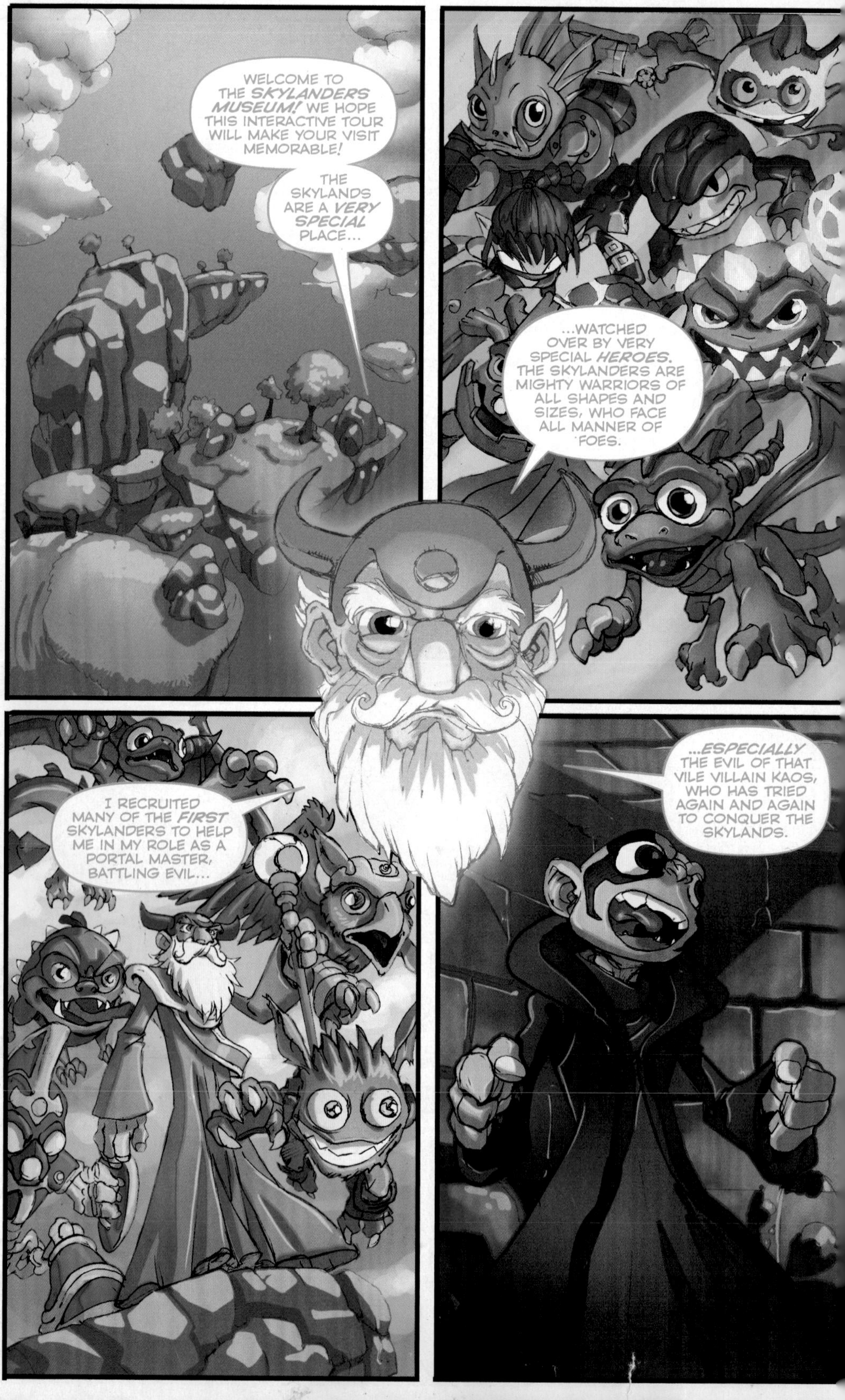
WELCOME TO THE SKYLANDERS MUSEUM! WE HOPE THIS INTERACTIVE TOUR WILL MAKE YOUR VISIT MEMORABLE!
THE SKYLANDS ARE A VERY SPECIAL PLACE...
...WATCHED OVER BY VERY SPECIAL HEROES. THE SKYLANDERS ARE MIGHTY WARRIORS OF ALL SHAPES AND SIZES, WHO FACE ALL MANNER OF FOES.
I RECRUITED MANY OF THE FIRST SKYLANDERS TO HELP ME IN MY ROLE AS A PORTAL MASTER, BATTLING EVIL...
...ESPECIALLY THE EVIL OF THAT VILE VILLAIN KAOS, WHO HAS TRIED AGAIN AND AGAIN TO CONQUER THE SKYLANDS.

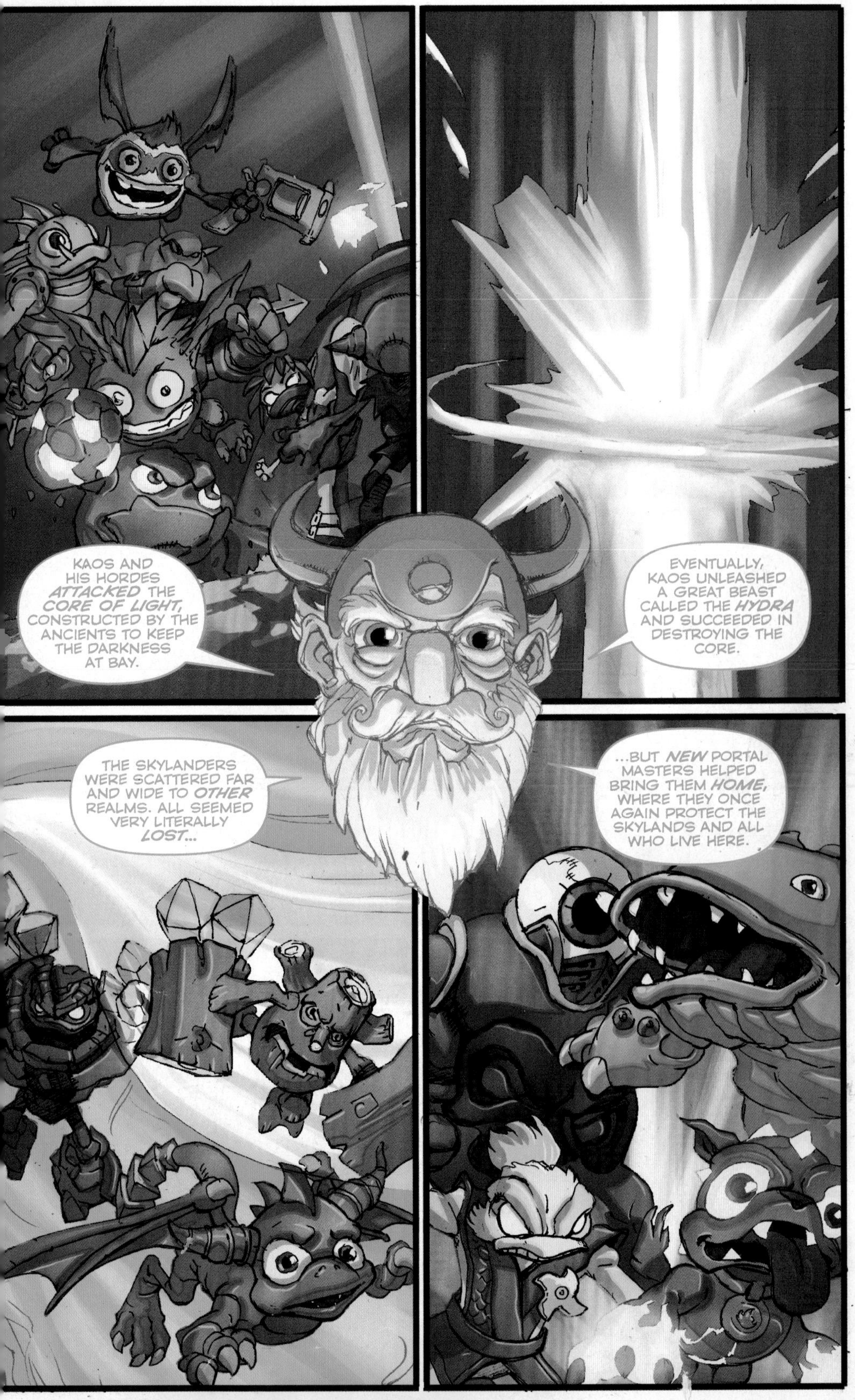
KAOS AND HIS HORDES ATTACKED THE CORE OF LIGHT, CONSTRUCTED BY THE ANCIENTS TO KEEP THE DARKNESS AT BAY.
EVENTUALLY, KAOS UNLEASHED A GREAT BEAST CALLED THE HYDRA AND SUCCEEDED IN DESTROYING THE CORE.
THE SKYLANDERS WERE SCATTERED FAR AND WIDE TO OTHER REALMS. ALL SEEMED VERY LITERALLY LOST...
...BUT NEW PORTAL MASTERS HELPED BRING THEM HOME, WHERE THEY ONCE AGAIN PROTECT THE SKYLANDS AND ALL WHO LIVE HERE.

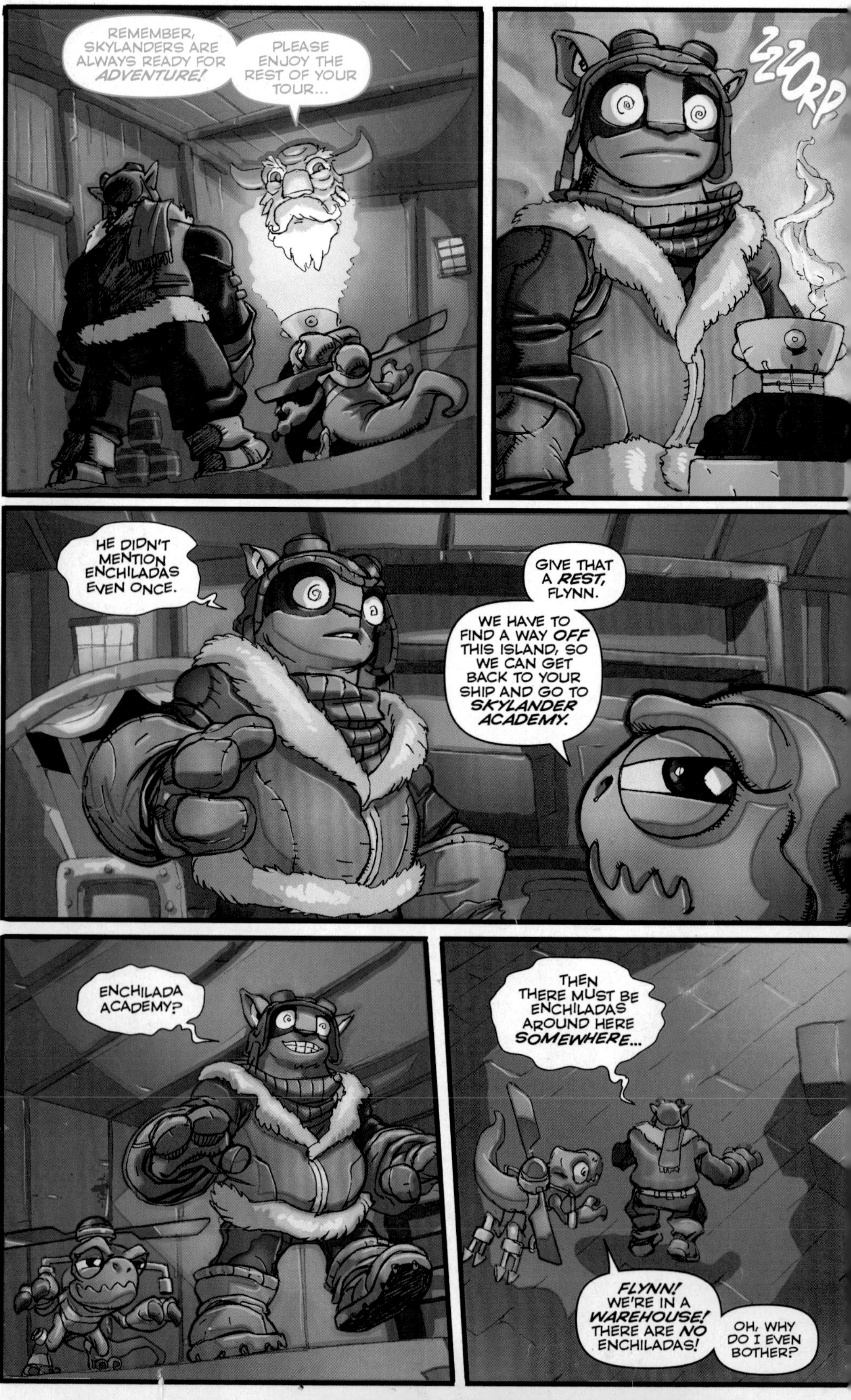
REMEMBER, SKYLANDERS ARE ALWAYS READY FOR ADVENTURE!
PLEASE ENJOY THE REST OF YOUR TOUR...
ZZZORP!
HE DIDN'T MENTION ENCHILADAS EVEN ONCE.
GIVE THAT A REST, FLYNN.
WE HAVE TO FIND A WAY OFF THIS ISLAND, SO WE CAN GET BACK TO YOUR SHIP AND GO TO SKYLANDER ACADEMY.
ENCHILADA ACADEMY?
THEN THERE MUST BE ENCHILADAS AROUND HERE SOMEWHERE...
FLYNN! WE'RE IN A WAREHOUSE! THERE ARE NO ENCHILADAS!
OH, WHY DO I EVEN BOTHER?

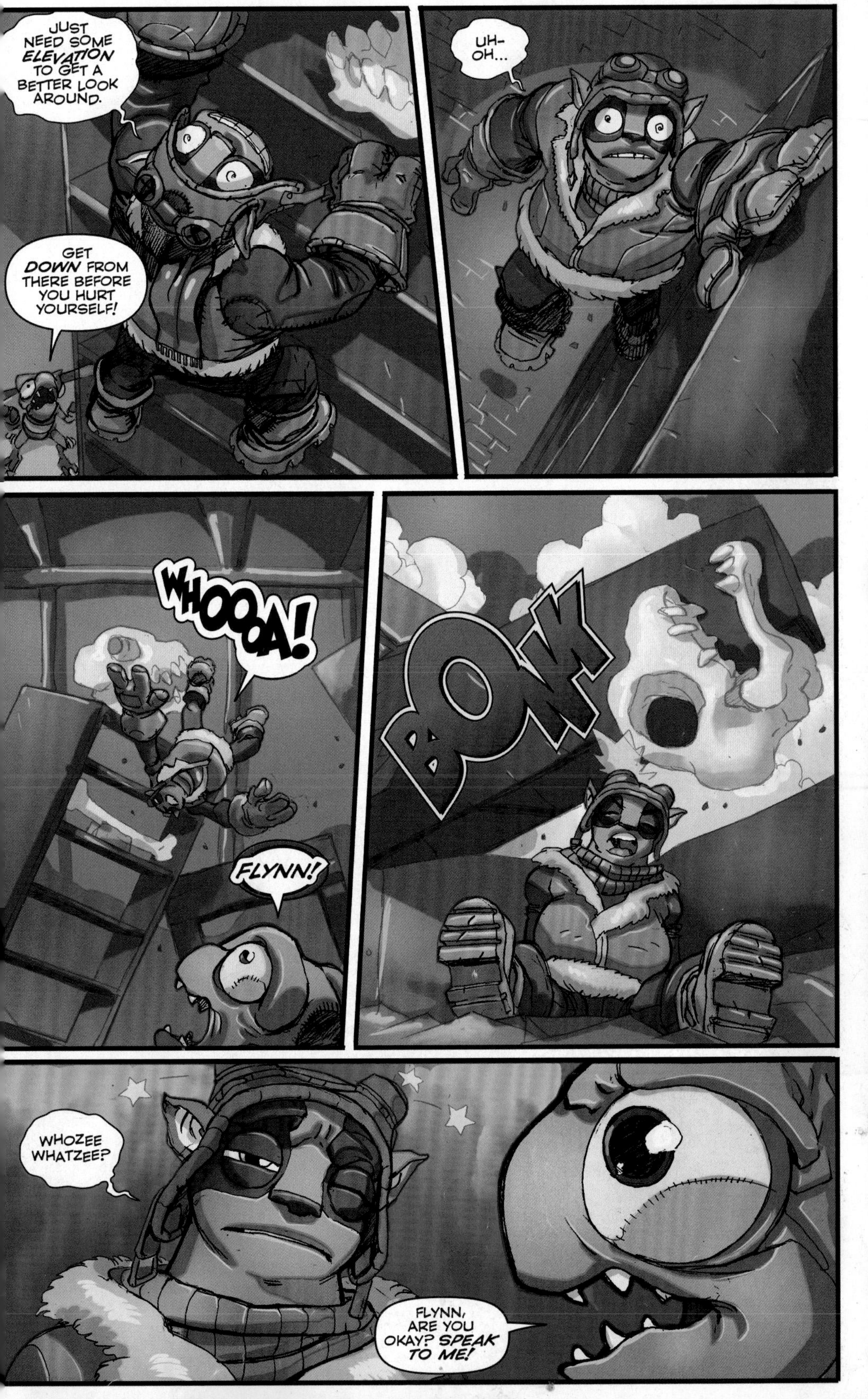
JUST NEED SOME ELEVATION TO GET A BETTER LOOK AROUND.
GET DOWN FROM THERE BEFORE YOU HURT YOURSELF!
UH-OH...
WHOOOA!
FLYNN!
BONK
WHOZEE WHATZEE?
FLYNN, ARE YOU OKAY? SPEAK TO ME!

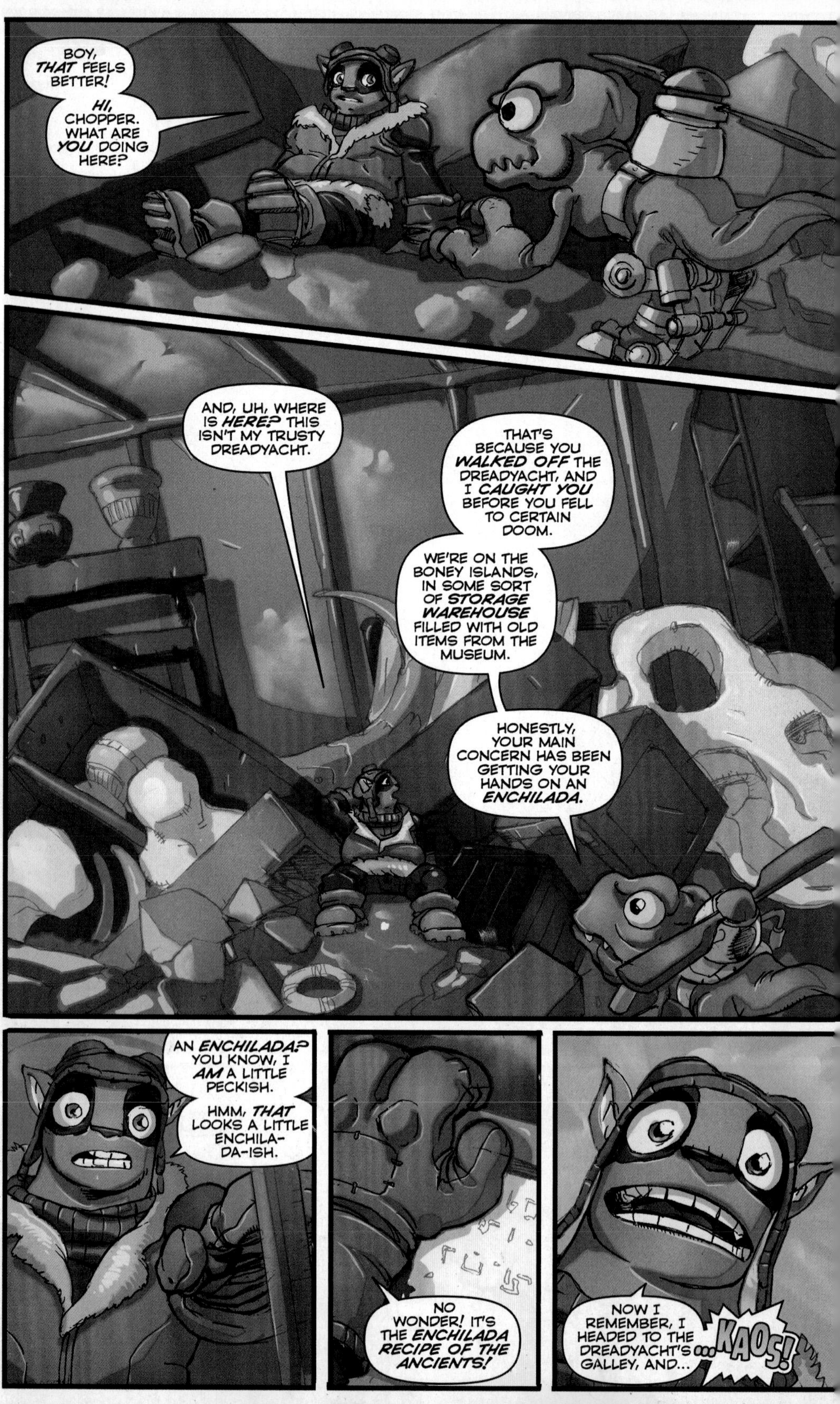
BOY, THAT FEELS BETTER!
HI, CHOPPER. WHAT ARE YOU DOING HERE?
AND, UH, WHERE IS HERE? THIS ISN'T MY TRUSTY DREADYACHT.
THAT'S BECAUSE YOU WALKED OFF THE DREADYACHT, AND I CAUGHT YOU BEFORE YOU FELL TO CERTAIN DOOM.
WE'RE ON THE BONEY ISLANDS, IN SOME SORT OF STORAGE WAREHOUSE FILLED WITH OLD ITEMS FROM THE MUSEUM.
HONESTLY, YOUR MAIN CONCERN HAS BEEN GETTING YOUR HANDS ON AN ENCHILADA.
AN ENCHILADA? YOU KNOW, I AM A LITTLE PECKISH.
HMM, THAT LOOKS A LITTLE ENCHILA-DA-ISH.
NO WONDER! IT'S THE ENCHILADA RECIPE OF THE ANCIENTS!
NOW I REMEMBER, I HEADED TO THE DREADYACHT'S GALLEY, AND...
KAOS!

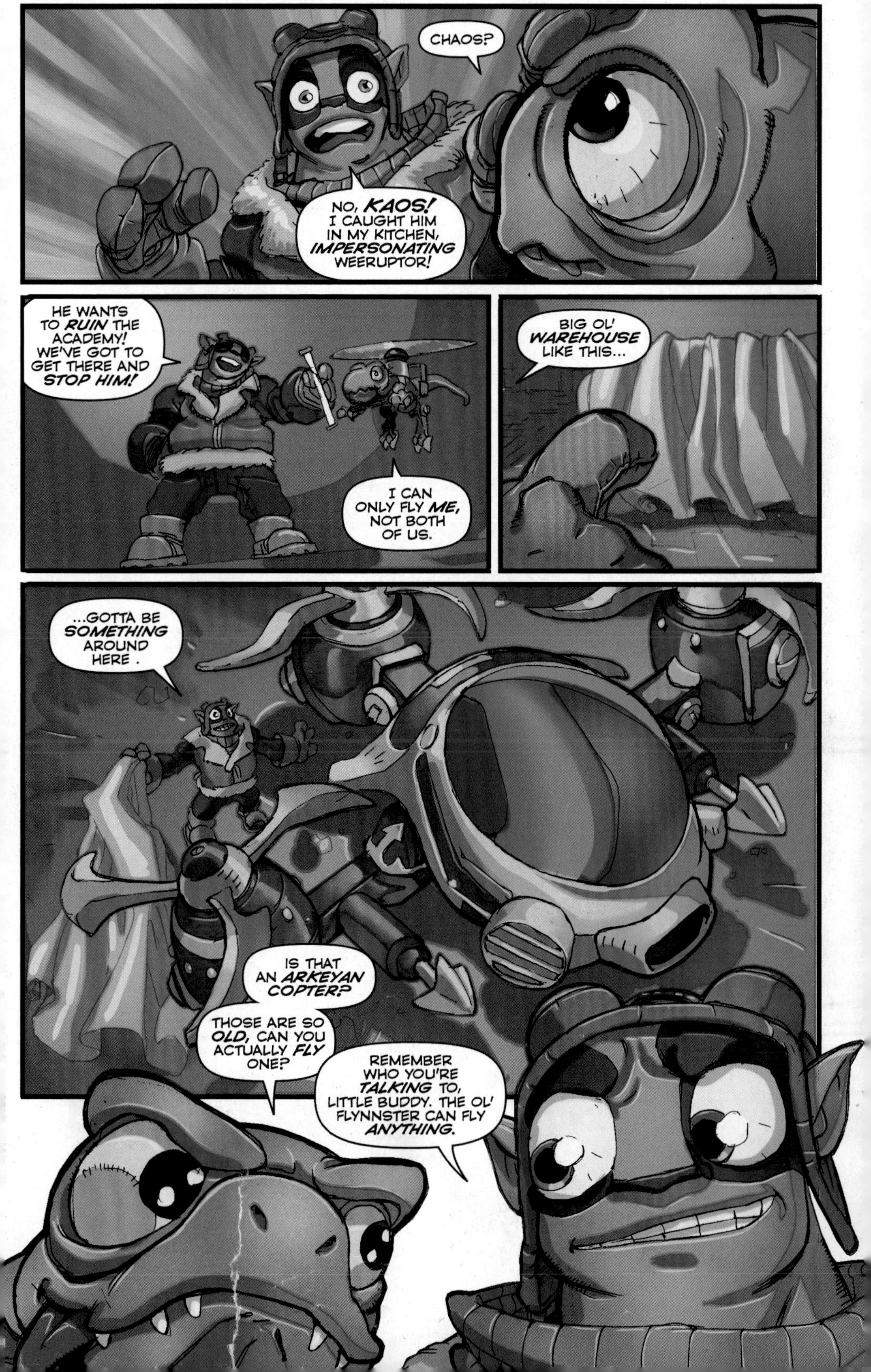
CHAOS?
NO, KAOS! I CAUGHT HIM IN MY KITCHEN, IMPERSONATING WEERUPTOR!
HE WANTS TO RUIN THE ACADEMY! WE'VE GOT TO GET THERE AND STOP HIM!
I CAN ONLY FLY ME, NOT BOTH OF US.
BIG OL' WAREHOUSE LIKE THIS...
...GOTTA BE SOMETHING AROUND HERE .
IS THAT AN ARKEYAN COPTER?
THOSE ARE SO OLD, CAN YOU ACTUALLY FLY ONE?
REMEMBER WHO YOU'RE TALKING TO, LITTLE BUDDY. THE OL' FLYNNSTER CAN FLY ANYTHING.

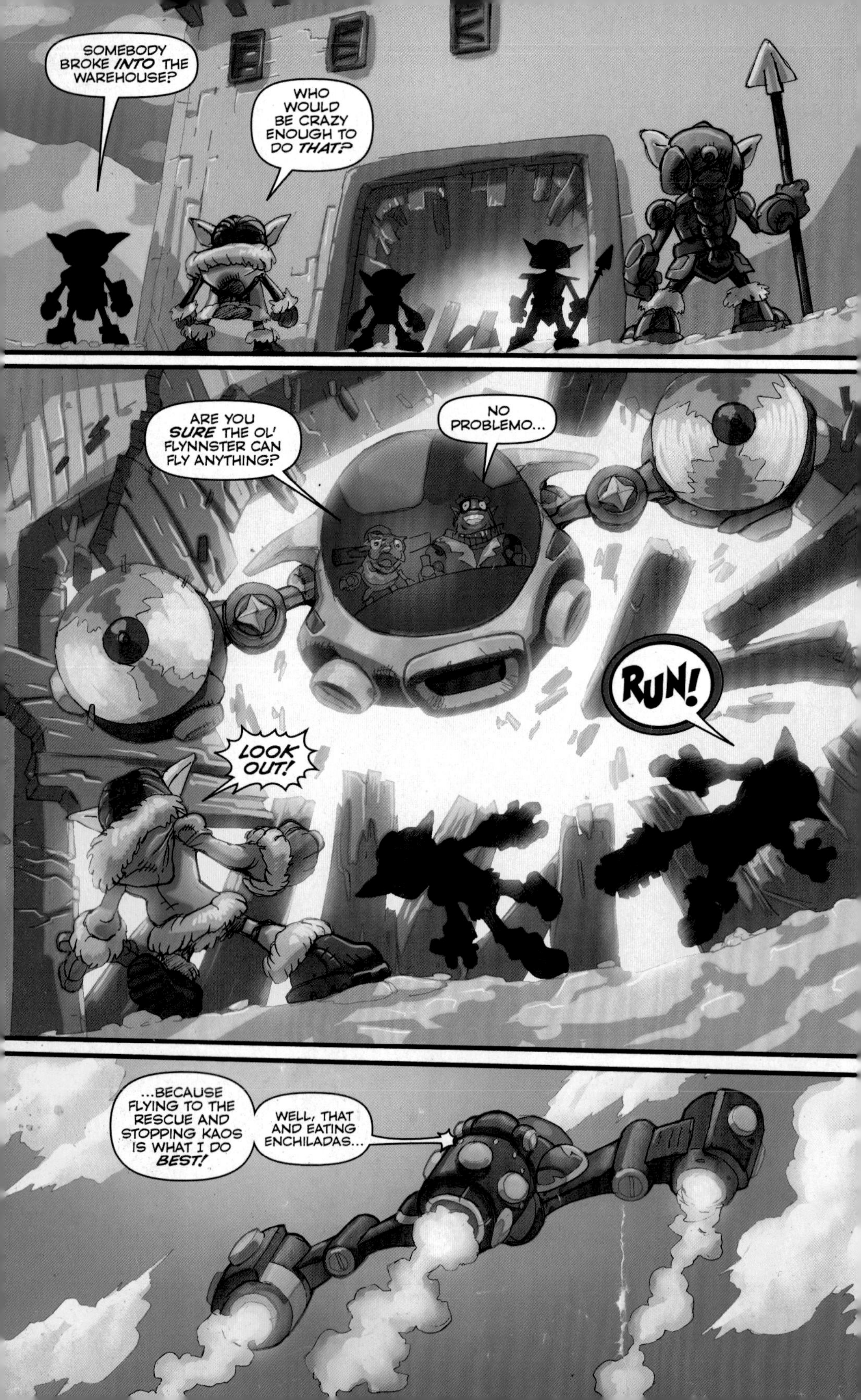
SOMEBODY BROKE *INTO* THE WAREHOUSE?
WHO WOULD BE CRAZY ENOUGH TO DO *THAT?*
ARE YOU *SURE* THE OL' FLYNNSTER CAN FLY ANYTHING?
NO PROBLEMO...
LOOK OUT!
RUN!
...BECAUSE FLYING TO THE RESCUE AND STOPPING KAOS IS WHAT I DO *BEST!*
WELL, THAT AND EATING ENCHILADAS...

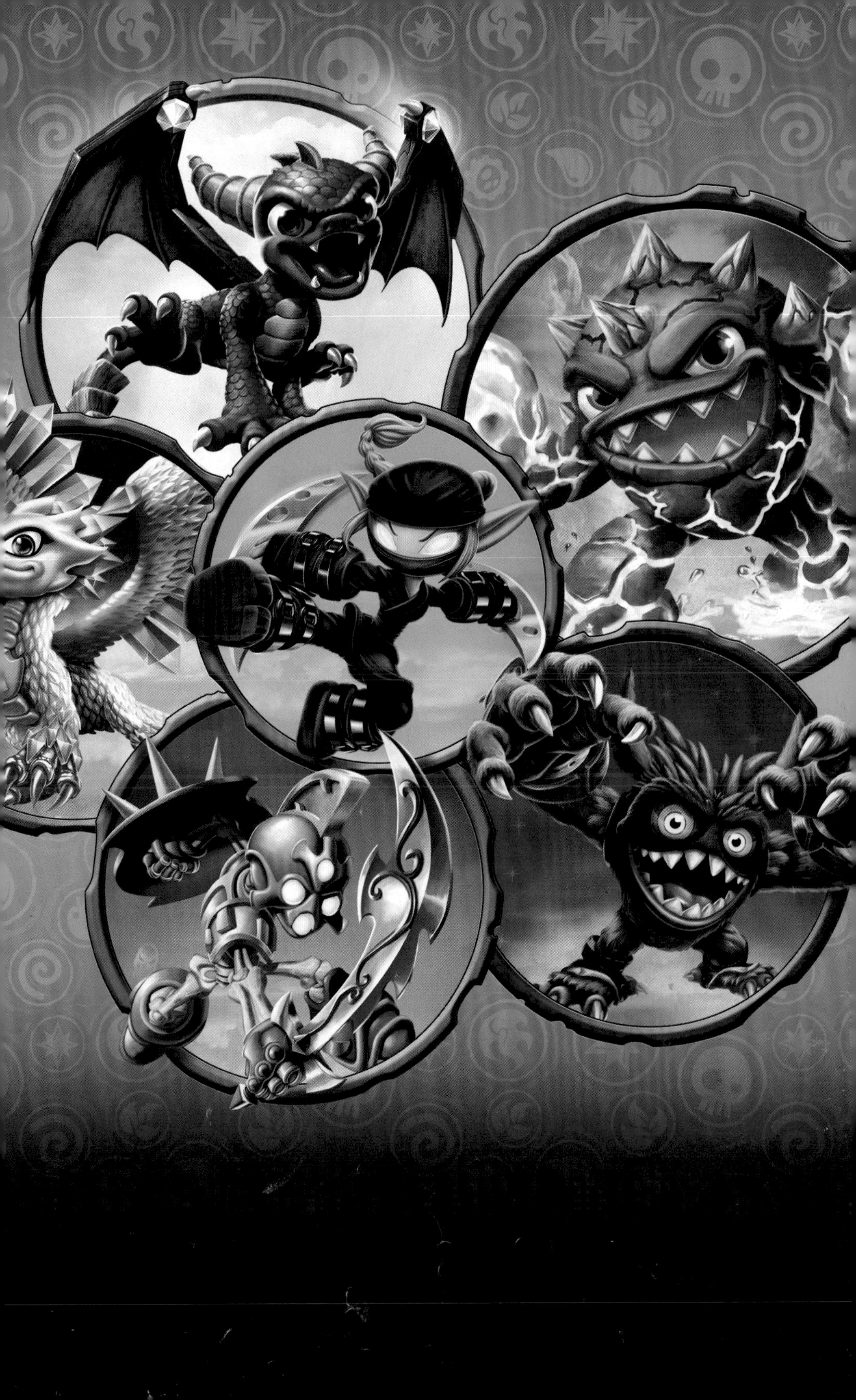

MINI BUT MIGHTY

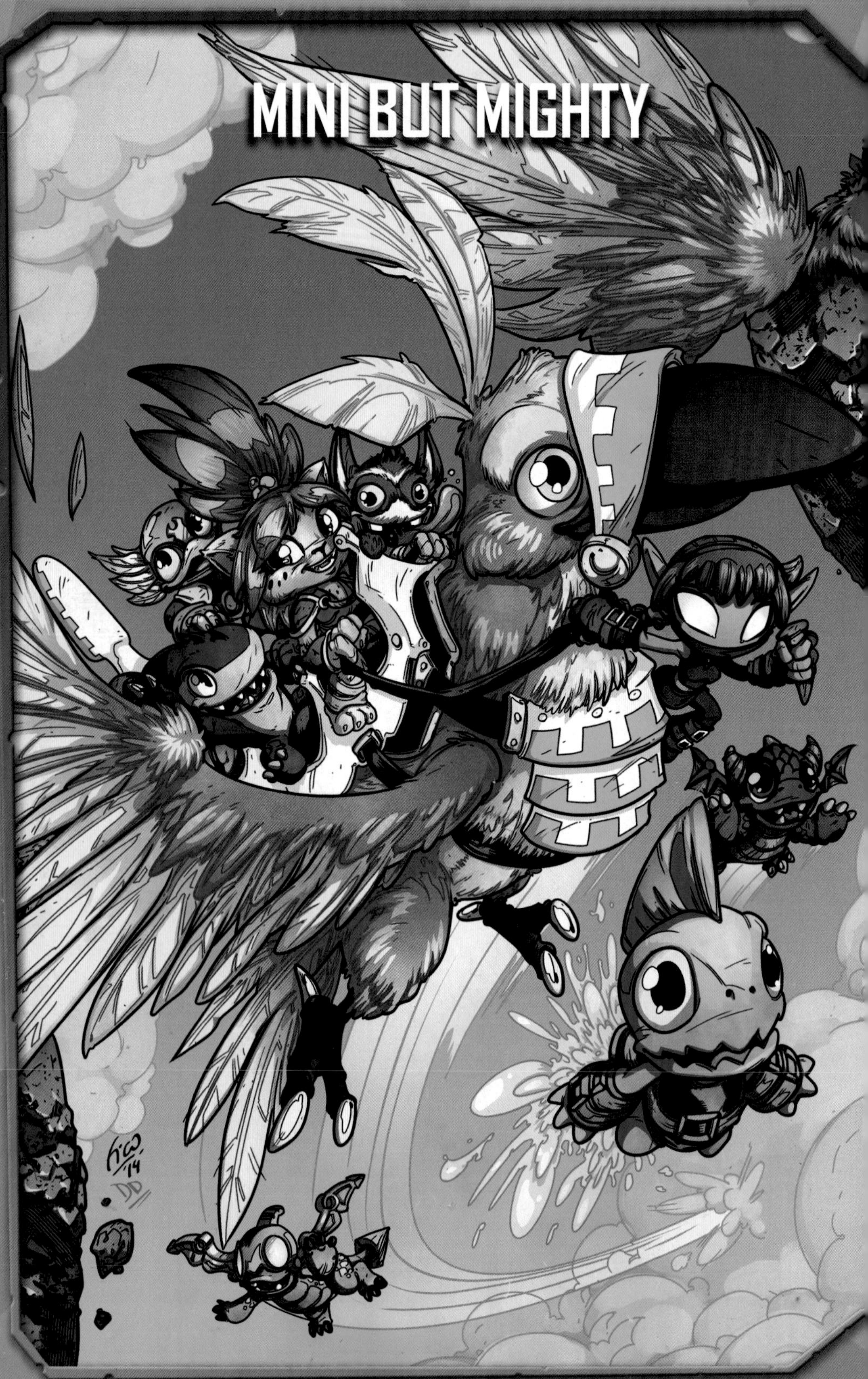

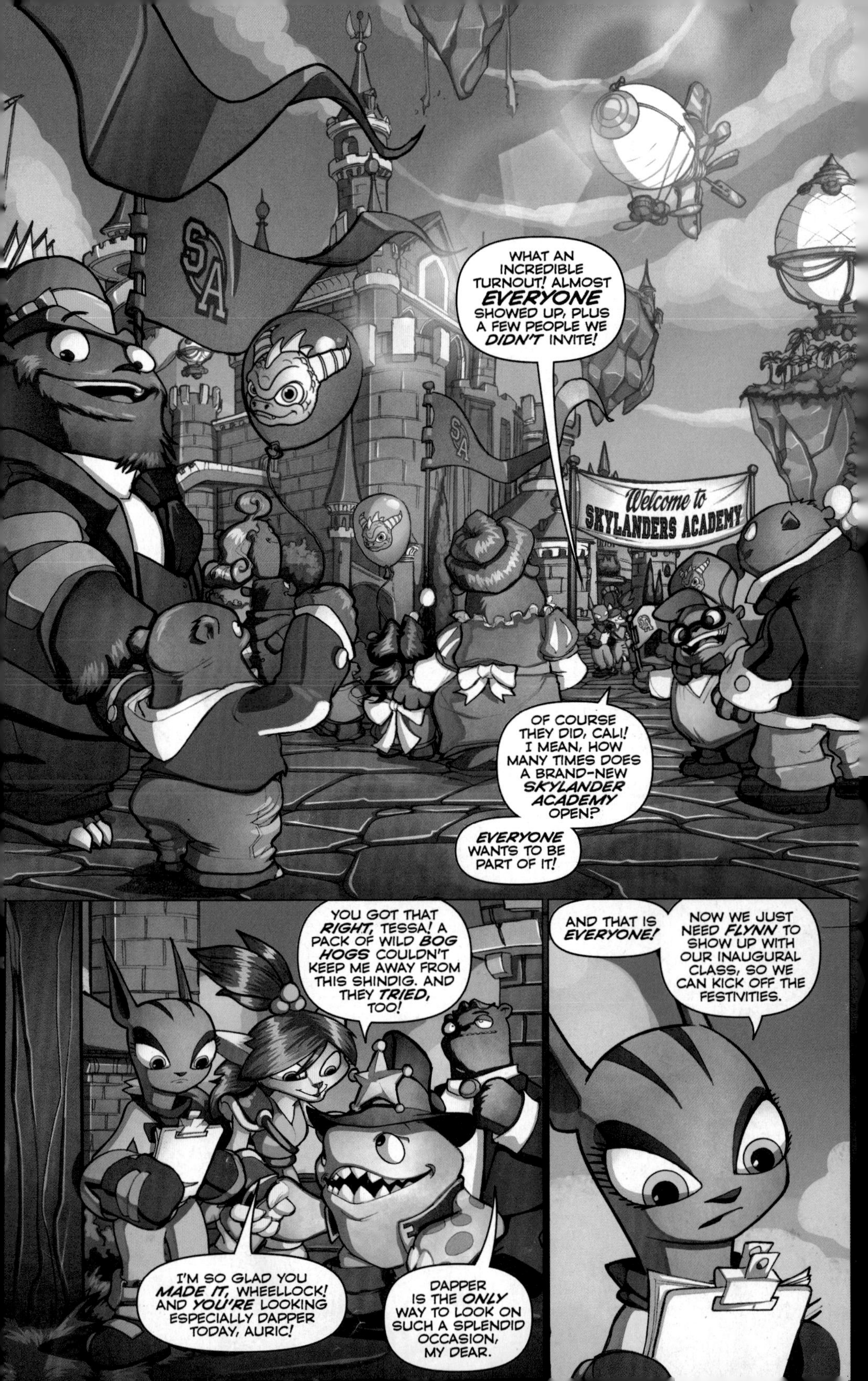
Welcome to
SKYLANDERS ACADEMY
WHAT AN INCREDIBLE TURNOUT! ALMOST EVERYONE SHOWED UP, PLUS A FEW PEOPLE WE DIDN'T INVITE!
OF COURSE THEY DID, CALI! I MEAN, HOW MANY TIMES DOES A BRAND-NEW SKYLANDER ACADEMY OPEN?
EVERYONE WANTS TO BE PART OF IT!
YOU GOT THAT RIGHT, TESSA! A PACK OF WILD BOG HOGS COULDN'T KEEP ME AWAY FROM THIS SHINDIG. AND THEY TRIED, TOO!
I'M SO GLAD YOU MADE IT, WHEELLOCK! AND YOU'RE LOOKING ESPECIALLY DAPPER TODAY, AURIC!
DAPPER IS THE ONLY WAY TO LOOK ON SUCH A SPLENDID OCCASION, MY DEAR.
AND THAT IS EVERYONE!
NOW WE JUST NEED FLYNN TO SHOW UP WITH OUR INAUGURAL CLASS, SO WE CAN KICK OFF THE FESTIVITIES.

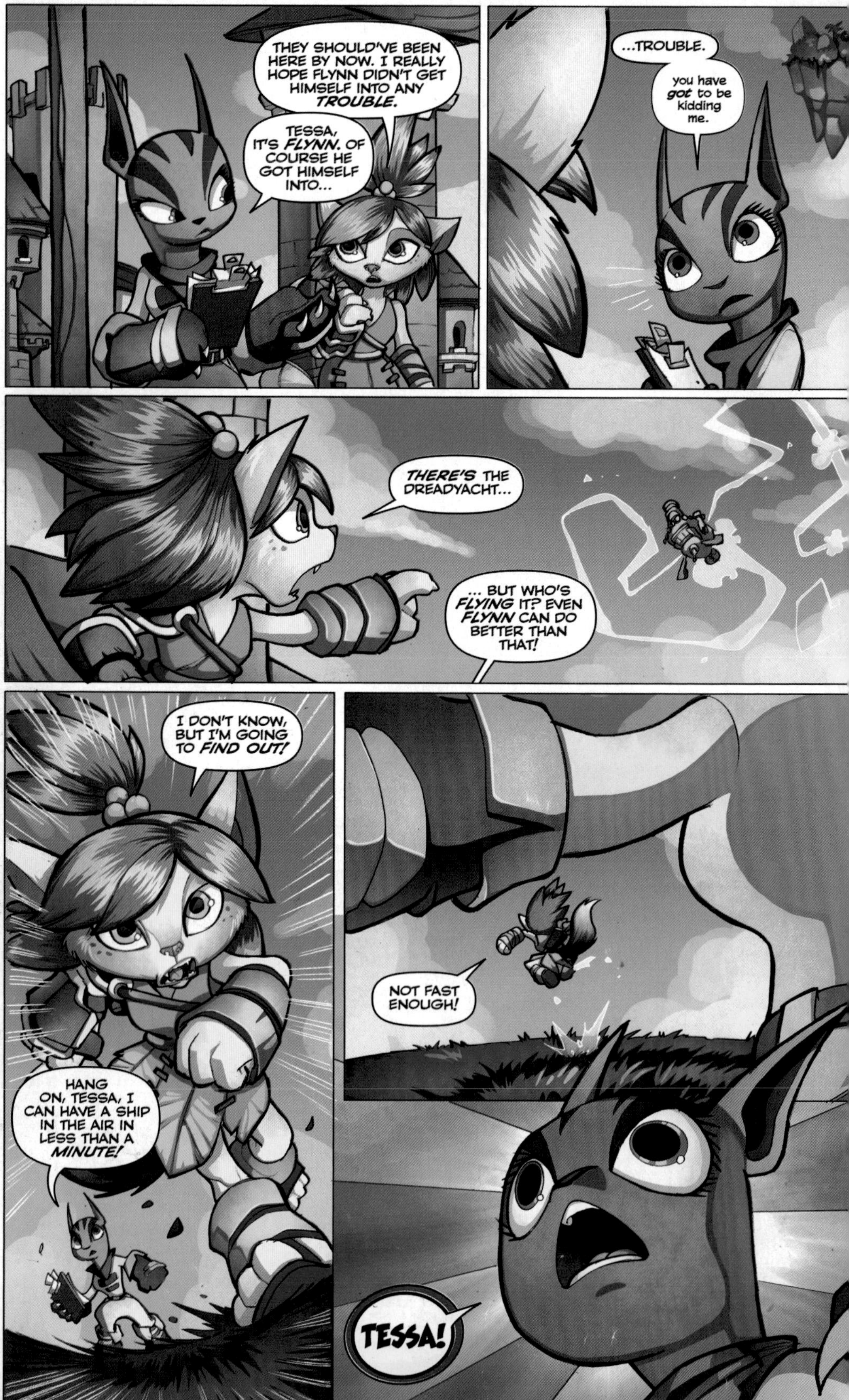
THEY SHOULD'VE BEEN HERE BY NOW. I REALLY HOPE FLYNN DIDN'T GET HIMSELF INTO ANY *TROUBLE.*
TESSA, IT'S *FLYNN.* OF COURSE HE GOT HIMSELF INTO...
...TROUBLE.
you have *got* to be kidding me.
THERE'S THE DREADYACHT...
... BUT WHO'S *FLYING* IT? EVEN *FLYNN* CAN DO BETTER THAN THAT!
I DON'T KNOW, BUT I'M GOING TO *FIND OUT!*
HANG ON, TESSA, I CAN HAVE A SHIP IN THE AIR IN LESS THAN A *MINUTE!*
NOT FAST ENOUGH!
TESSA!

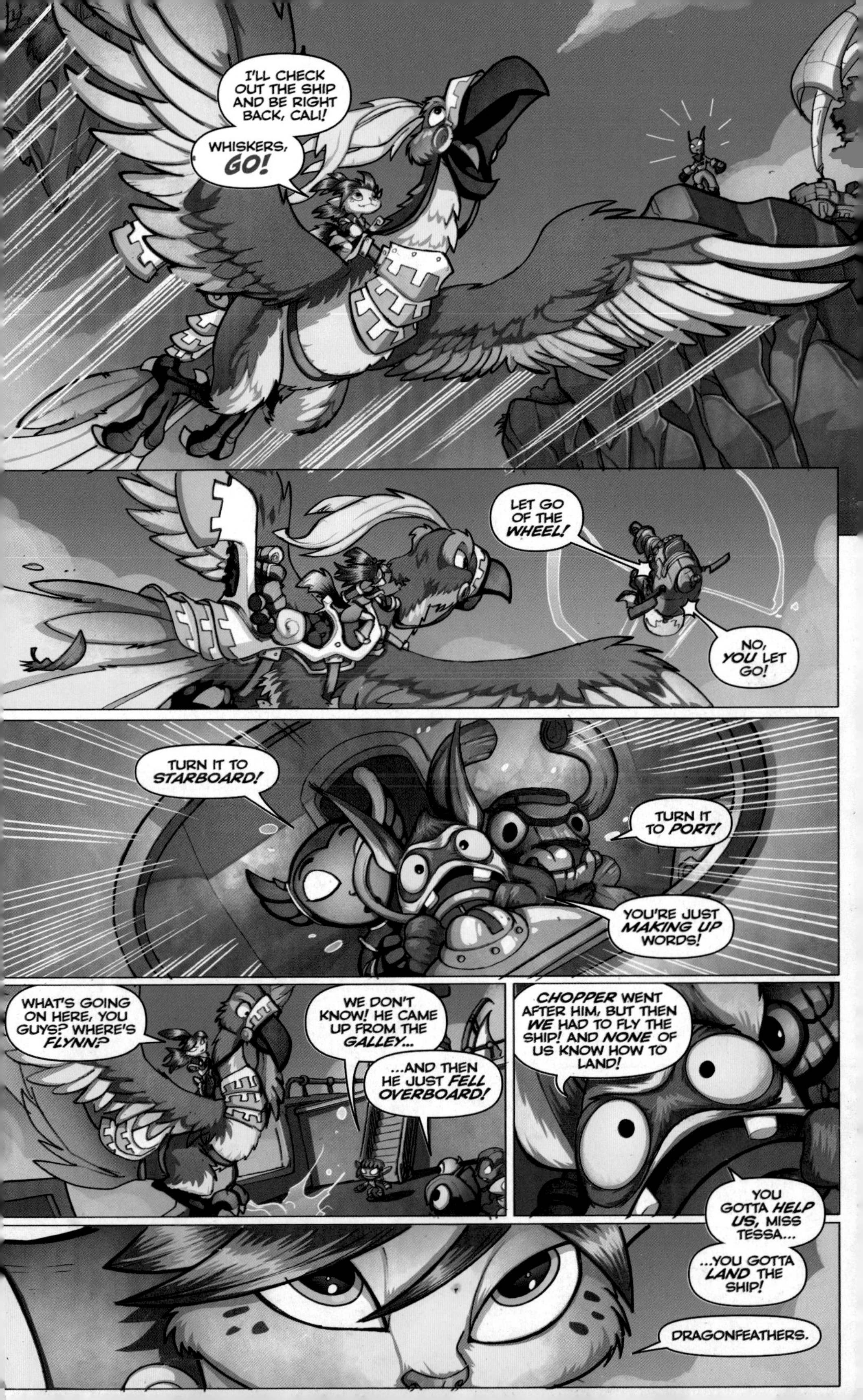
I'LL CHECK OUT THE SHIP AND BE RIGHT BACK, CALI!
WHISKERS, GO!
LET GO OF THE WHEEL!
NO, YOU LET GO!
TURN IT TO STARBOARD!
TURN IT TO PORT!
YOU'RE JUST MAKING UP WORDS!
WHAT'S GOING ON HERE, YOU GUYS? WHERE'S FLYNN?
WE DON'T KNOW! HE CAME UP FROM THE GALLEY...
...AND THEN HE JUST FELL OVERBOARD!
CHOPPER WENT AFTER HIM, BUT THEN WE HAD TO FLY THE SHIP! AND NONE OF US KNOW HOW TO LAND!
YOU GOTTA HELP US, MISS TESSA...
...YOU GOTTA LAND THE SHIP!
DRAGONFEATHERS.

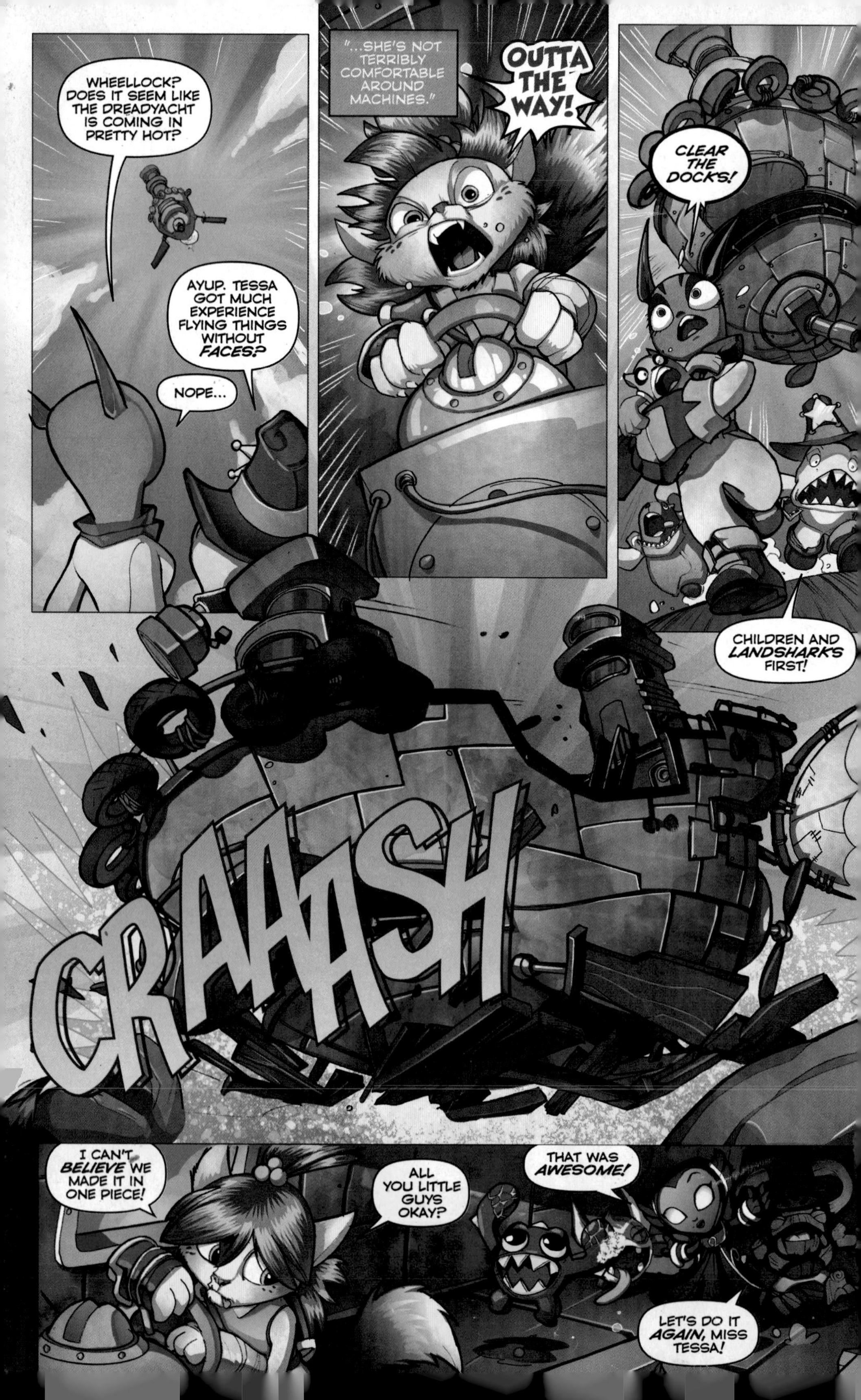
WHEELLOCK? DOES IT SEEM LIKE THE DREADYACHT IS COMING IN PRETTY HOT?
AYUP. TESSA GOT MUCH EXPERIENCE FLYING THINGS WITHOUT FACES?
NOPE...
"...SHE'S NOT TERRIBLY COMFORTABLE AROUND MACHINES."
OUTTA THE WAY!
CLEAR THE DOCKS!
CHILDREN AND LANDSHARKS FIRST!
CRAAASH
I CAN'T BELIEVE WE MADE IT IN ONE PIECE!
ALL YOU LITTLE GUYS OKAY?
THAT WAS AWESOME!
LET'S DO IT AGAIN, MISS TESSA!

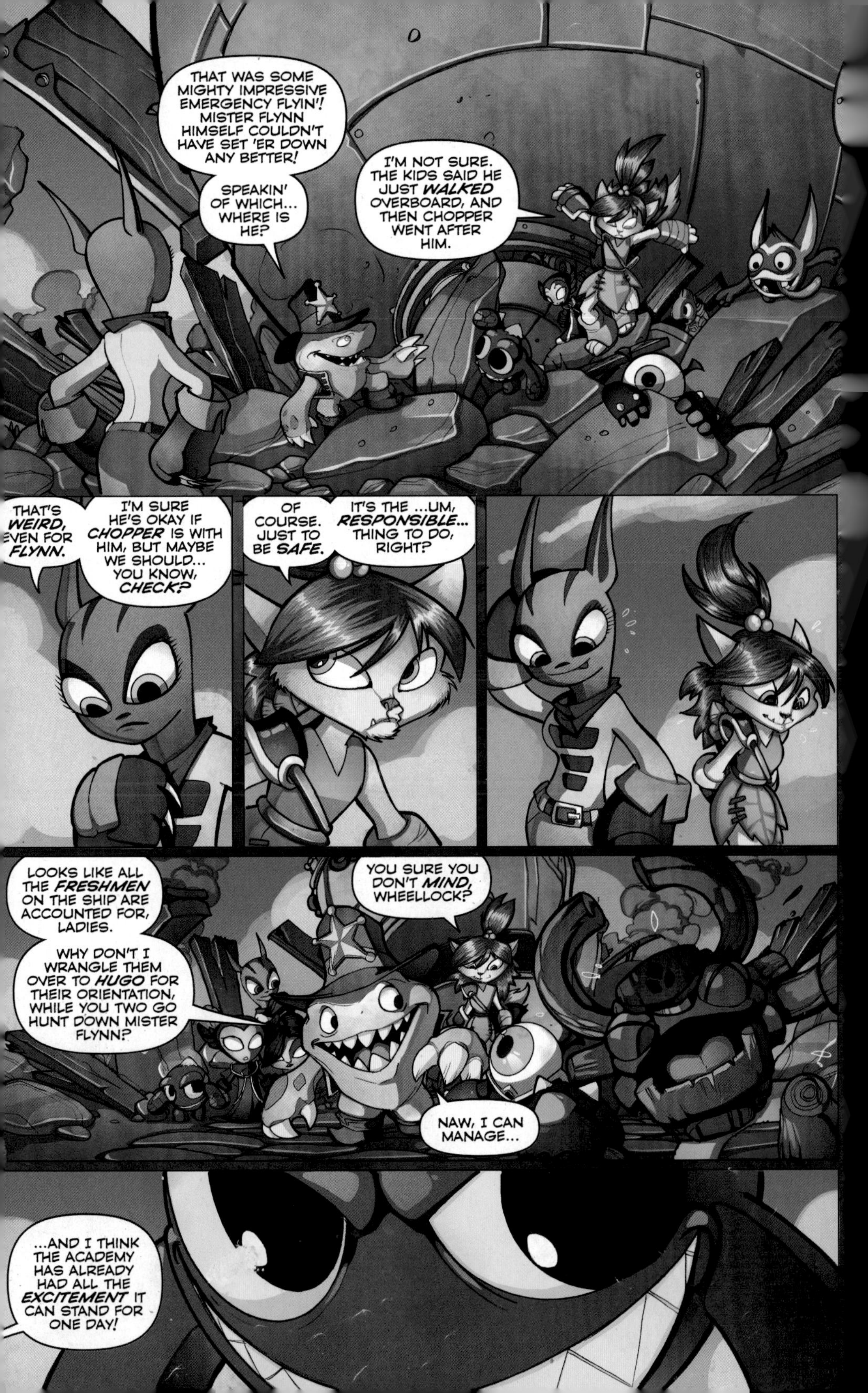
THAT WAS SOME MIGHTY IMPRESSIVE EMERGENCY FLYIN'! MISTER FLYNN HIMSELF COULDN'T HAVE SET 'ER DOWN ANY BETTER!
SPEAKIN' OF WHICH... WHERE IS HE?
I'M NOT SURE. THE KIDS SAID HE JUST WALKED OVERBOARD, AND THEN CHOPPER WENT AFTER HIM.
THAT'S WEIRD, EVEN FOR FLYNN.
I'M SURE HE'S OKAY IF CHOPPER IS WITH HIM, BUT MAYBE WE SHOULD... YOU KNOW, CHECK?
OF COURSE. JUST TO BE SAFE.
IT'S THE ...UM, RESPONSIBLE... THING TO DO, RIGHT?
LOOKS LIKE ALL THE FRESHMEN ON THE SHIP ARE ACCOUNTED FOR, LADIES.
WHY DON'T I WRANGLE THEM OVER TO HUGO FOR THEIR ORIENTATION, WHILE YOU TWO GO HUNT DOWN MISTER FLYNN?
YOU SURE YOU DON'T MIND, WHEELLOCK?
NAW, I CAN MANAGE...
...AND I THINK THE ACADEMY HAS ALREADY HAD ALL THE EXCITEMENT IT CAN STAND FOR ONE DAY!

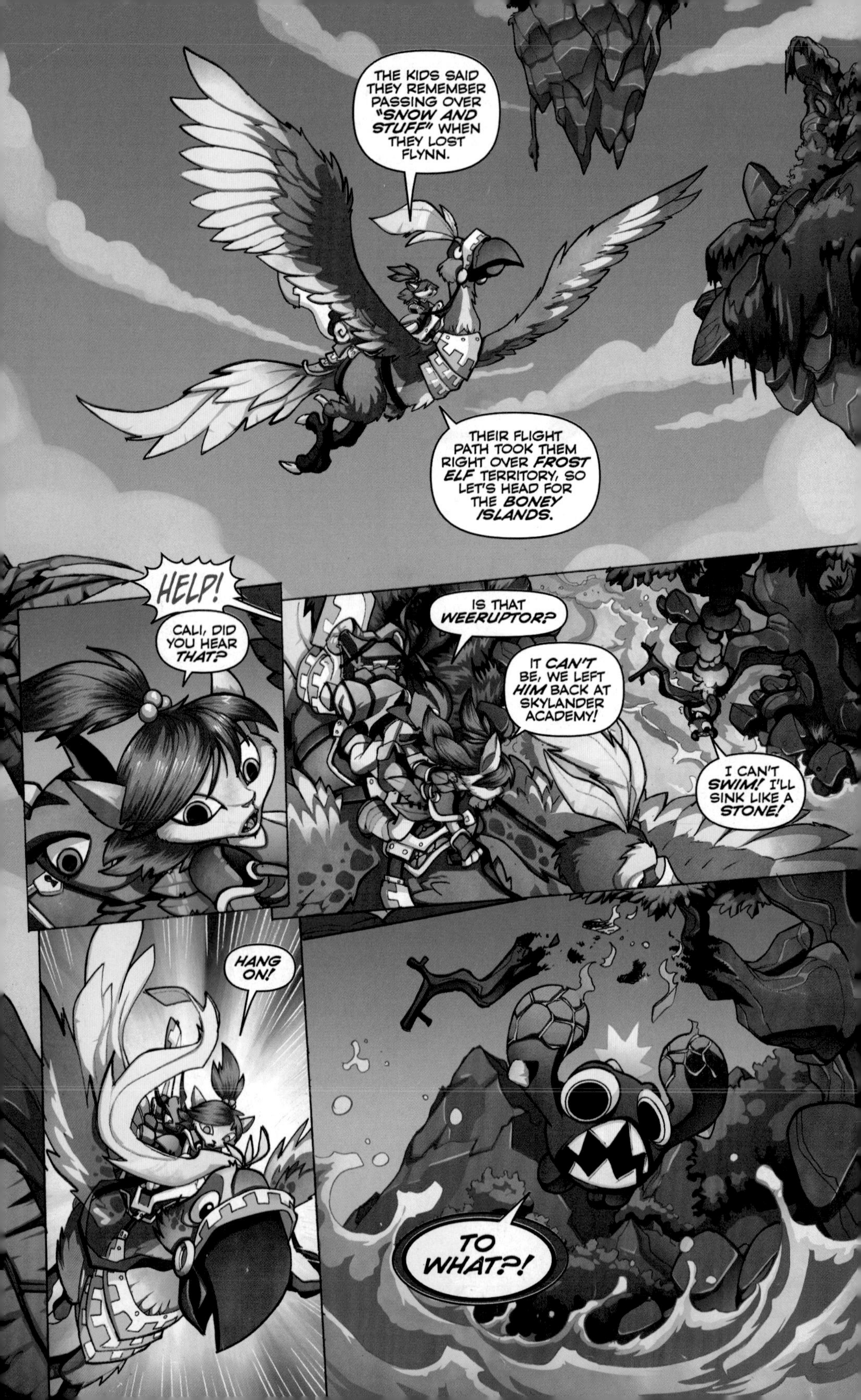
THE KIDS SAID THEY REMEMBER PASSING OVER "SNOW AND STUFF" WHEN THEY LOST FLYNN.
THEIR FLIGHT PATH TOOK THEM RIGHT OVER FROST ELF TERRITORY, SO LET'S HEAD FOR THE BONEY ISLANDS.
HELP!
CALI, DID YOU HEAR THAT?
IS THAT WEERUPTOR?
IT CAN'T BE, WE LEFT HIM BACK AT SKYLANDER ACADEMY!
I CAN'T SWIM! I'LL SINK LIKE A STONE!
HANG ON!
TO WHAT?!

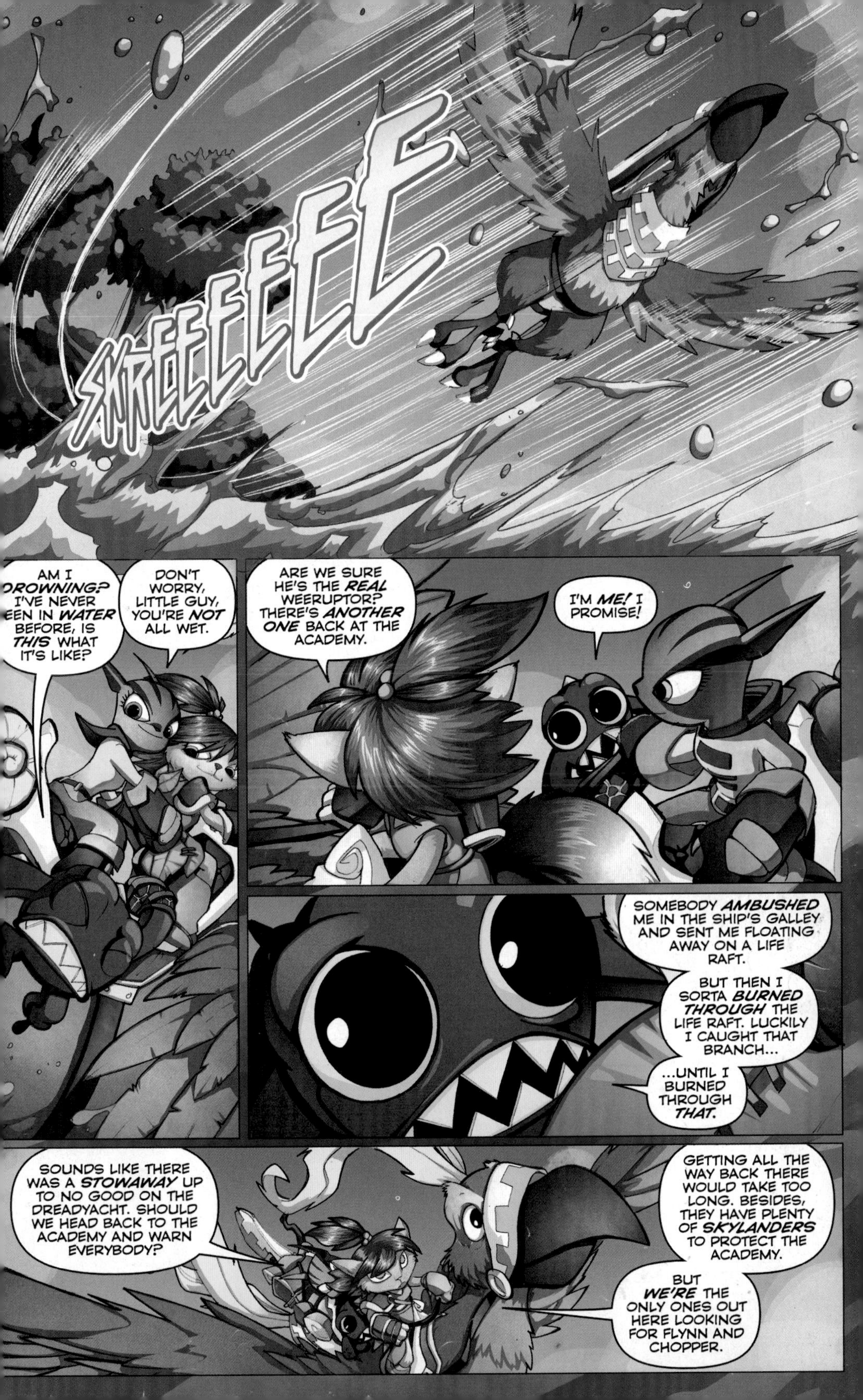
SKREEEEEE
AM I DROWNING? I'VE NEVER BEEN IN WATER BEFORE, IS THIS WHAT IT'S LIKE?
DON'T WORRY, LITTLE GUY, YOU'RE NOT ALL WET.
ARE WE SURE HE'S THE REAL WEERUPTOR? THERE'S ANOTHER ONE BACK AT THE ACADEMY.
I'M ME! I PROMISE!
SOMEBODY AMBUSHED ME IN THE SHIP'S GALLEY AND SENT ME FLOATING AWAY ON A LIFE RAFT.
BUT THEN I SORTA BURNED THROUGH THE LIFE RAFT. LUCKILY I CAUGHT THAT BRANCH...
...UNTIL I BURNED THROUGH THAT.
SOUNDS LIKE THERE WAS A STOWAWAY UP TO NO GOOD ON THE DREADYACHT. SHOULD WE HEAD BACK TO THE ACADEMY AND WARN EVERYBODY?
GETTING ALL THE WAY BACK THERE WOULD TAKE TOO LONG. BESIDES, THEY HAVE PLENTY OF SKYLANDERS TO PROTECT THE ACADEMY.
BUT WE'RE THE ONLY ONES OUT HERE LOOKING FOR FLYNN AND CHOPPER.

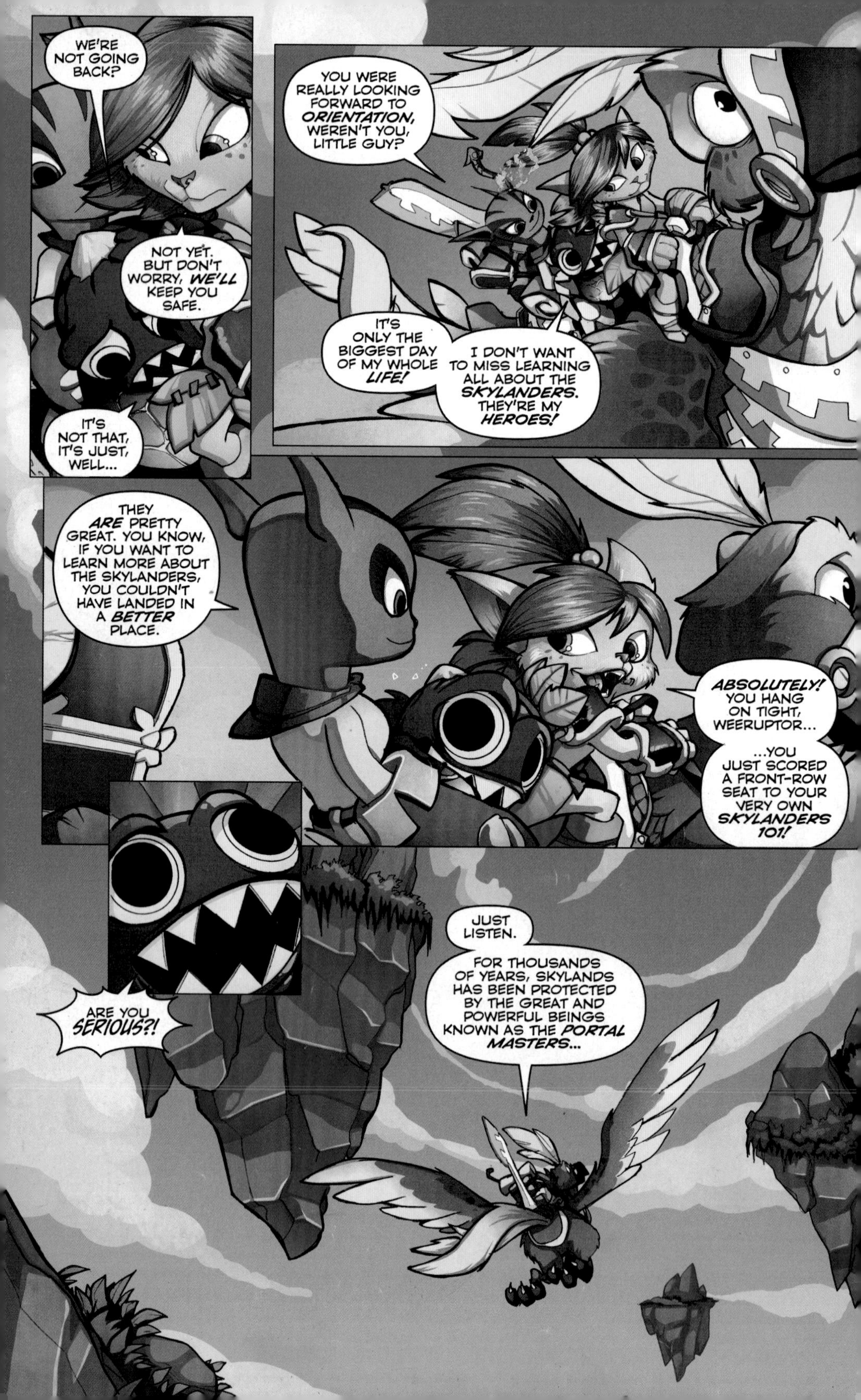
WE'RE NOT GOING BACK?
NOT YET. BUT DON'T WORRY, WE'LL KEEP YOU SAFE.
IT'S NOT THAT, IT'S JUST, WELL...
YOU WERE REALLY LOOKING FORWARD TO ORIENTATION, WEREN'T YOU, LITTLE GUY?
IT'S ONLY THE BIGGEST DAY OF MY WHOLE LIFE!
I DON'T WANT TO MISS LEARNING ALL ABOUT THE SKYLANDERS. THEY'RE MY HEROES!
THEY ARE PRETTY GREAT. YOU KNOW, IF YOU WANT TO LEARN MORE ABOUT THE SKYLANDERS, YOU COULDN'T HAVE LANDED IN A BETTER PLACE.
ABSOLUTELY! YOU HANG ON TIGHT, WEERUPTOR...
...YOU JUST SCORED A FRONT-ROW SEAT TO YOUR VERY OWN SKYLANDERS 101!
ARE YOU SERIOUS?!
JUST LISTEN.
FOR THOUSANDS OF YEARS, SKYLANDS HAS BEEN PROTECTED BY THE GREAT AND POWERFUL BEINGS KNOWN AS THE PORTAL MASTERS...

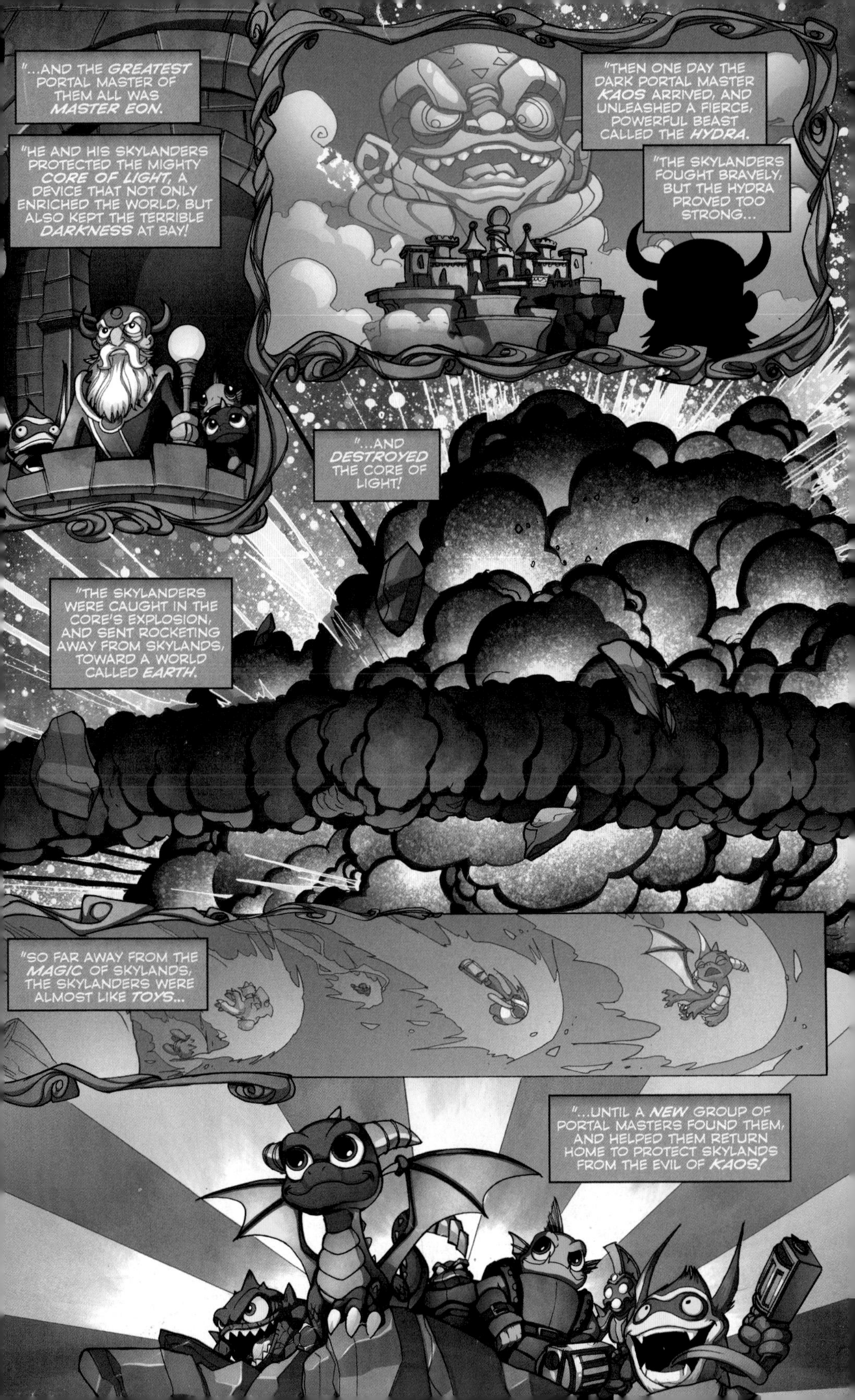
"...AND THE GREATEST PORTAL MASTER OF THEM ALL WAS MASTER EON.
"HE AND HIS SKYLANDERS PROTECTED THE MIGHTY CORE OF LIGHT, A DEVICE THAT NOT ONLY ENRICHED THE WORLD, BUT ALSO KEPT THE TERRIBLE DARKNESS AT BAY!
"THEN ONE DAY THE DARK PORTAL MASTER KAOS ARRIVED, AND UNLEASHED A FIERCE, POWERFUL BEAST CALLED THE HYDRA.
"THE SKYLANDERS FOUGHT BRAVELY, BUT THE HYDRA PROVED TOO STRONG...
"...AND DESTROYED THE CORE OF LIGHT!
"THE SKYLANDERS WERE CAUGHT IN THE CORE'S EXPLOSION, AND SENT ROCKETING AWAY FROM SKYLANDS, TOWARD A WORLD CALLED EARTH.
"SO FAR AWAY FROM THE MAGIC OF SKYLANDS, THE SKYLANDERS WERE ALMOST LIKE TOYS...
"...UNTIL A NEW GROUP OF PORTAL MASTERS FOUND THEM, AND HELPED THEM RETURN HOME TO PROTECT SKYLANDS FROM THE EVIL OF KAOS!

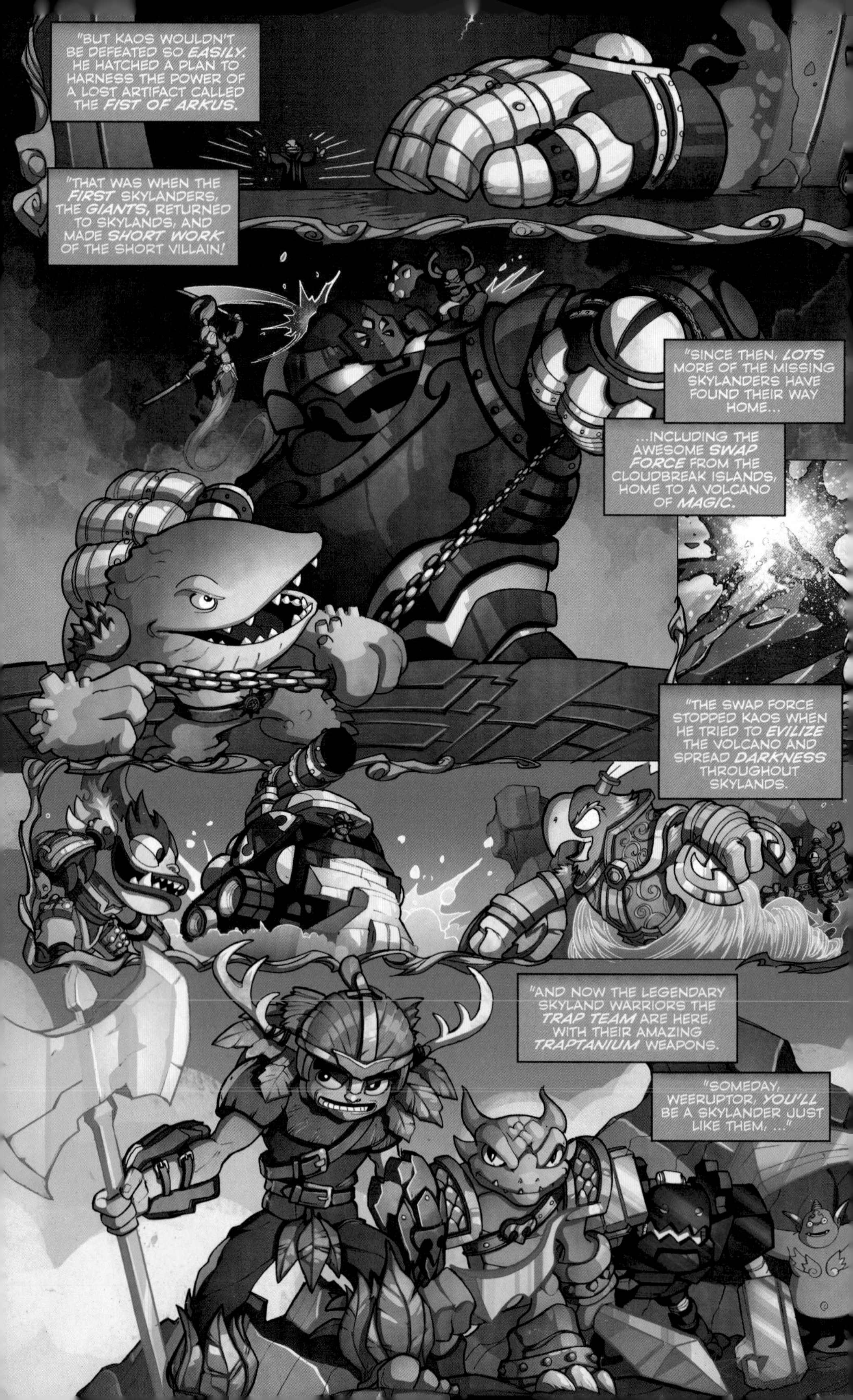
"BUT KAOS WOULDN'T BE DEFEATED SO EASILY. HE HATCHED A PLAN TO HARNESS THE POWER OF A LOST ARTIFACT CALLED THE FIST OF ARKUS.
"THAT WAS WHEN THE FIRST SKYLANDERS, THE GIANTS, RETURNED TO SKYLANDS, AND MADE SHORT WORK OF THE SHORT VILLAIN!
"SINCE THEN, LOTS MORE OF THE MISSING SKYLANDERS HAVE FOUND THEIR WAY HOME...
...INCLUDING THE AWESOME SWAP FORCE FROM THE CLOUDBREAK ISLANDS, HOME TO A VOLCANO OF MAGIC.
"THE SWAP FORCE STOPPED KAOS WHEN HE TRIED TO EVILIZE THE VOLCANO AND SPREAD DARKNESS THROUGHOUT SKYLANDS.
"AND NOW THE LEGENDARY SKYLAND WARRIORS THE TRAP TEAM ARE HERE, WITH THEIR AMAZING TRAPTANIUM WEAPONS.
"SOMEDAY, WEERUPTOR, YOU'LL BE A SKYLANDER JUST LIKE THEM, ..."

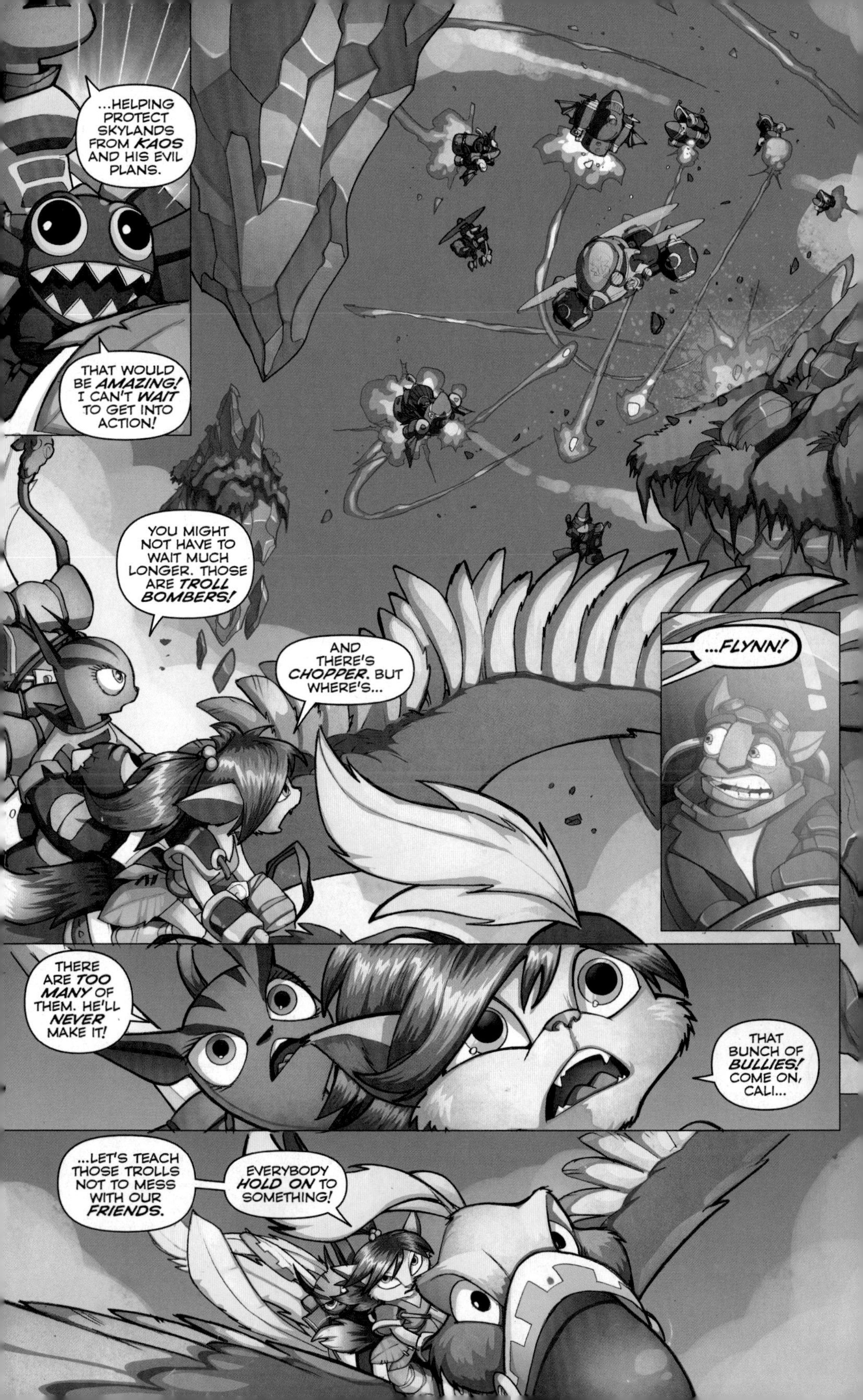
...HELPING PROTECT SKYLANDS FROM KAOS AND HIS EVIL PLANS.
THAT WOULD BE AMAZING! I CAN'T WAIT TO GET INTO ACTION!
YOU MIGHT NOT HAVE TO WAIT MUCH LONGER. THOSE ARE TROLL BOMBERS!
AND THERE'S CHOPPER. BUT WHERE'S...
...FLYNN!
THERE ARE TOO MANY OF THEM. HE'LL NEVER MAKE IT!
THAT BUNCH OF BULLIES! COME ON, CALI...
...LET'S TEACH THOSE TROLLS NOT TO MESS WITH OUR FRIENDS.
EVERYBODY HOLD ON TO SOMETHING!

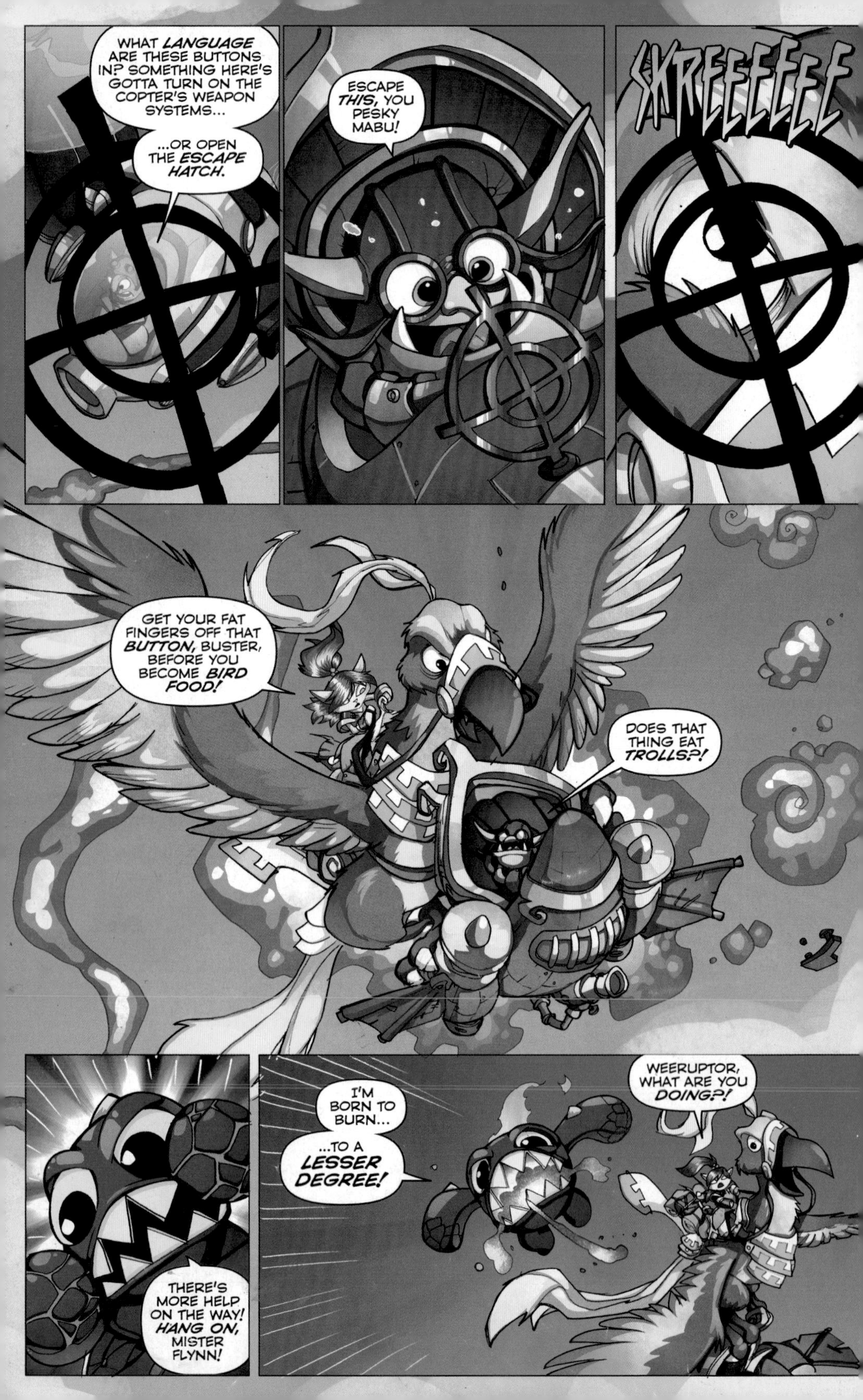
WHAT LANGUAGE ARE THESE BUTTONS IN? SOMETHING HERE'S GOTTA TURN ON THE COPTER'S WEAPON SYSTEMS...
...OR OPEN THE ESCAPE HATCH.
ESCAPE THIS, YOU PESKY MABU!
SKREEEEEE
GET YOUR FAT FINGERS OFF THAT BUTTON, BUSTER, BEFORE YOU BECOME BIRD FOOD!
DOES THAT THING EAT TROLLS?!
THERE'S MORE HELP ON THE WAY! HANG ON, MISTER FLYNN!
I'M BORN TO BURN...
...TO A LESSER DEGREE!
WEERUPTOR, WHAT ARE YOU DOING?!

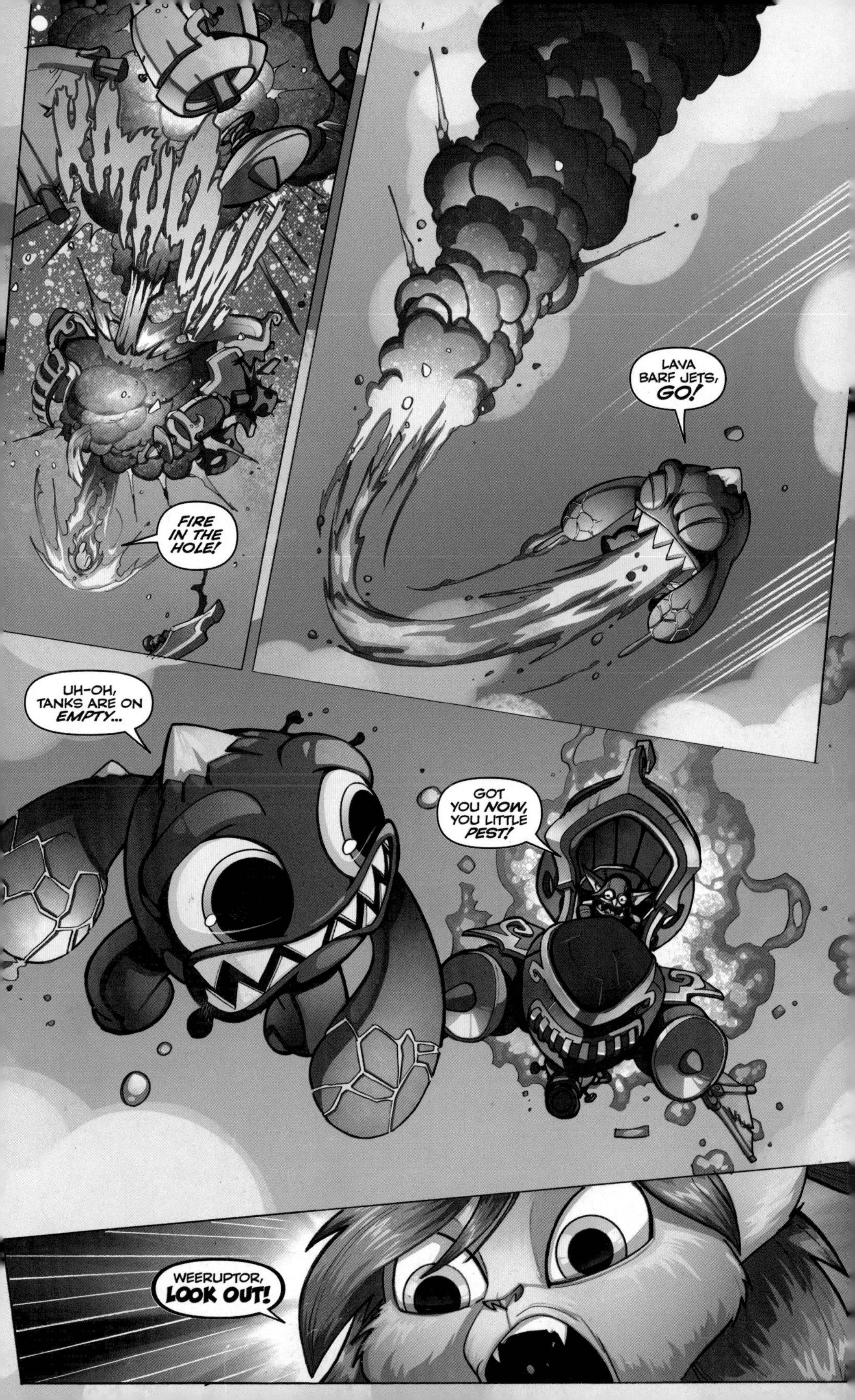
FIRE IN THE HOLE!
LAVA BARF JETS, GO!
UH-OH, TANKS ARE ON EMPTY...
GOT YOU NOW, YOU LITTLE PEST!
WEERUPTOR, LOOK OUT!

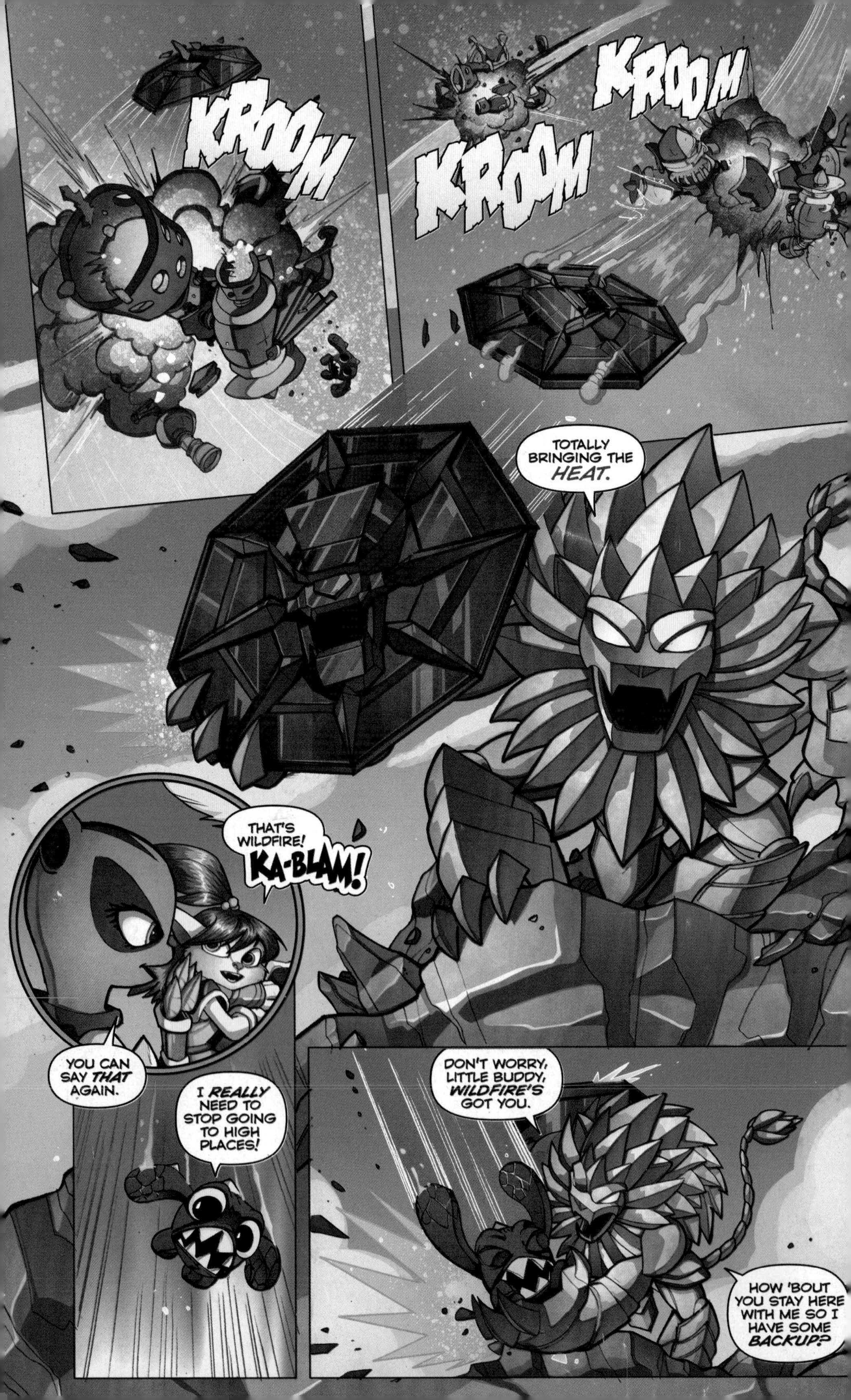

KROOM
KROOM
KROOM
TOTALLY BRINGING THE HEAT.
THAT'S WILDFIRE! KA-BLAM!
YOU CAN SAY THAT AGAIN.
I REALLY NEED TO STOP GOING TO HIGH PLACES!
DON'T WORRY, LITTLE BUDDY, WILDFIRE'S GOT YOU.
HOW 'BOUT YOU STAY HERE WITH ME SO I HAVE SOME BACKUP?

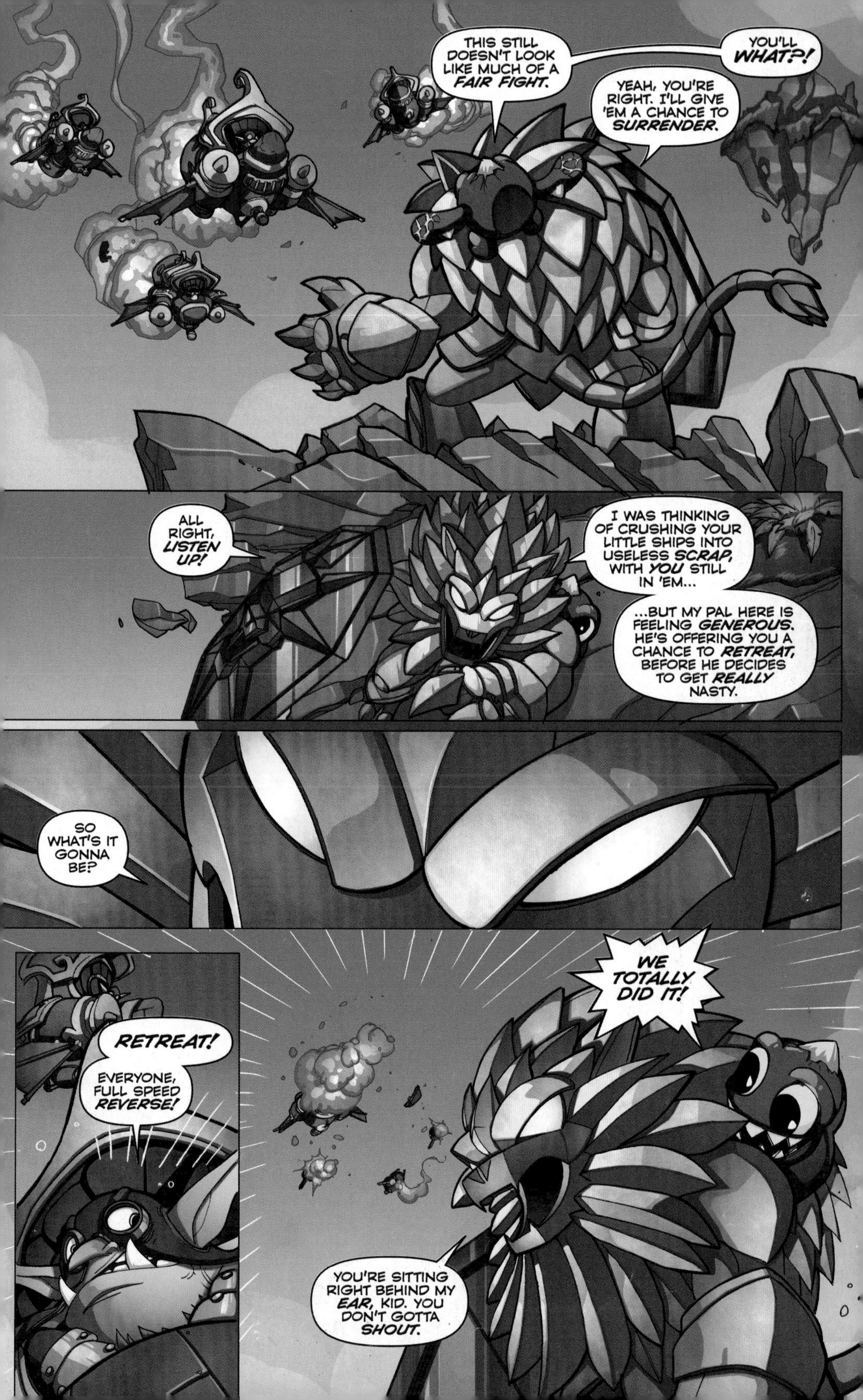
THIS STILL DOESN'T LOOK LIKE MUCH OF A FAIR FIGHT.
YOU'LL WHAT?!
YEAH, YOU'RE RIGHT. I'LL GIVE 'EM A CHANCE TO SURRENDER.
ALL RIGHT, LISTEN UP!
I WAS THINKING OF CRUSHING YOUR LITTLE SHIPS INTO USELESS SCRAP, WITH YOU STILL IN 'EM...
...BUT MY PAL HERE IS FEELING GENEROUS. HE'S OFFERING YOU A CHANCE TO RETREAT, BEFORE HE DECIDES TO GET REALLY NASTY.
SO WHAT'S IT GONNA BE?
RETREAT!
EVERYONE, FULL SPEED REVERSE!
WE TOTALLY DID IT!
YOU'RE SITTING RIGHT BEHIND MY EAR, KID. YOU DON'T GOTTA SHOUT.

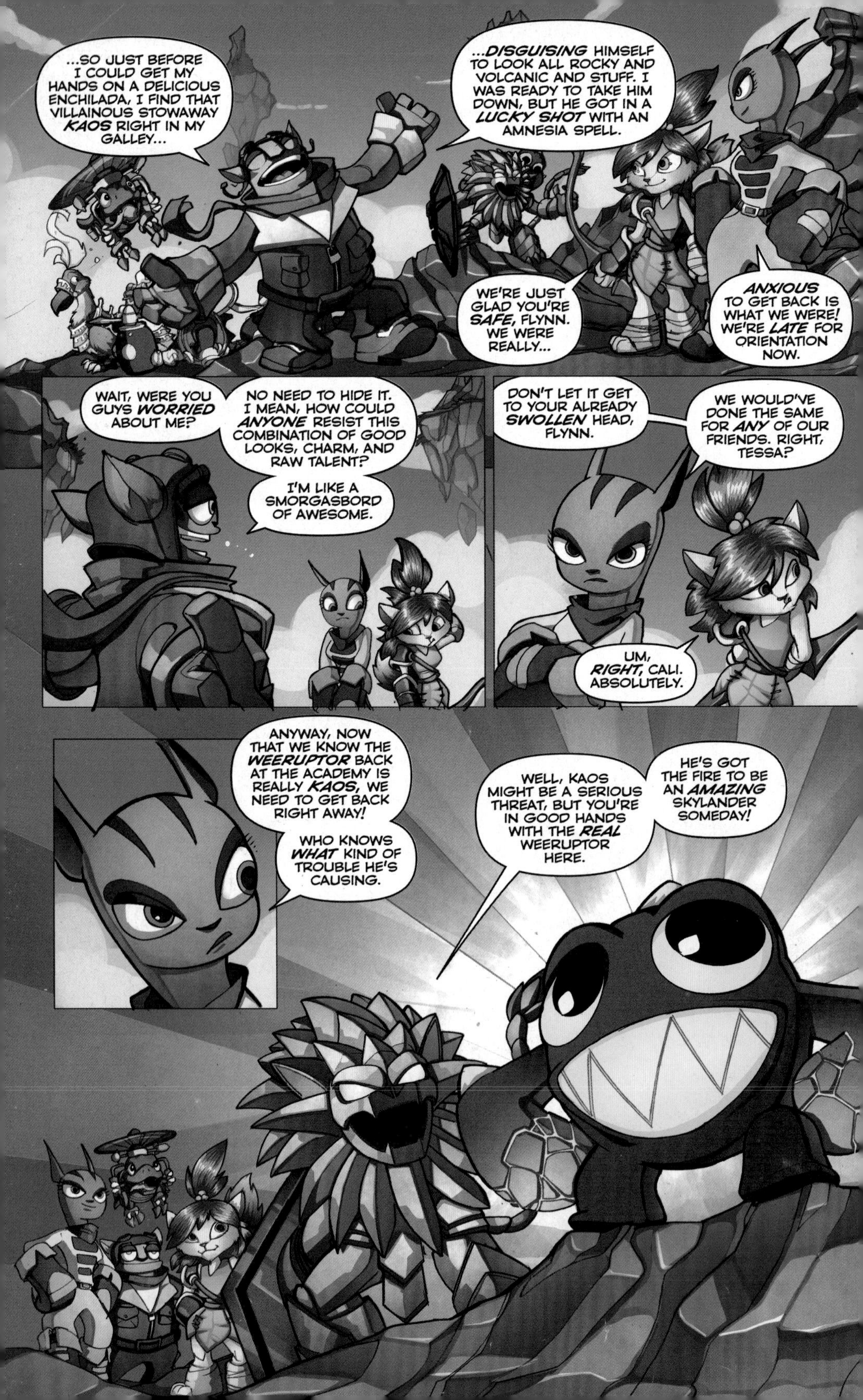
...SO JUST BEFORE I COULD GET MY HANDS ON A DELICIOUS ENCHILADA, I FIND THAT VILLAINOUS STOWAWAY KAOS RIGHT IN MY GALLEY...
...DISGUISING HIMSELF TO LOOK ALL ROCKY AND VOLCANIC AND STUFF. I WAS READY TO TAKE HIM DOWN, BUT HE GOT IN A LUCKY SHOT WITH AN AMNESIA SPELL.
WE'RE JUST GLAD YOU'RE SAFE, FLYNN. WE WERE REALLY...
ANXIOUS TO GET BACK IS WHAT WE WERE! WE'RE LATE FOR ORIENTATION NOW.
WAIT, WERE YOU GUYS WORRIED ABOUT ME?
NO NEED TO HIDE IT. I MEAN, HOW COULD ANYONE RESIST THIS COMBINATION OF GOOD LOOKS, CHARM, AND RAW TALENT?
I'M LIKE A SMORGASBORD OF AWESOME.
DON'T LET IT GET TO YOUR ALREADY SWOLLEN HEAD, FLYNN.
WE WOULD'VE DONE THE SAME FOR ANY OF OUR FRIENDS. RIGHT, TESSA?
UM, RIGHT, CALI. ABSOLUTELY.
ANYWAY, NOW THAT WE KNOW THE WEERUPTOR BACK AT THE ACADEMY IS REALLY KAOS, WE NEED TO GET BACK RIGHT AWAY!
WHO KNOWS WHAT KIND OF TROUBLE HE'S CAUSING.
WELL, KAOS MIGHT BE A SERIOUS THREAT, BUT YOU'RE IN GOOD HANDS WITH THE REAL WEERUPTOR HERE.
HE'S GOT THE FIRE TO BE AN AMAZING SKYLANDER SOMEDAY!

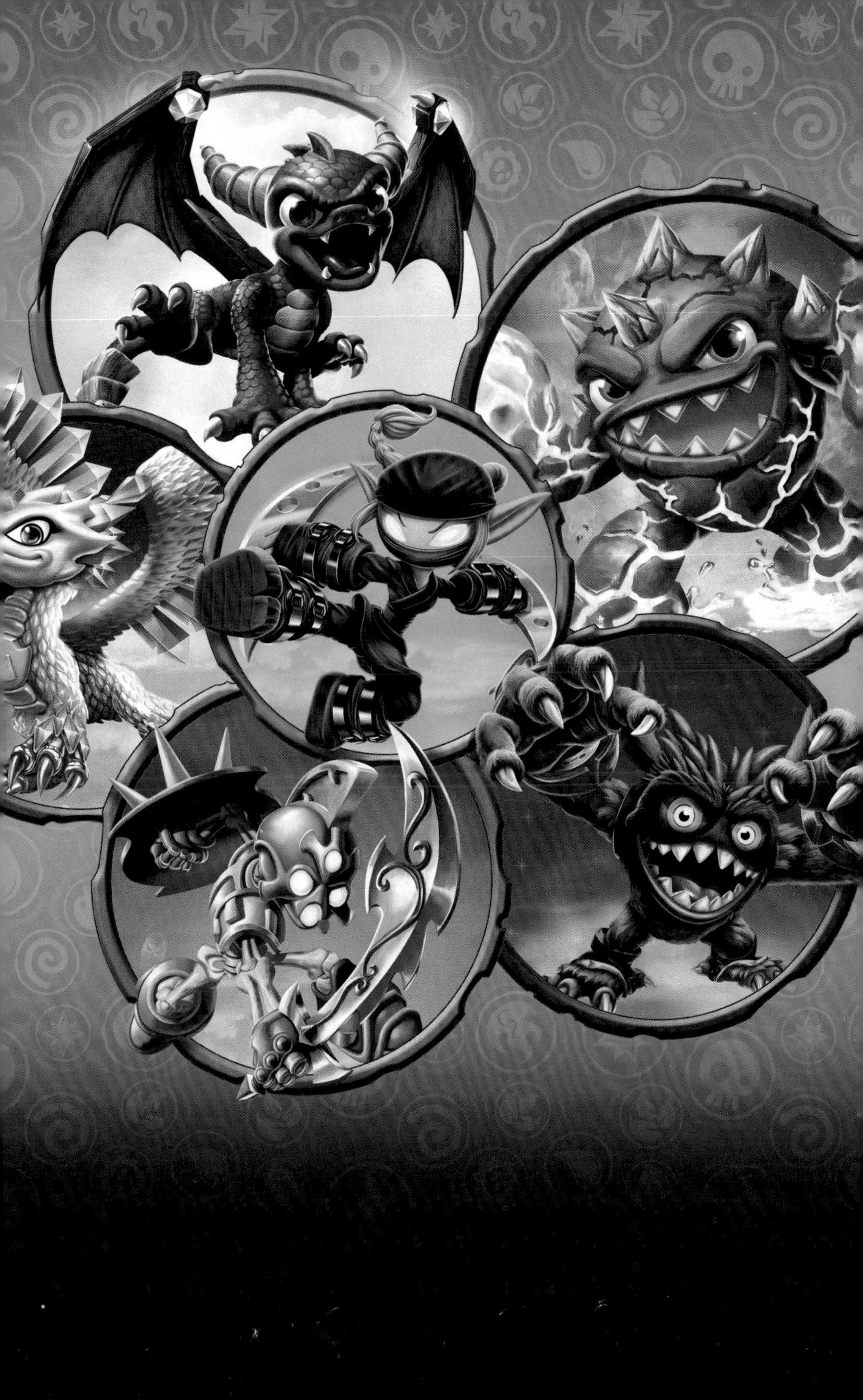

WELCOME TO SKYLANDER ACADEMY

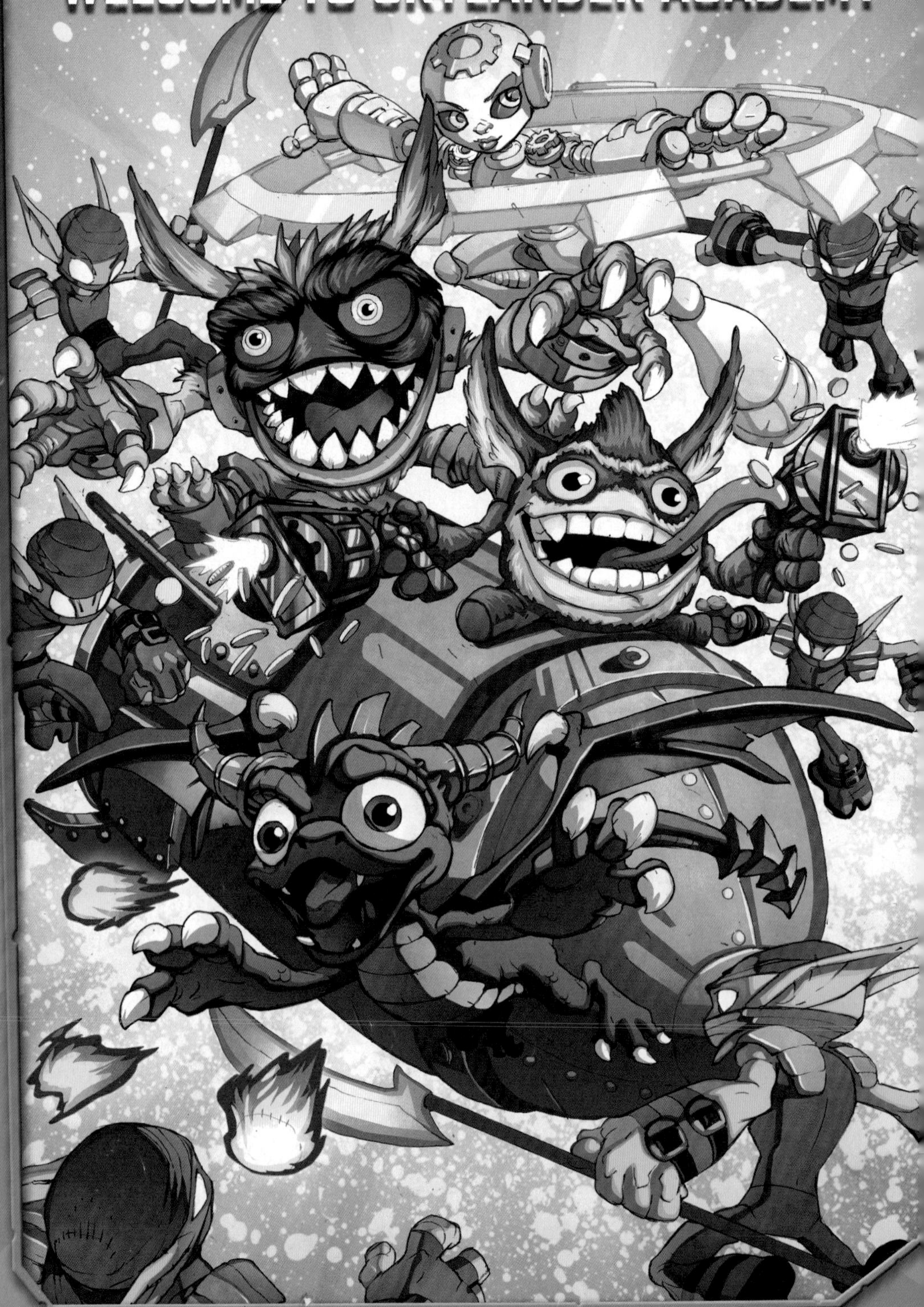

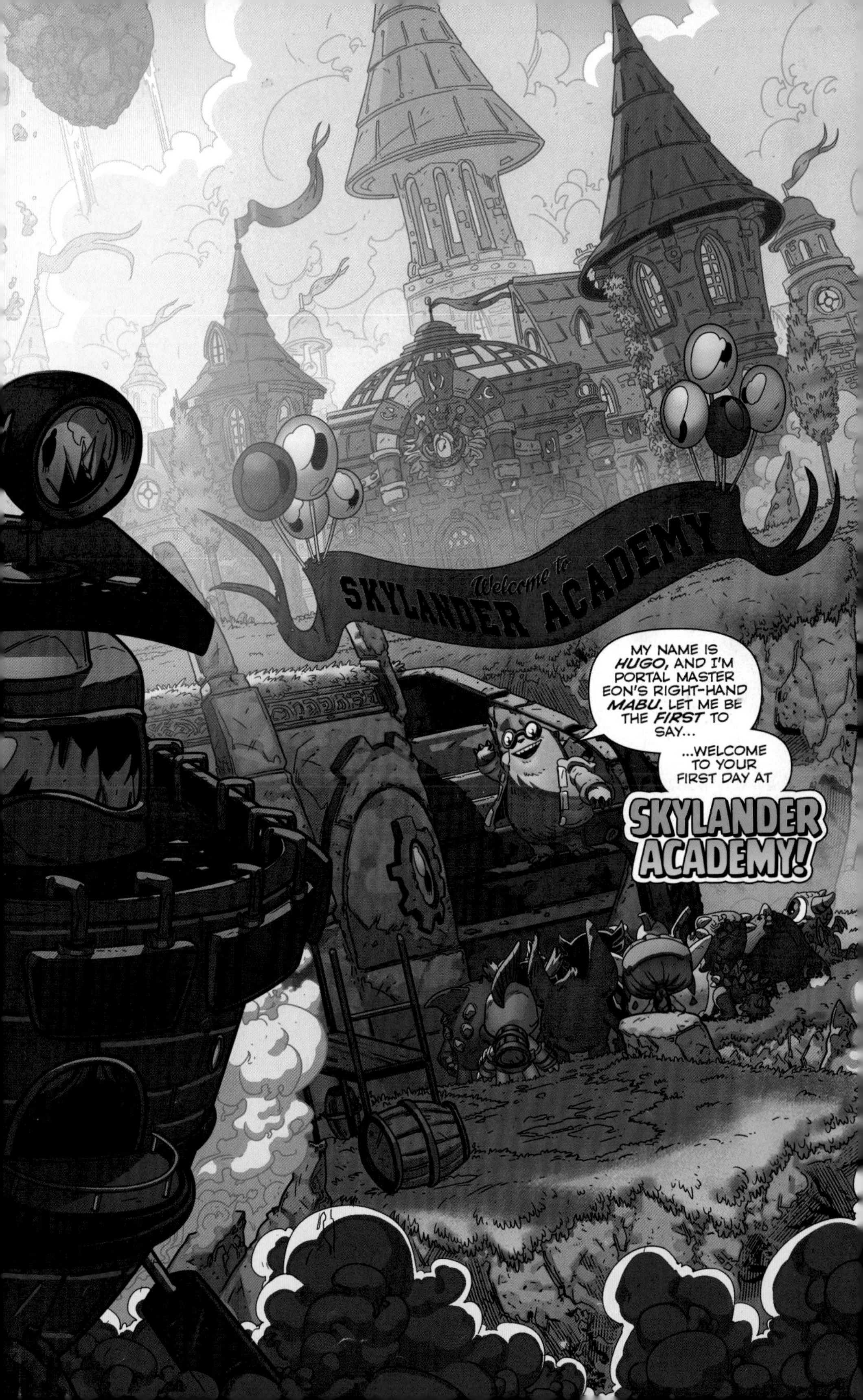

Welcome to
SKYLANDER ACADEMY
MY NAME IS HUGO, AND I'M PORTAL MASTER EON'S RIGHT-HAND MABU. LET ME BE THE FIRST TO SAY...
...WELCOME TO YOUR FIRST DAY AT
SKYLANDER ACADEMY!

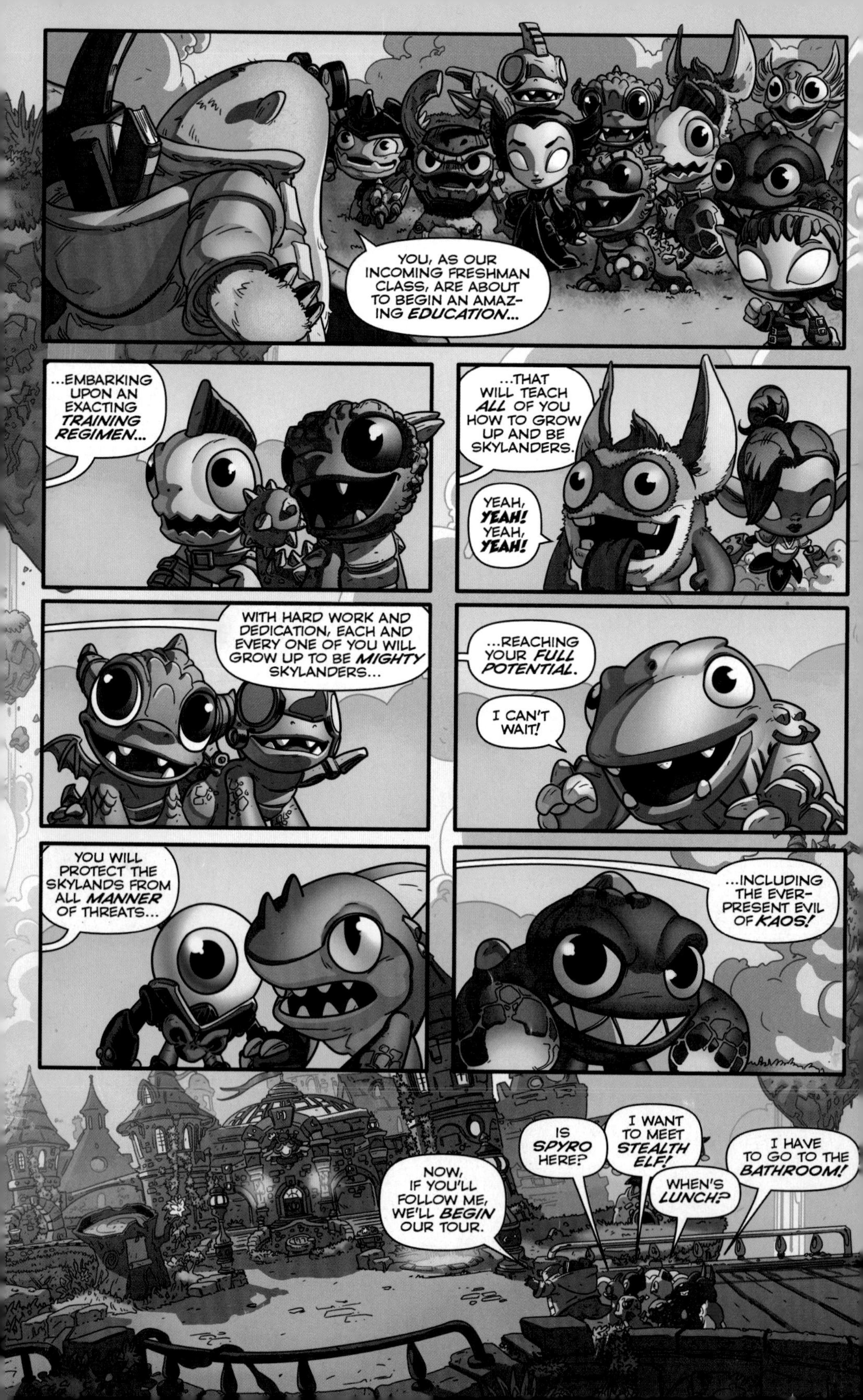
YOU, AS OUR INCOMING FRESHMAN CLASS, ARE ABOUT TO BEGIN AN AMAZ-ING *EDUCATION*...
...EMBARKING UPON AN EXACTING *TRAINING REGIMEN*...
...THAT WILL TEACH *ALL* OF YOU HOW TO GROW UP AND BE SKYLANDERS.
YEAH, **YEAH!** YEAH, **YEAH!**
WITH HARD WORK AND DEDICATION, EACH AND EVERY ONE OF YOU WILL GROW UP TO BE *MIGHTY* SKYLANDERS...
...REACHING YOUR *FULL POTENTIAL*.
I CAN'T WAIT!
YOU WILL PROTECT THE SKYLANDS FROM ALL *MANNER* OF THREATS...
...INCLUDING THE EVER-PRESENT EVIL OF *KAOS!*
NOW, IF YOU'LL FOLLOW ME, WE'LL *BEGIN* OUR TOUR.
IS *SPYRO* HERE?
I WANT TO MEET *STEALTH ELF!*
WHEN'S *LUNCH?*
I HAVE TO GO TO THE *BATHROOM!*

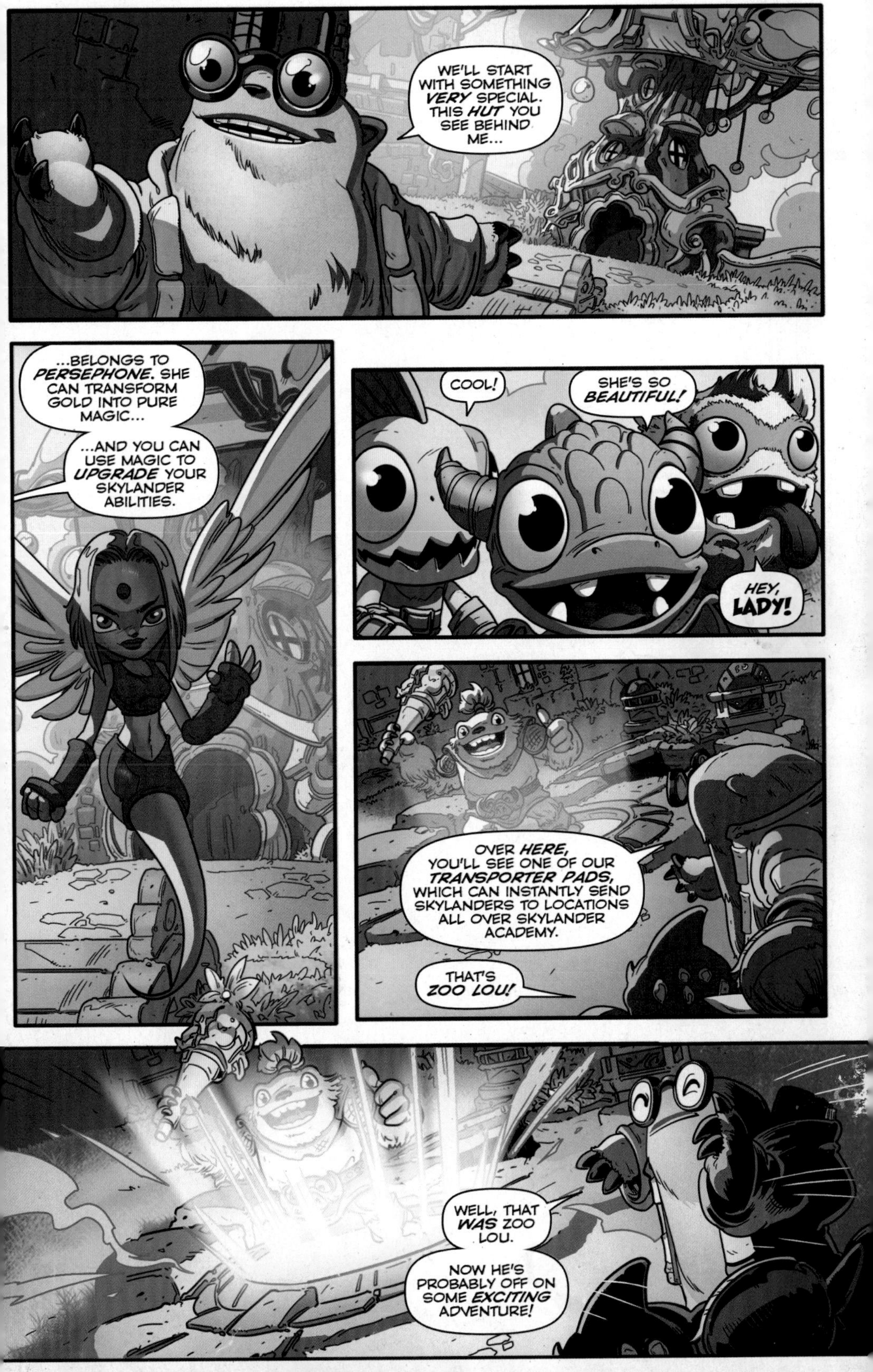
WE'LL START WITH SOMETHING VERY SPECIAL. THIS HUT YOU SEE BEHIND ME...
...BELONGS TO PERSEPHONE. SHE CAN TRANSFORM GOLD INTO PURE MAGIC...
...AND YOU CAN USE MAGIC TO UPGRADE YOUR SKYLANDER ABILITIES.
COOL!
SHE'S SO BEAUTIFUL!
HEY, LADY!
OVER HERE, YOU'LL SEE ONE OF OUR TRANSPORTER PADS, WHICH CAN INSTANTLY SEND SKYLANDERS TO LOCATIONS ALL OVER SKYLANDER ACADEMY.
THAT'S ZOO LOU!
WELL, THAT WAS ZOO LOU.
NOW HE'S PROBABLY OFF ON SOME EXCITING ADVENTURE!

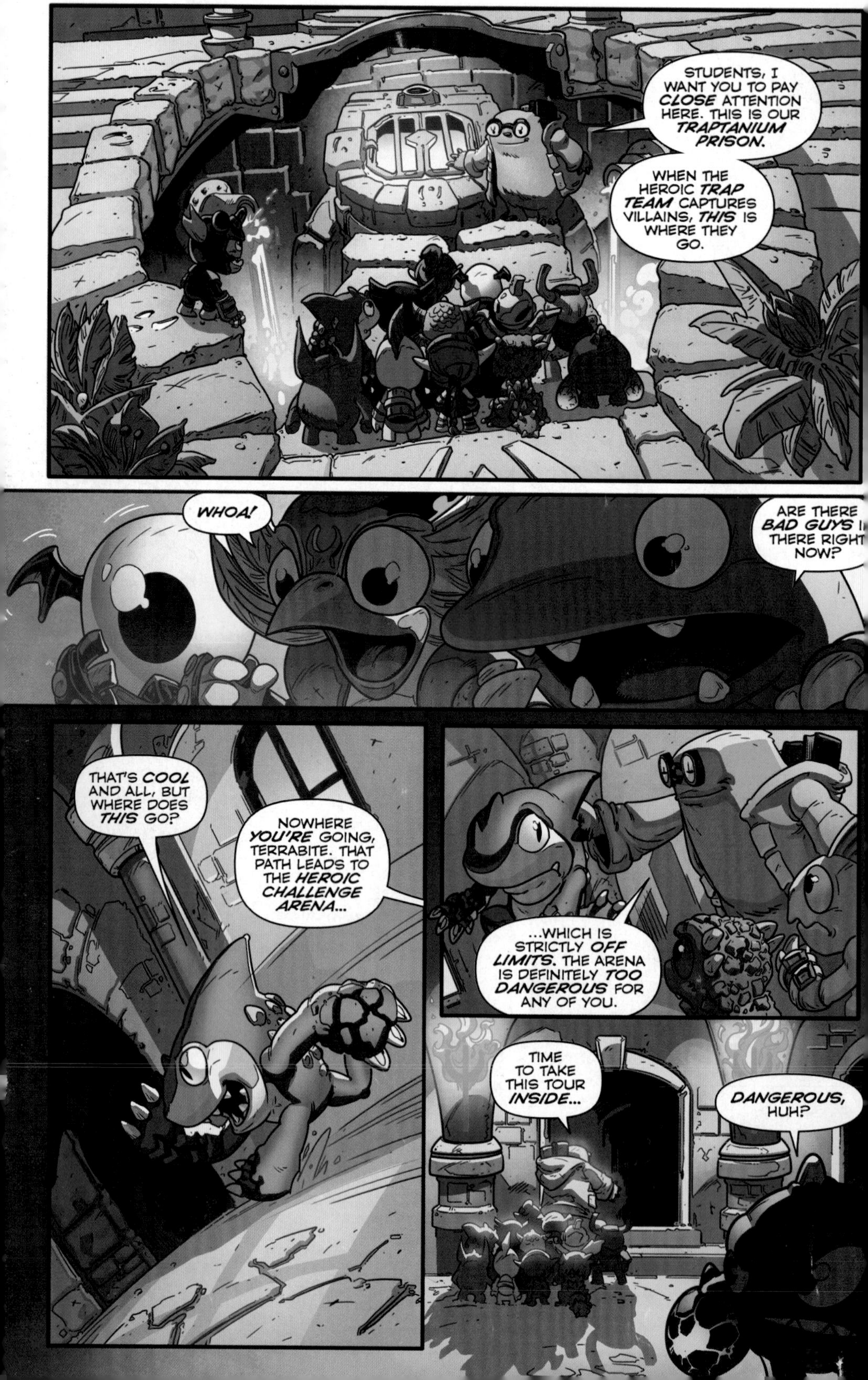
STUDENTS, I WANT YOU TO PAY CLOSE ATTENTION HERE. THIS IS OUR TRAPTANIUM PRISON.
WHEN THE HEROIC TRAP TEAM CAPTURES VILLAINS, THIS IS WHERE THEY GO.
WHOA!
ARE THERE BAD GUYS I THERE RIGHT NOW?
THAT'S COOL AND ALL, BUT WHERE DOES THIS GO?
NOWHERE YOU'RE GOING, TERRABITE. THAT PATH LEADS TO THE HEROIC CHALLENGE ARENA...
...WHICH IS STRICTLY OFF LIMITS. THE ARENA IS DEFINITELY TOO DANGEROUS FOR ANY OF YOU.
TIME TO TAKE THIS TOUR INSIDE...
DANGEROUS, HUH?

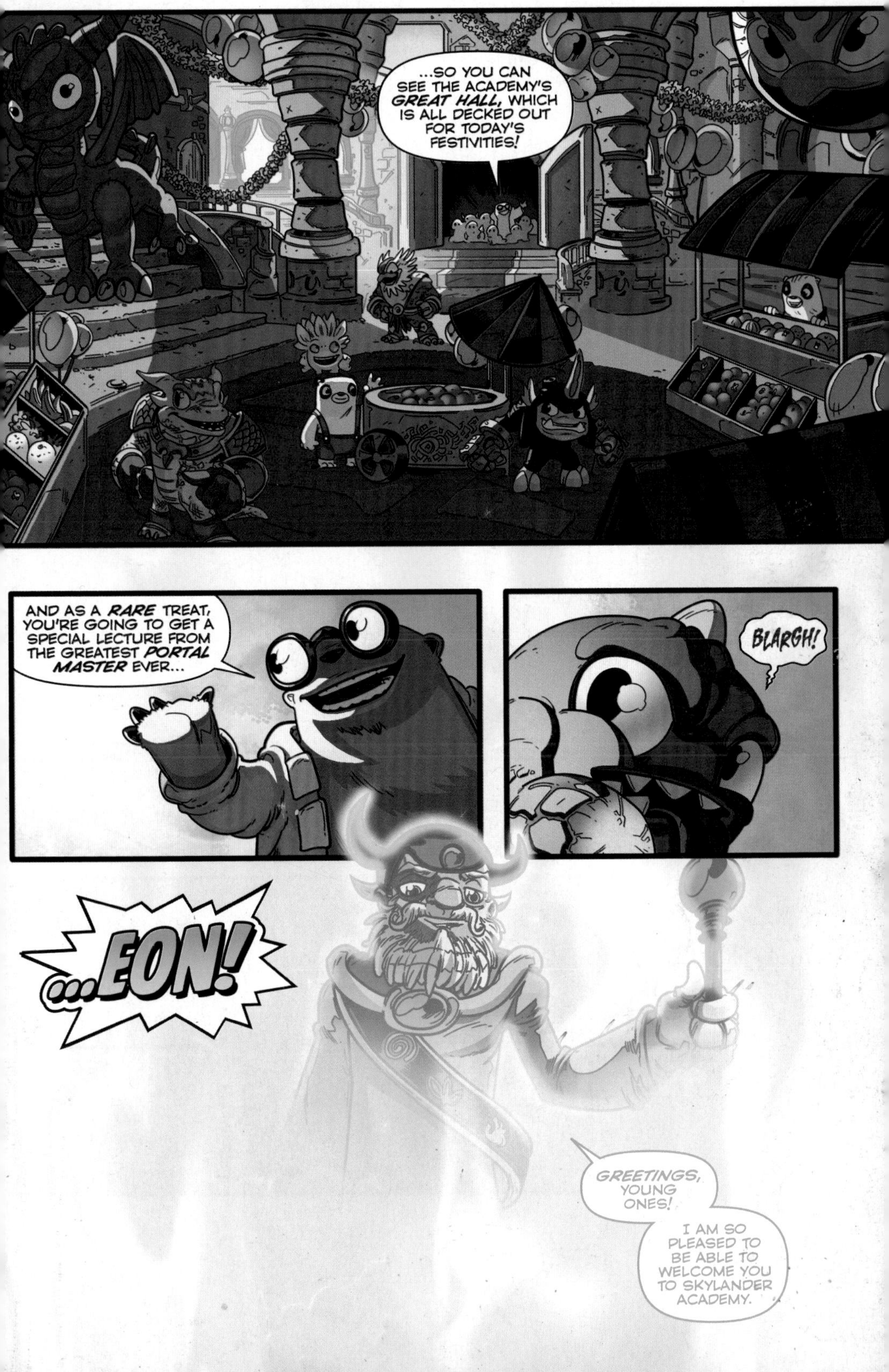
...SO YOU CAN SEE THE ACADEMY'S GREAT HALL, WHICH IS ALL DECKED OUT FOR TODAY'S FESTIVITIES!
AND AS A RARE TREAT, YOU'RE GOING TO GET A SPECIAL LECTURE FROM THE GREATEST PORTAL MASTER EVER...
BLARGH!
...EON!
GREETINGS, YOUNG ONES!
I AM SO PLEASED TO BE ABLE TO WELCOME YOU TO SKYLANDER ACADEMY.

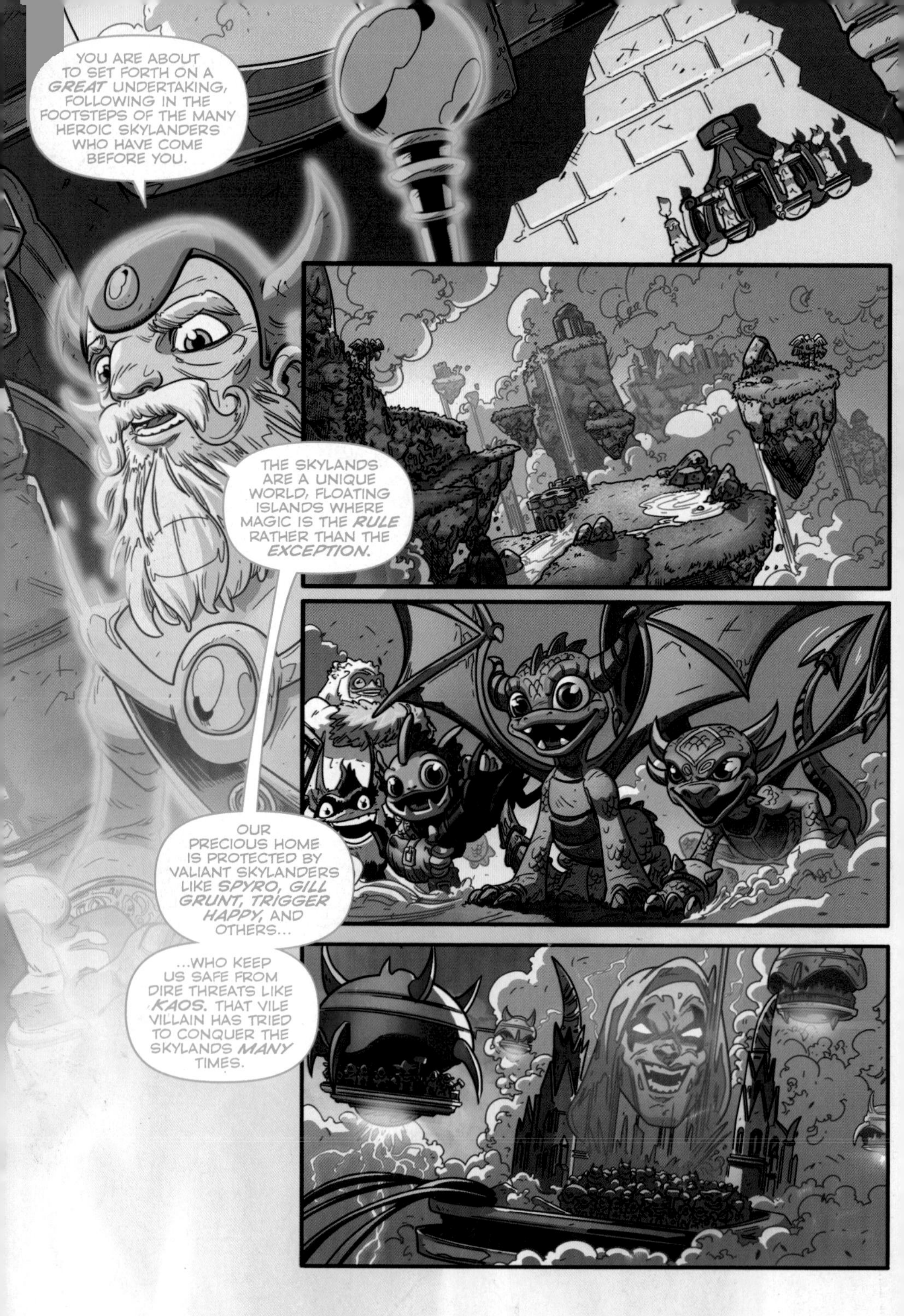
YOU ARE ABOUT TO SET FORTH ON A GREAT UNDERTAKING, FOLLOWING IN THE FOOTSTEPS OF THE MANY HEROIC SKYLANDERS WHO HAVE COME BEFORE YOU.
THE SKYLANDS ARE A UNIQUE WORLD, FLOATING ISLANDS WHERE MAGIC IS THE RULE RATHER THAN THE EXCEPTION.
OUR PRECIOUS HOME IS PROTECTED BY VALIANT SKYLANDERS LIKE SPYRO, GILL GRUNT, TRIGGER HAPPY, AND OTHERS...
...WHO KEEP US SAFE FROM DIRE THREATS LIKE KAOS. THAT VILE VILLAIN HAS TRIED TO CONQUER THE SKYLANDS MANY TIMES.

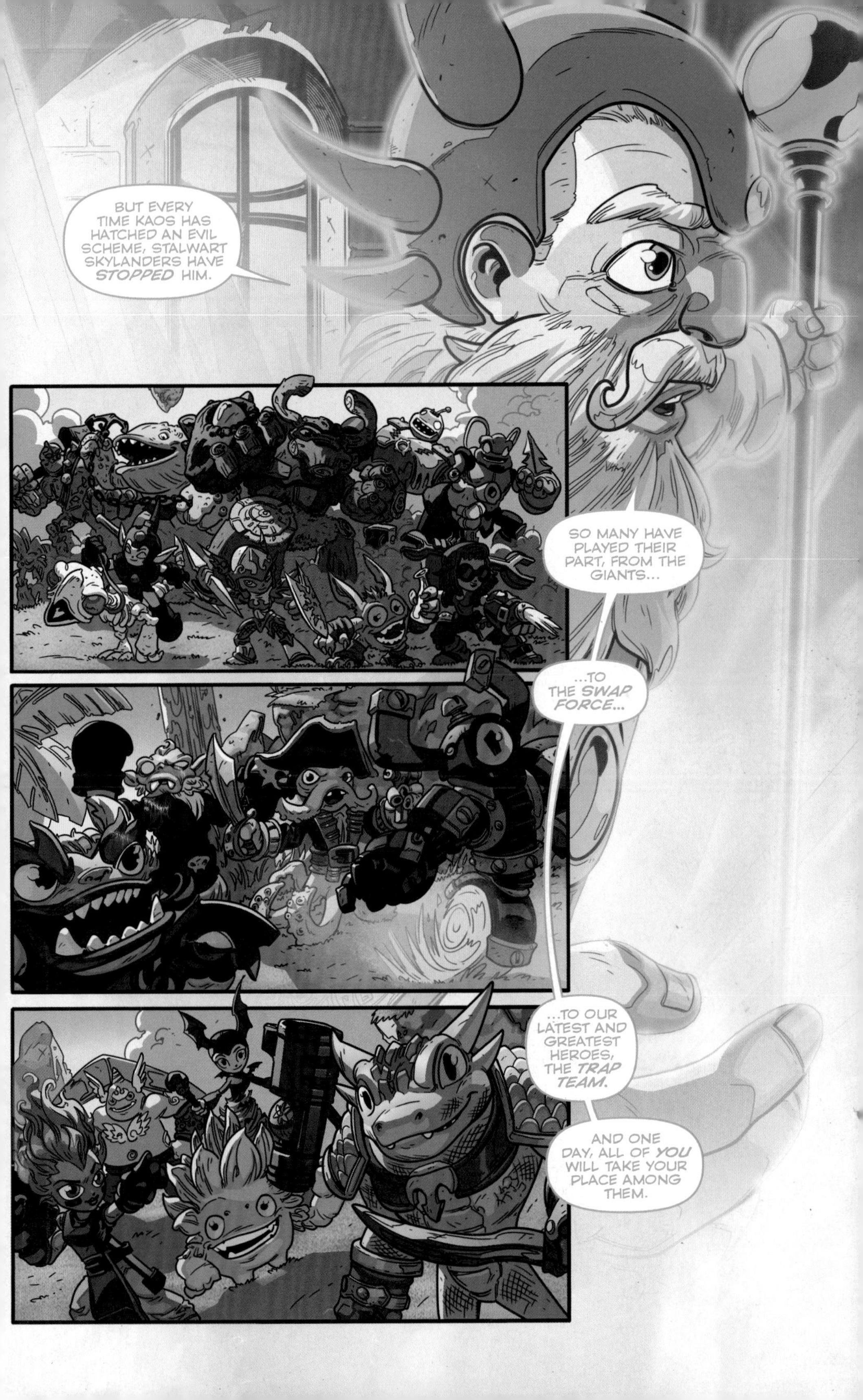
BUT EVERY TIME KAOS HAS HATCHED AN EVIL SCHEME, STALWART SKYLANDERS HAVE STOPPED HIM.
SO MANY HAVE PLAYED THEIR PART, FROM THE GIANTS...
...TO THE SWAP FORCE...
...TO OUR LATEST AND GREATEST HEROES, THE TRAP TEAM.
AND ONE DAY, ALL OF YOU WILL TAKE YOUR PLACE AMONG THEM.

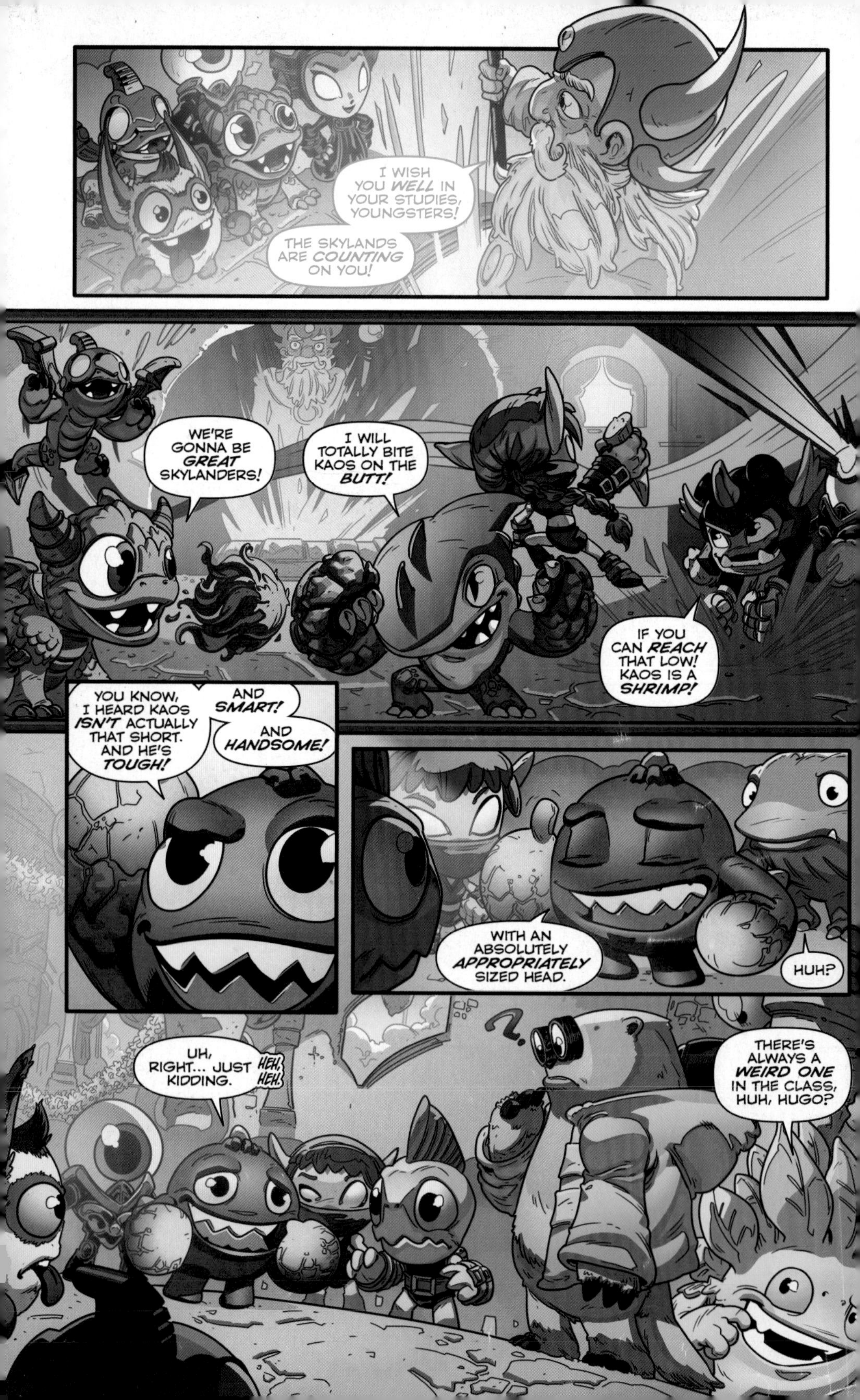
I WISH YOU WELL IN YOUR STUDIES, YOUNGSTERS!
THE SKYLANDS ARE COUNTING ON YOU!
WE'RE GONNA BE GREAT SKYLANDERS!
I WILL TOTALLY BITE KAOS ON THE BUTT!
IF YOU CAN REACH THAT LOW! KAOS IS A SHRIMP!
YOU KNOW, I HEARD KAOS ISN'T ACTUALLY THAT SHORT. AND HE'S TOUGH!
AND SMART!
AND HANDSOME!
WITH AN ABSOLUTELY APPROPRIATELY SIZED HEAD.
HUH?
UH, RIGHT... JUST KIDDING.
HEH, HEH.
THERE'S ALWAYS A WEIRD ONE IN THE CLASS, HUH, HUGO?

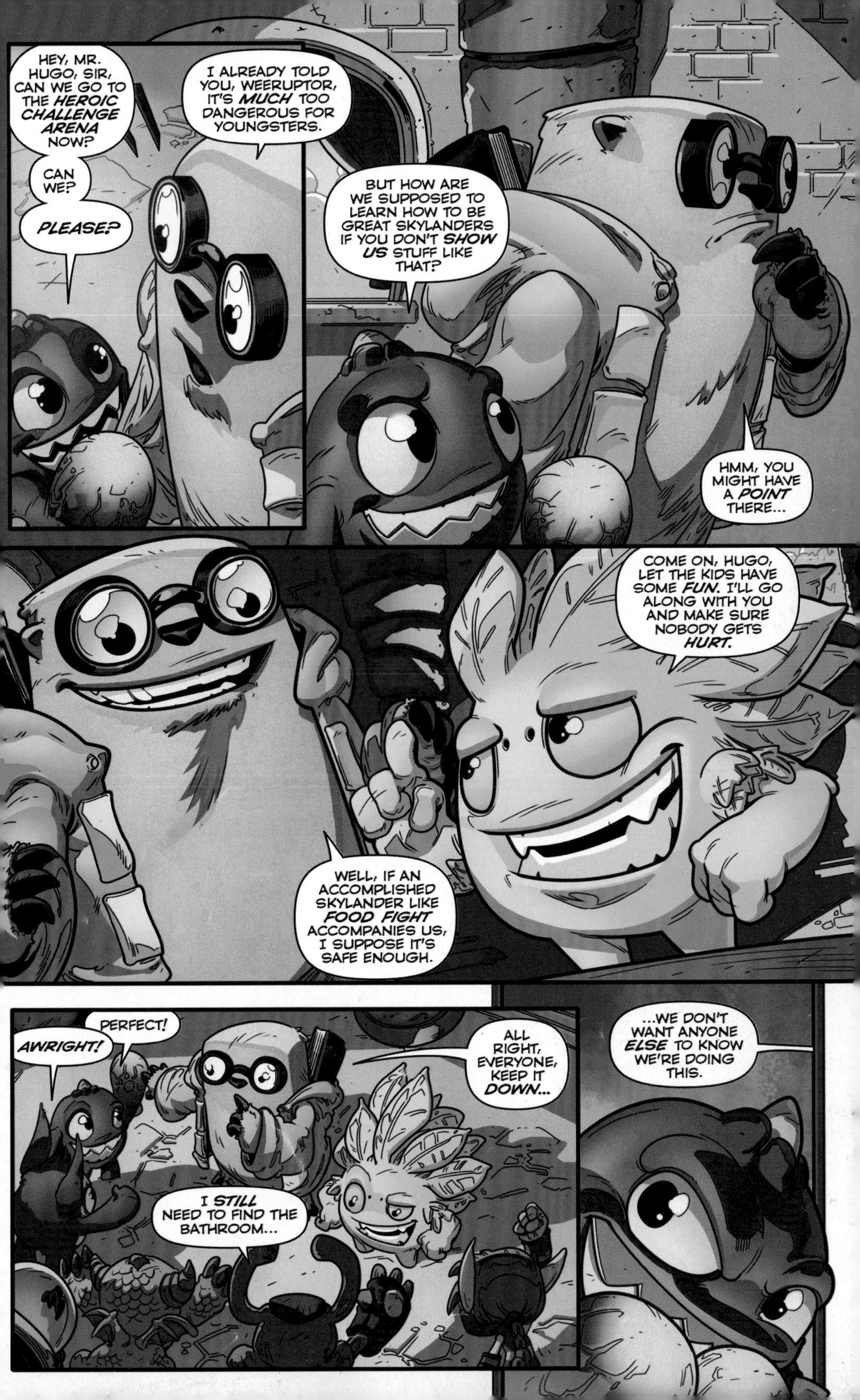
HEY, MR. HUGO, SIR, CAN WE GO TO THE HEROIC CHALLENGE ARENA NOW?
CAN WE?
PLEASE?
I ALREADY TOLD YOU, WEERUPTOR, IT'S MUCH TOO DANGEROUS FOR YOUNGSTERS.
BUT HOW ARE WE SUPPOSED TO LEARN HOW TO BE GREAT SKYLANDERS IF YOU DON'T SHOW US STUFF LIKE THAT?
HMM, YOU MIGHT HAVE A POINT THERE...
COME ON, HUGO, LET THE KIDS HAVE SOME FUN. I'LL GO ALONG WITH YOU AND MAKE SURE NOBODY GETS HURT.
WELL, IF AN ACCOMPLISHED SKYLANDER LIKE FOOD FIGHT ACCOMPANIES US, I SUPPOSE IT'S SAFE ENOUGH.
AWRIGHT!
PERFECT!
ALL RIGHT, EVERYONE, KEEP IT DOWN...
I STILL NEED TO FIND THE BATHROOM...
...WE DON'T WANT ANYONE ELSE TO KNOW WE'RE DOING THIS.

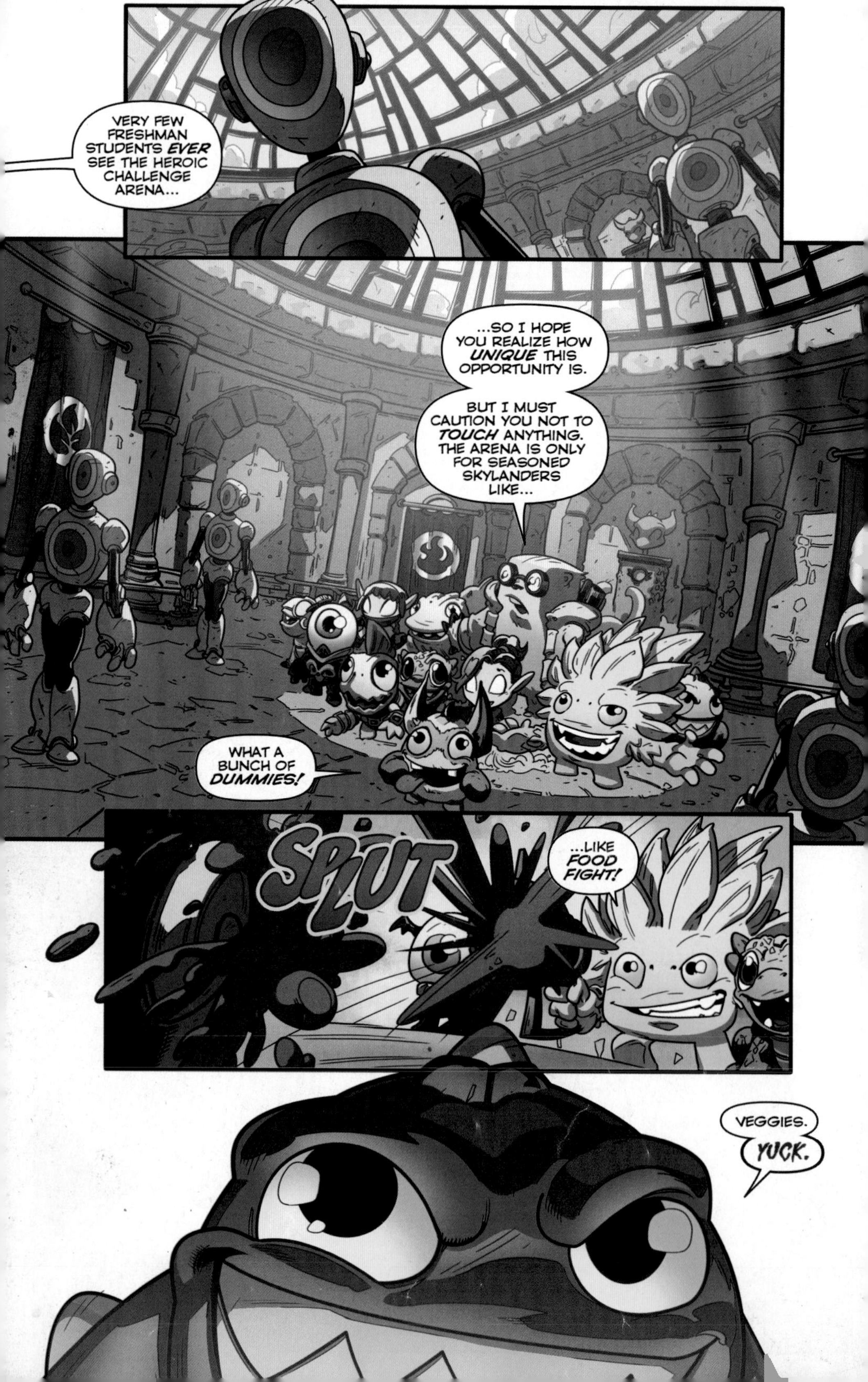
VERY FEW FRESHMAN STUDENTS EVER SEE THE HEROIC CHALLENGE ARENA...
...SO I HOPE YOU REALIZE HOW UNIQUE THIS OPPORTUNITY IS.
BUT I MUST CAUTION YOU NOT TO TOUCH ANYTHING. THE ARENA IS ONLY FOR SEASONED SKYLANDERS LIKE...
WHAT A BUNCH OF DUMMIES!
SPLUT
...LIKE FOOD FIGHT!
VEGGIES.
YUCK.

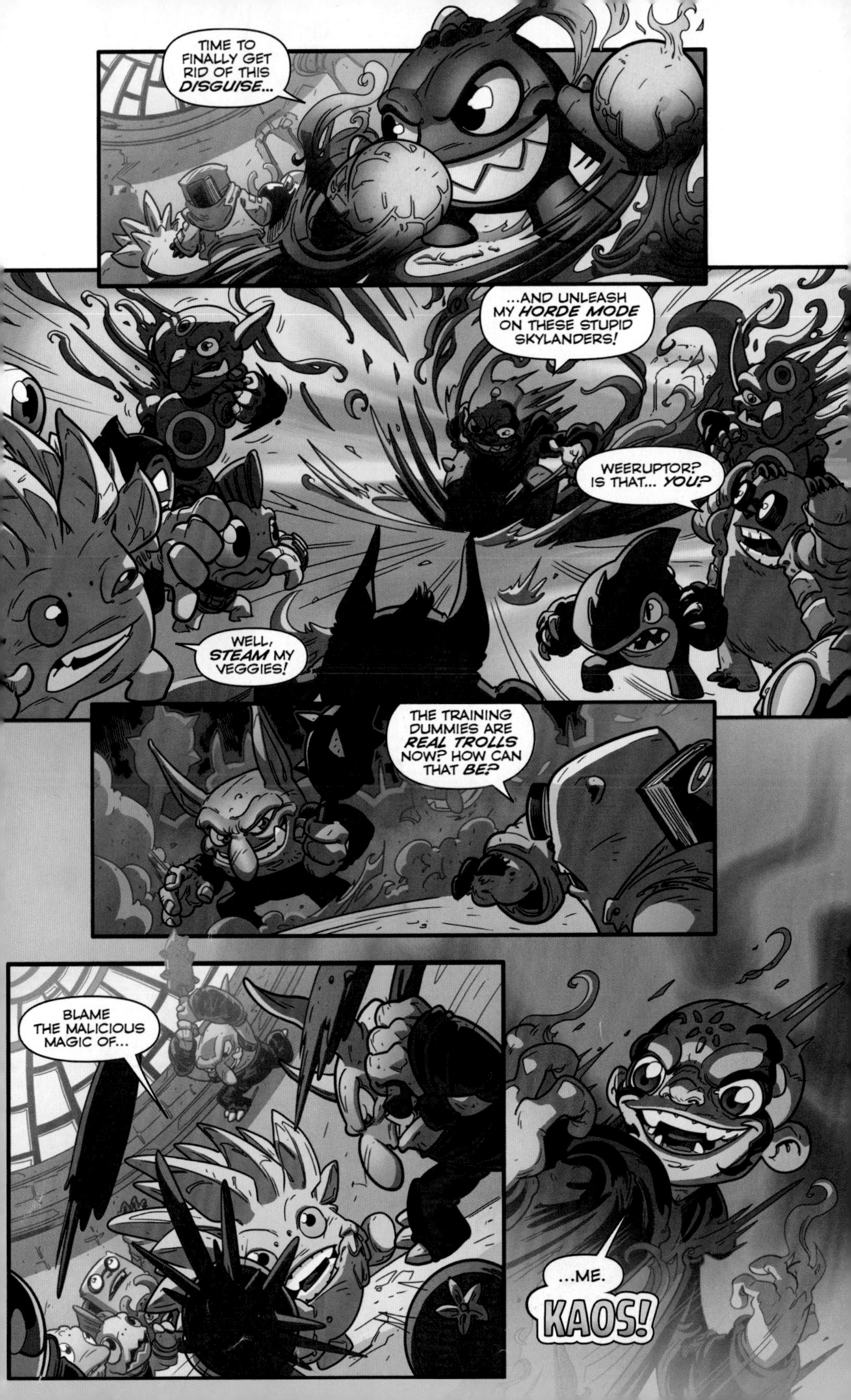
TIME TO FINALLY GET RID OF THIS *DISGUISE*...
...AND UNLEASH MY *HORDE MODE* ON THESE STUPID SKYLANDERS!
WEERUPTOR? IS THAT... *YOU?*
WELL, *STEAM* MY VEGGIES!
THE TRAINING DUMMIES ARE *REAL TROLLS* NOW? HOW CAN THAT *BE?*
BLAME THE MALICIOUS MAGIC OF...
...ME.
KAOS!

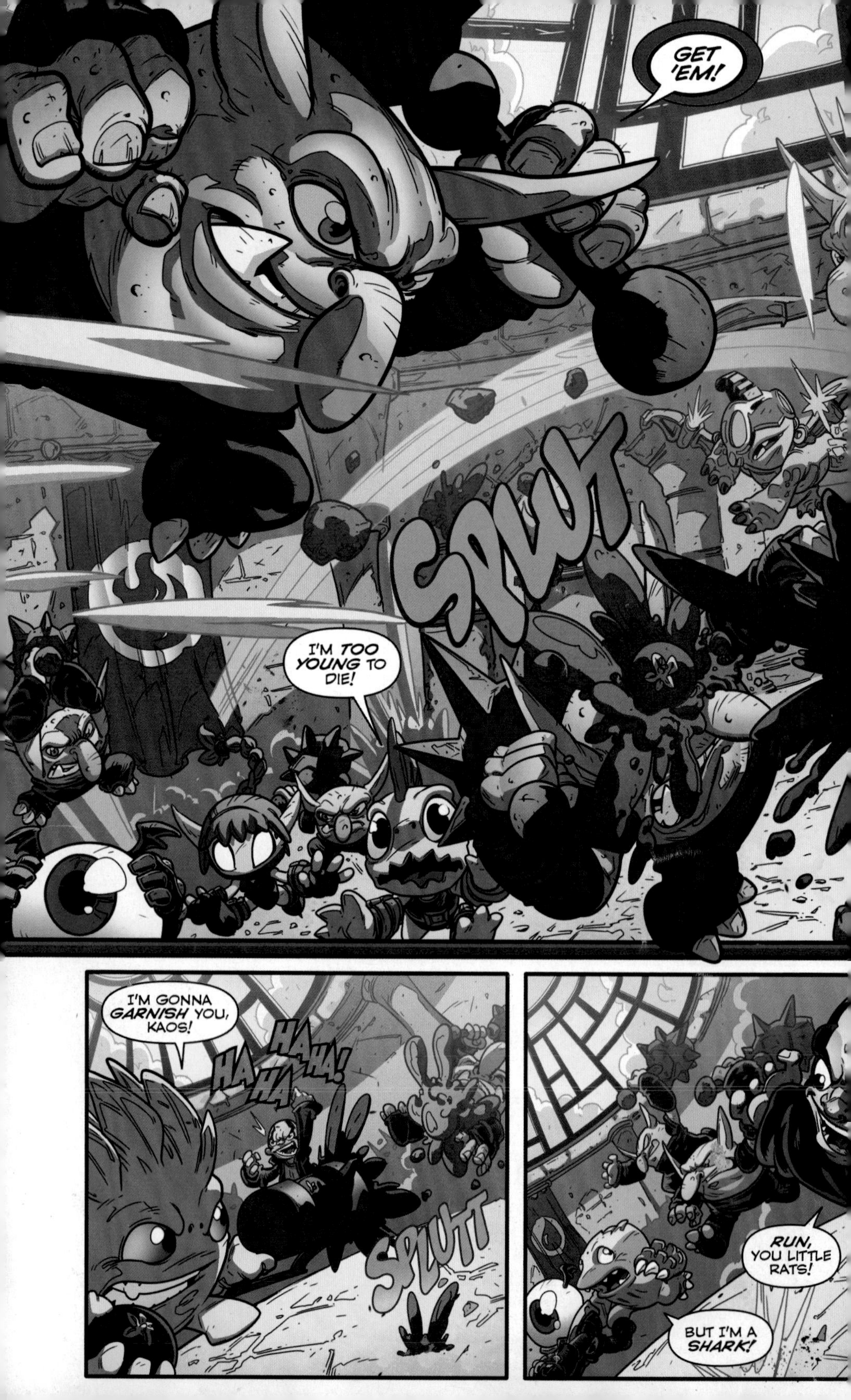
GET 'EM!
SPLUT
I'M *TOO YOUNG* TO DIE!
I'M GONNA *GARNISH* YOU, KAOS!
HA HA HA HA!
SPLUTT
RUN, YOU LITTLE RATS!
BUT I'M A *SHARK!*

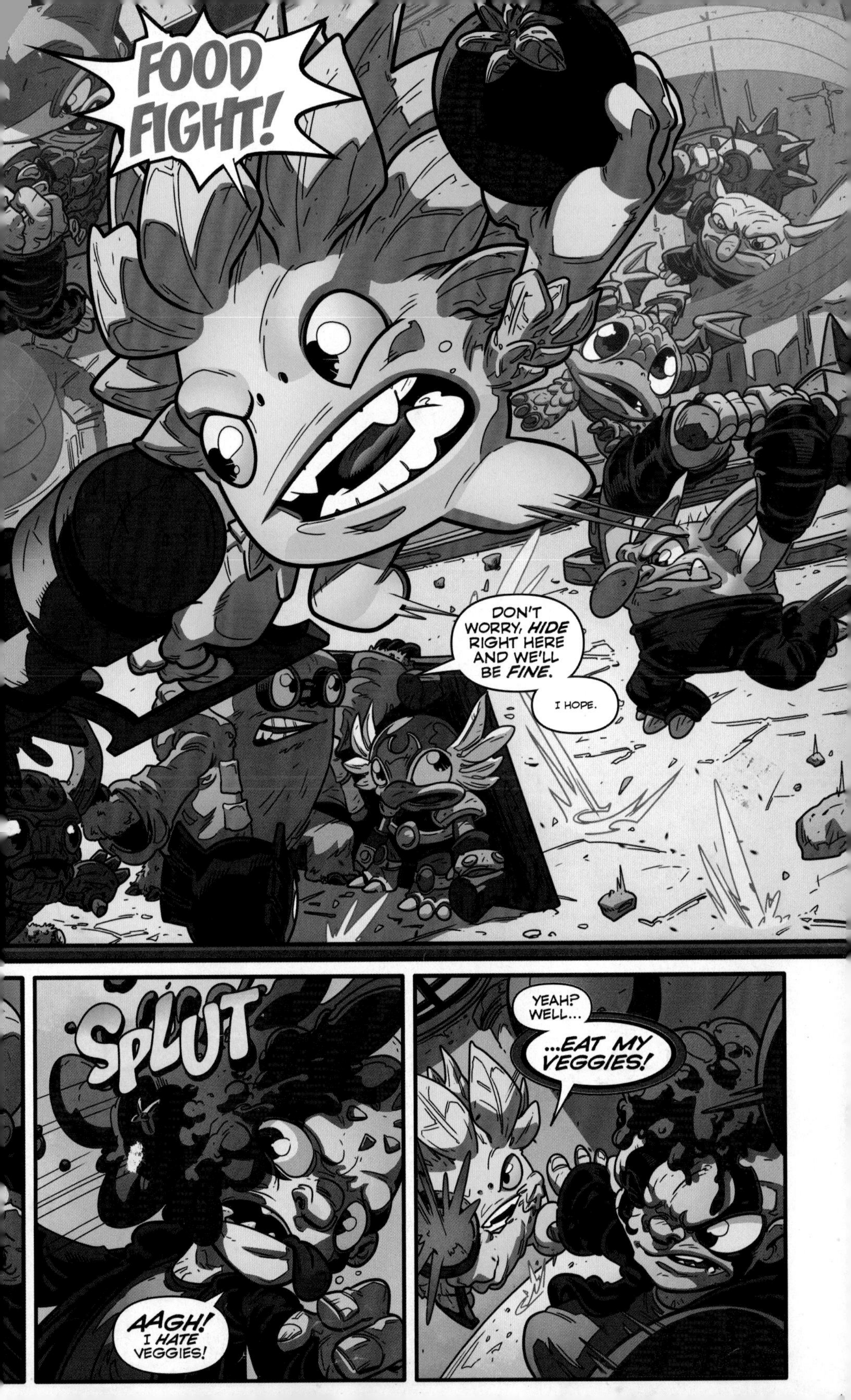
FOOD FIGHT!
DON'T WORRY, HIDE RIGHT HERE AND WE'LL BE FINE.
I HOPE.
SPLUT
AAGH! I HATE VEGGIES!
YEAH? WELL...
...EAT MY VEGGIES!

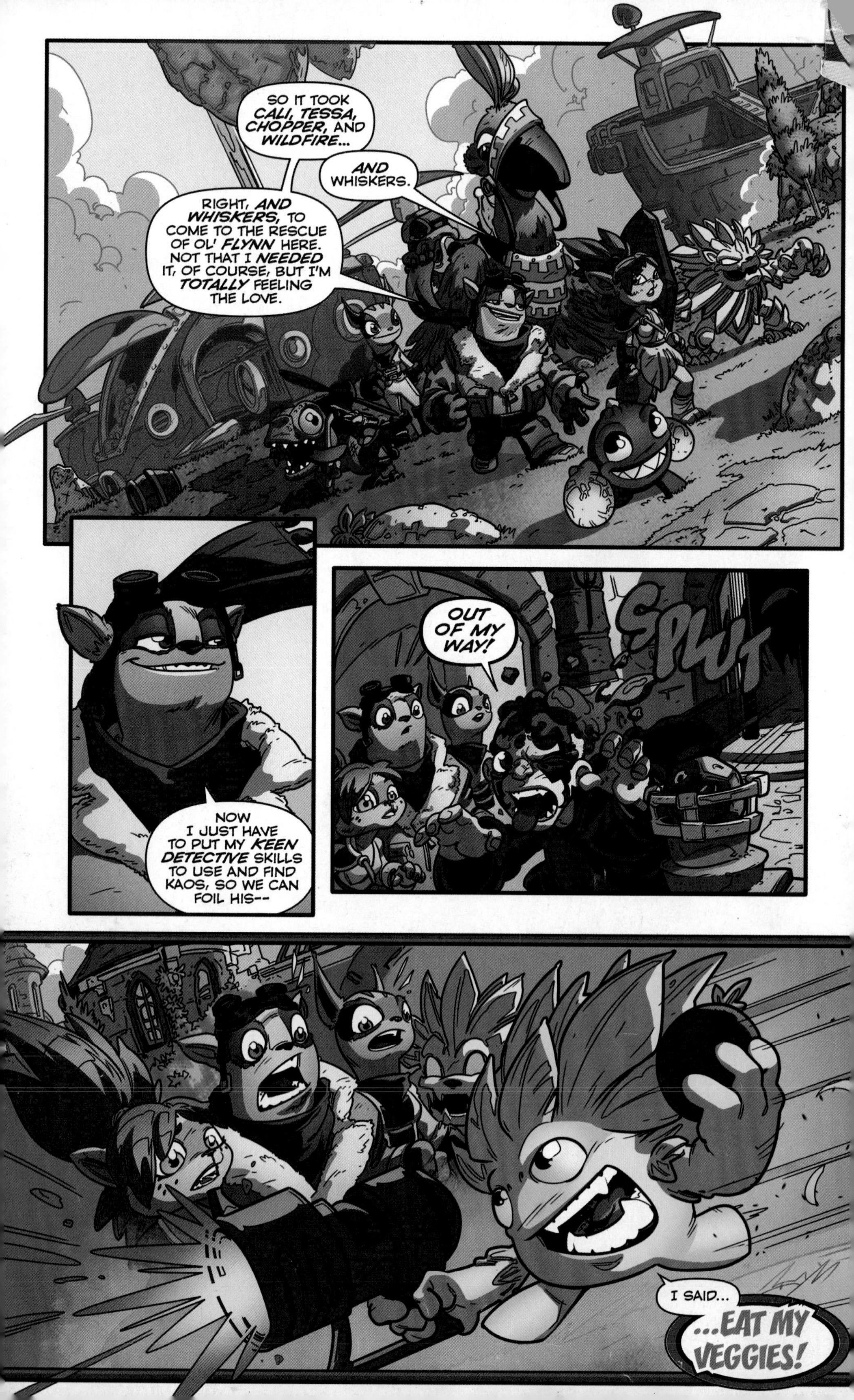
SO IT TOOK CALI, TESSA, CHOPPER, AND WILDFIRE...
AND WHISKERS.
RIGHT, AND WHISKERS, TO COME TO THE RESCUE OF OL' FLYNN HERE. NOT THAT I NEEDED IT, OF COURSE, BUT I'M TOTALLY FEELING THE LOVE.
NOW I JUST HAVE TO PUT MY KEEN DETECTIVE SKILLS TO USE AND FIND KAOS, SO WE CAN FOIL HIS--
OUT OF MY WAY!
SPLUT
I SAID...
...EAT MY VEGGIES!

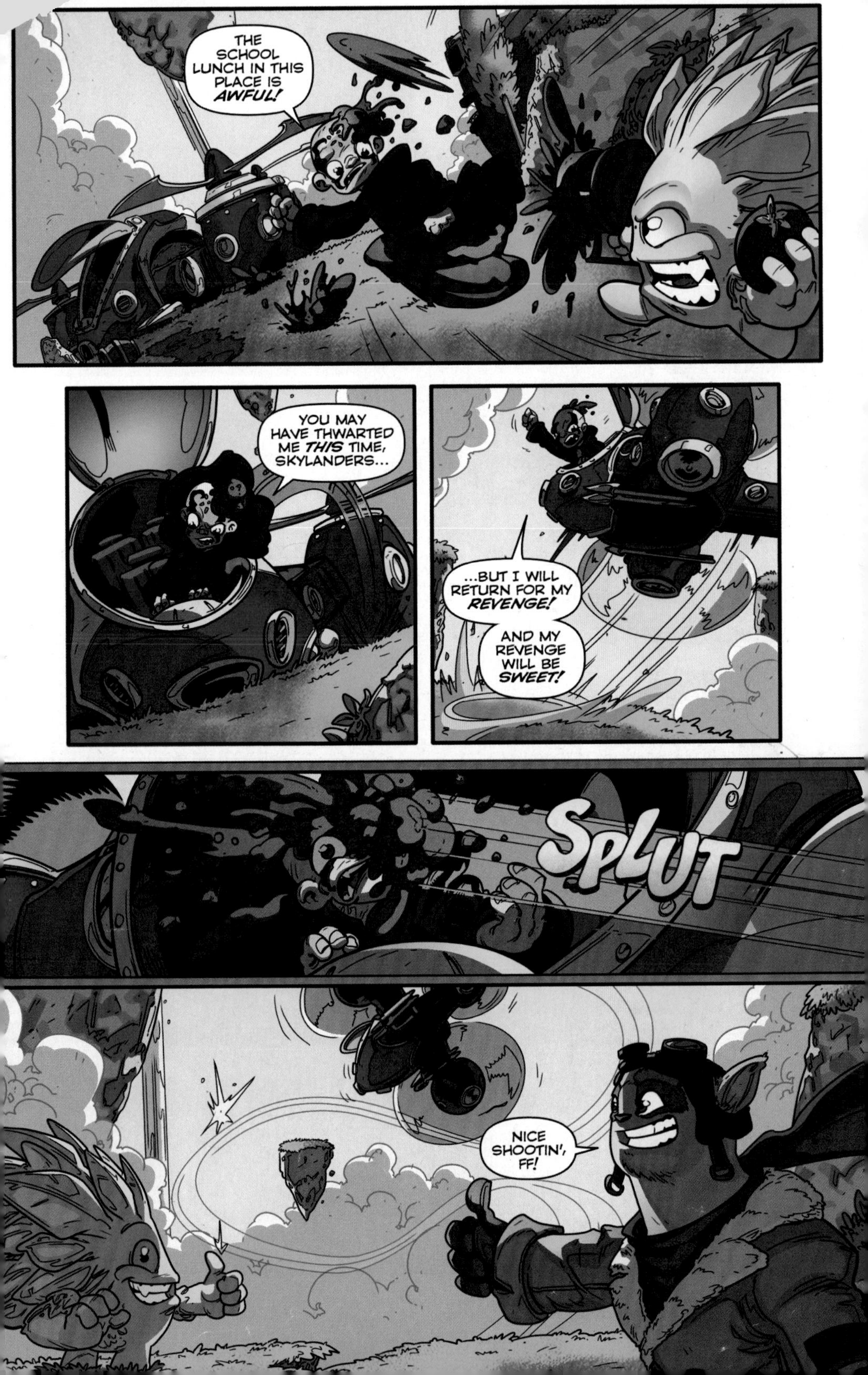
THE SCHOOL LUNCH IN THIS PLACE IS AWFUL!
YOU MAY HAVE THWARTED ME THIS TIME, SKYLANDERS...
...BUT I WILL RETURN FOR MY REVENGE!
AND MY REVENGE WILL BE SWEET!
SPLUT
NICE SHOOTIN', FF!

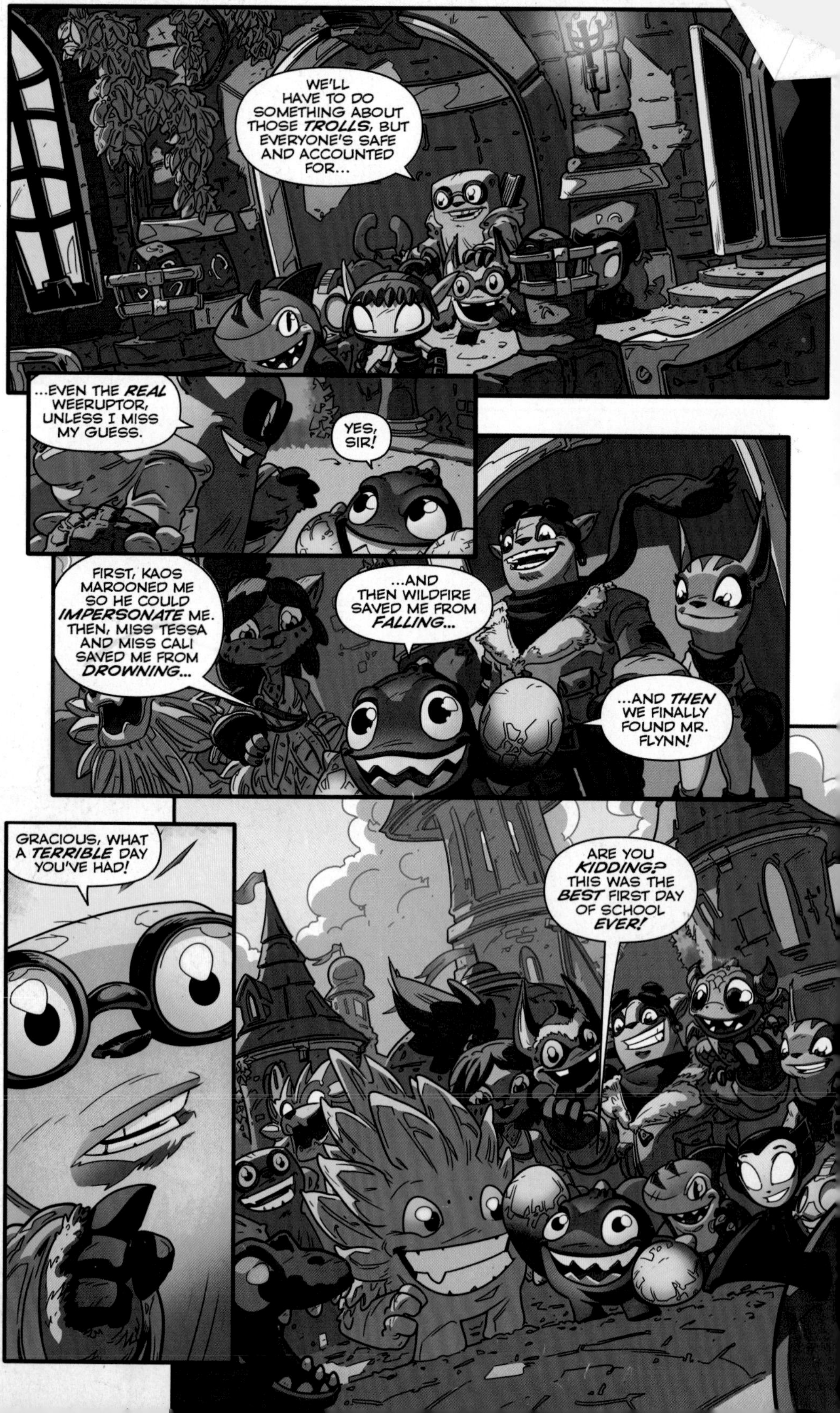
WE'LL HAVE TO DO SOMETHING ABOUT THOSE TROLLS, BUT EVERYONE'S SAFE AND ACCOUNTED FOR...
...EVEN THE REAL WEERUPTOR, UNLESS I MISS MY GUESS.
YES, SIR!
FIRST, KAOS MAROONED ME SO HE COULD IMPERSONATE ME. THEN, MISS TESSA AND MISS CALI SAVED ME FROM DROWNING...
...AND THEN WILDFIRE SAVED ME FROM FALLING...
...AND THEN WE FINALLY FOUND MR. FLYNN!
GRACIOUS, WHAT A TERRIBLE DAY YOU'VE HAD!
ARE YOU KIDDING? THIS WAS THE BEST FIRST DAY OF SCHOOL EVER!

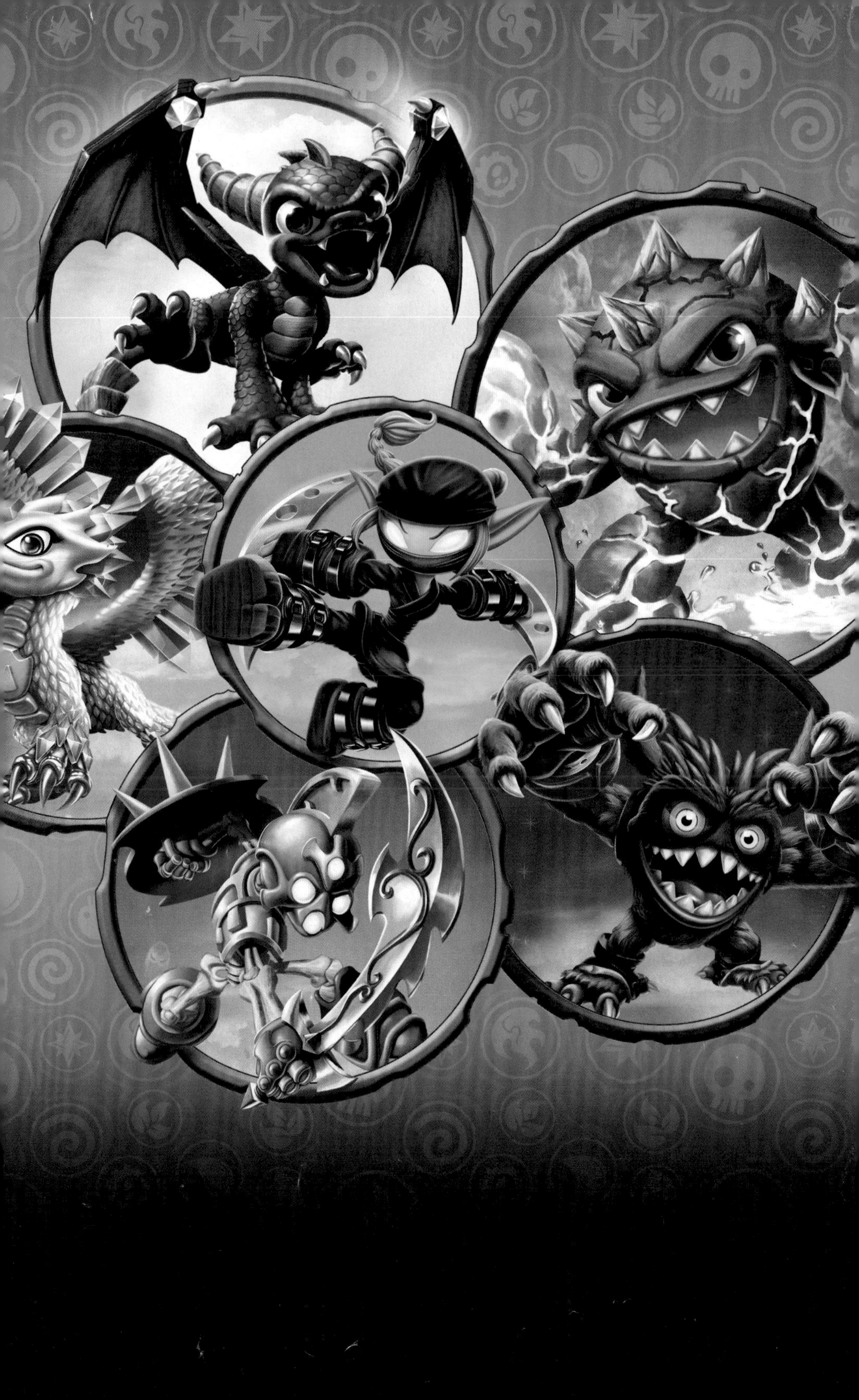

THE TRAP MASTERS

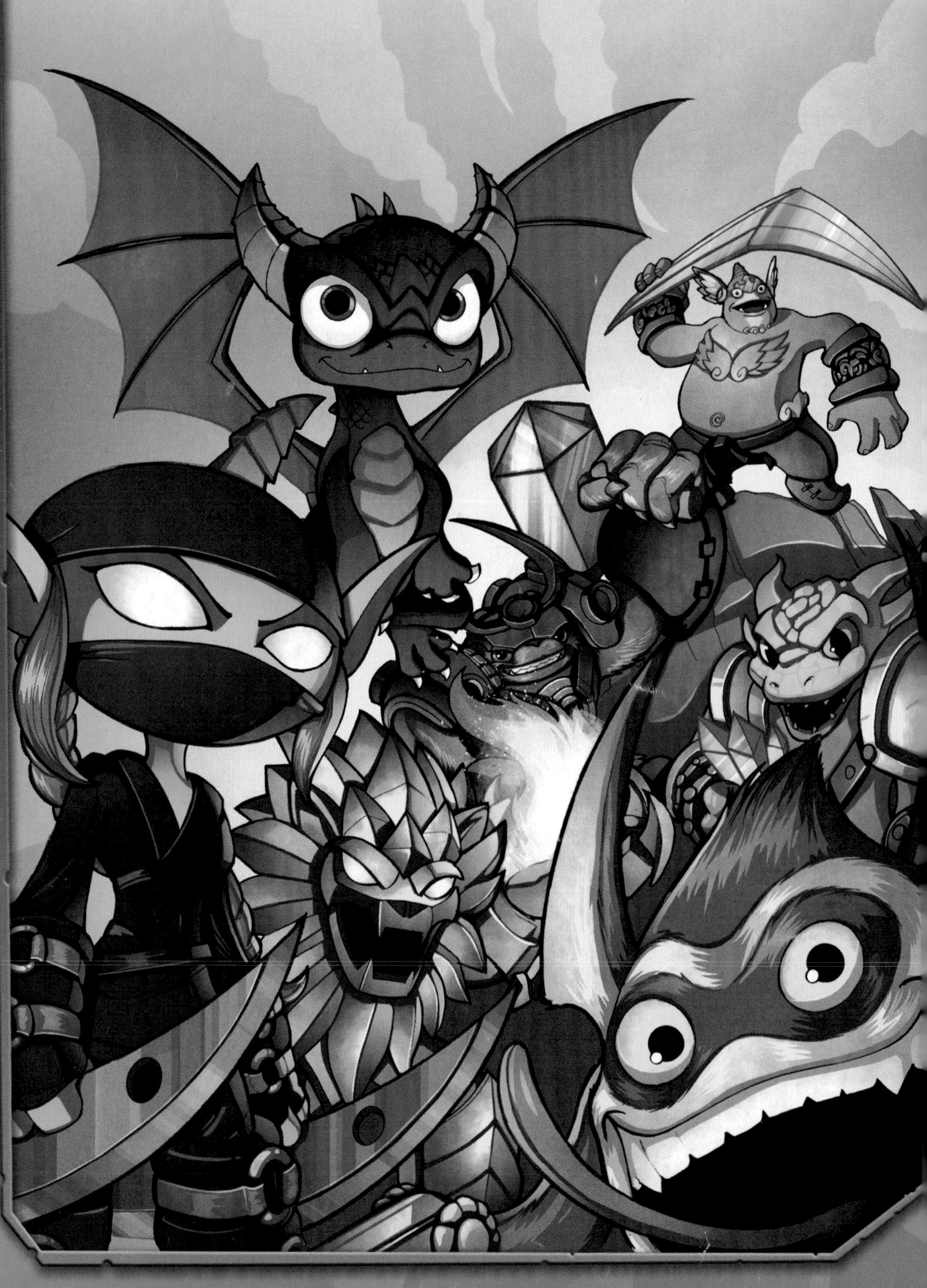

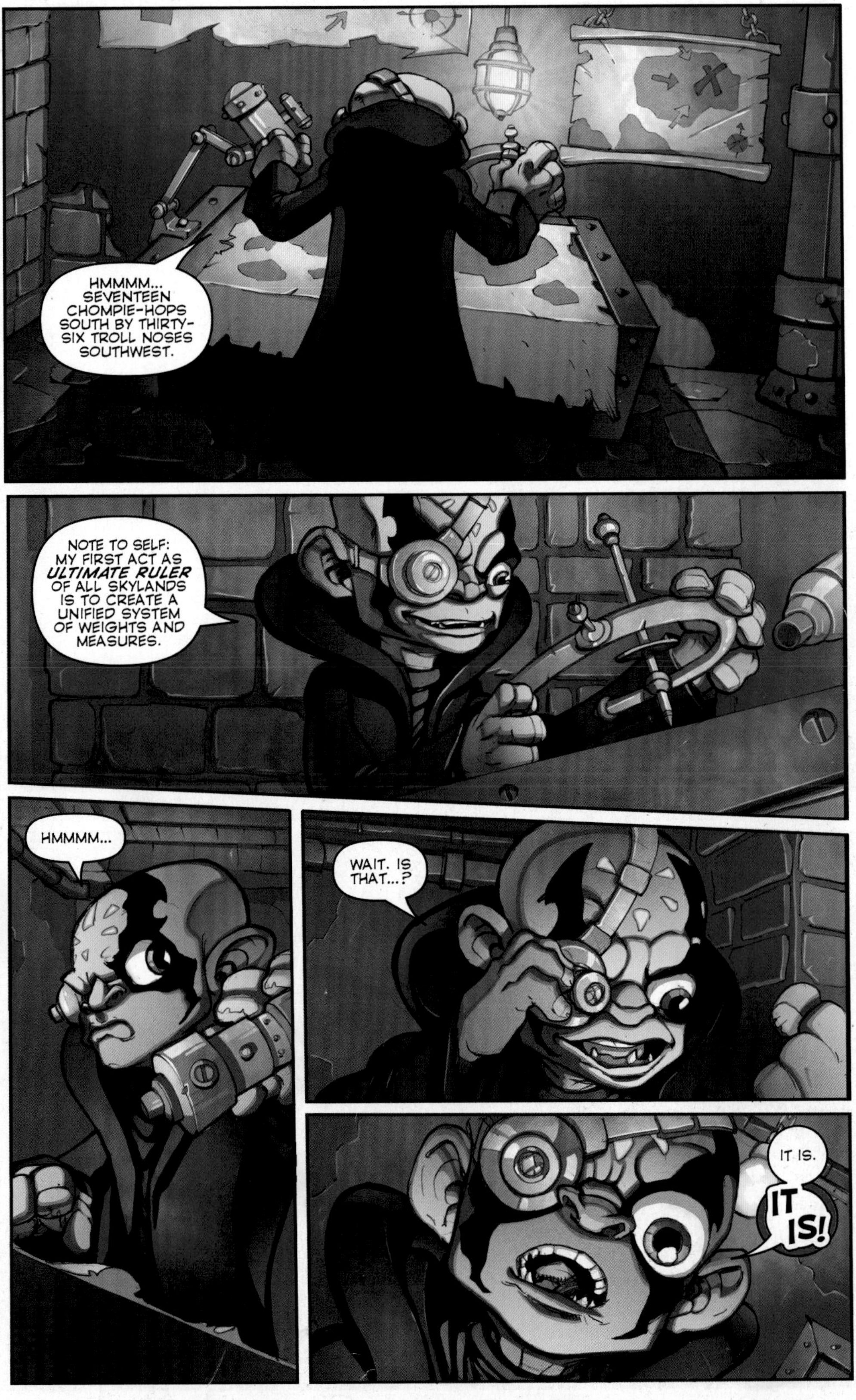
HMMMM... SEVENTEEN CHOMPIE-HOPS SOUTH BY THIRTY-SIX TROLL NOSES SOUTHWEST.
NOTE TO SELF: MY FIRST ACT AS *ULTIMATE RULER* OF ALL SKYLANDS IS TO CREATE A UNIFIED SYSTEM OF WEIGHTS AND MEASURES.
HMMMM...
WAIT. IS THAT...?
IT IS.
IT IS!

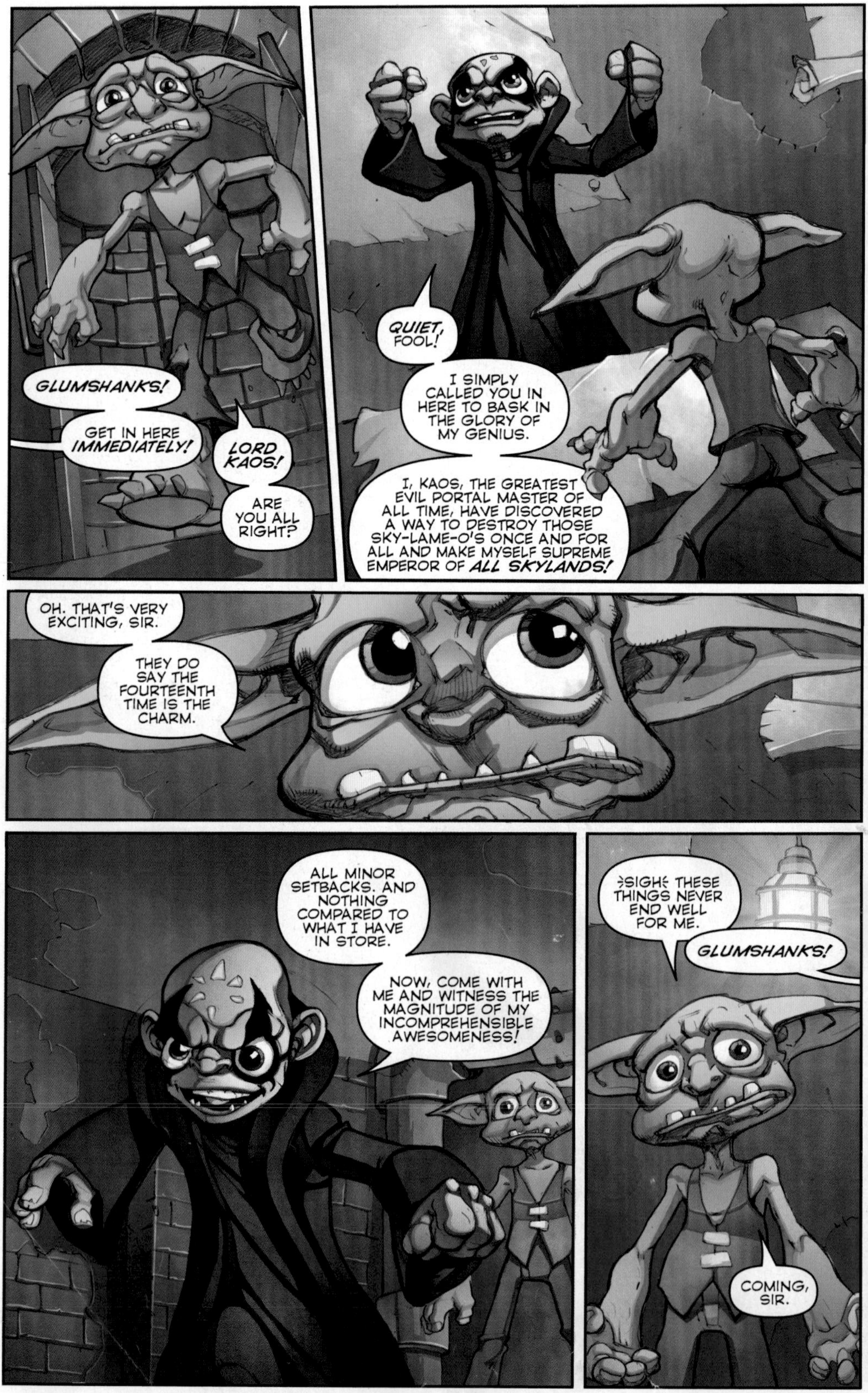
GLUMSHANKS!
GET IN HERE IMMEDIATELY!
LORD KAOS!
ARE YOU ALL RIGHT?
QUIET, FOOL!
I SIMPLY CALLED YOU IN HERE TO BASK IN THE GLORY OF MY GENIUS.
I, KAOS, THE GREATEST EVIL PORTAL MASTER OF ALL TIME, HAVE DISCOVERED A WAY TO DESTROY THOSE SKY-LAME-O'S ONCE AND FOR ALL AND MAKE MYSELF SUPREME EMPEROR OF ALL SKYLANDS!
OH. THAT'S VERY EXCITING, SIR.
THEY DO SAY THE FOURTEENTH TIME IS THE CHARM.
ALL MINOR SETBACKS. AND NOTHING COMPARED TO WHAT I HAVE IN STORE.
NOW, COME WITH ME AND WITNESS THE MAGNITUDE OF MY INCOMPREHENSIBLE AWESOMENESS!
SIGH THESE THINGS NEVER END WELL FOR ME.
GLUMSHANKS!
COMING, SIR.

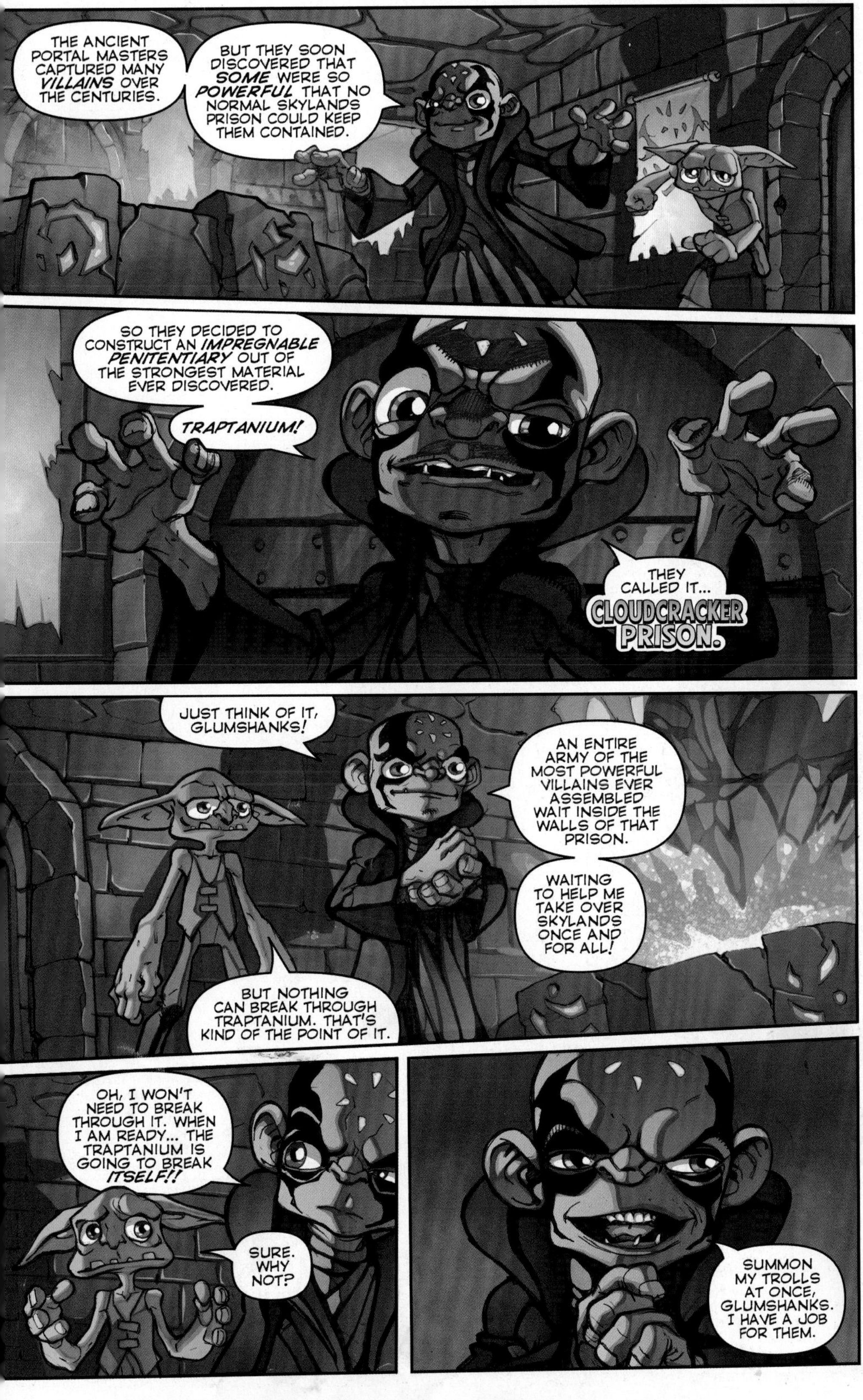

THE ANCIENT PORTAL MASTERS CAPTURED MANY *VILLAINS* OVER THE CENTURIES.
BUT THEY SOON DISCOVERED THAT *SOME* WERE SO *POWERFUL* THAT NO NORMAL SKYLANDS PRISON COULD KEEP THEM CONTAINED.
SO THEY DECIDED TO CONSTRUCT AN *IMPREGNABLE PENITENTIARY* OUT OF THE STRONGEST MATERIAL EVER DISCOVERED.
TRAPTANIUM!
THEY CALLED IT... CLOUDCRACKER PRISON.
JUST THINK OF IT, GLUMSHANKS!
AN ENTIRE ARMY OF THE MOST POWERFUL VILLAINS EVER ASSEMBLED WAIT INSIDE THE WALLS OF THAT PRISON.
WAITING TO HELP ME TAKE OVER SKYLANDS ONCE AND FOR ALL!
BUT NOTHING CAN BREAK THROUGH TRAPTANIUM. THAT'S KIND OF THE POINT OF IT.
OH, I WON'T NEED TO BREAK THROUGH IT. WHEN I AM READY... THE TRAPTANIUM IS GOING TO BREAK *ITSELF!!*
SURE. WHY NOT?
SUMMON MY TROLLS AT ONCE, GLUMSHANKS. I HAVE A JOB FOR THEM.

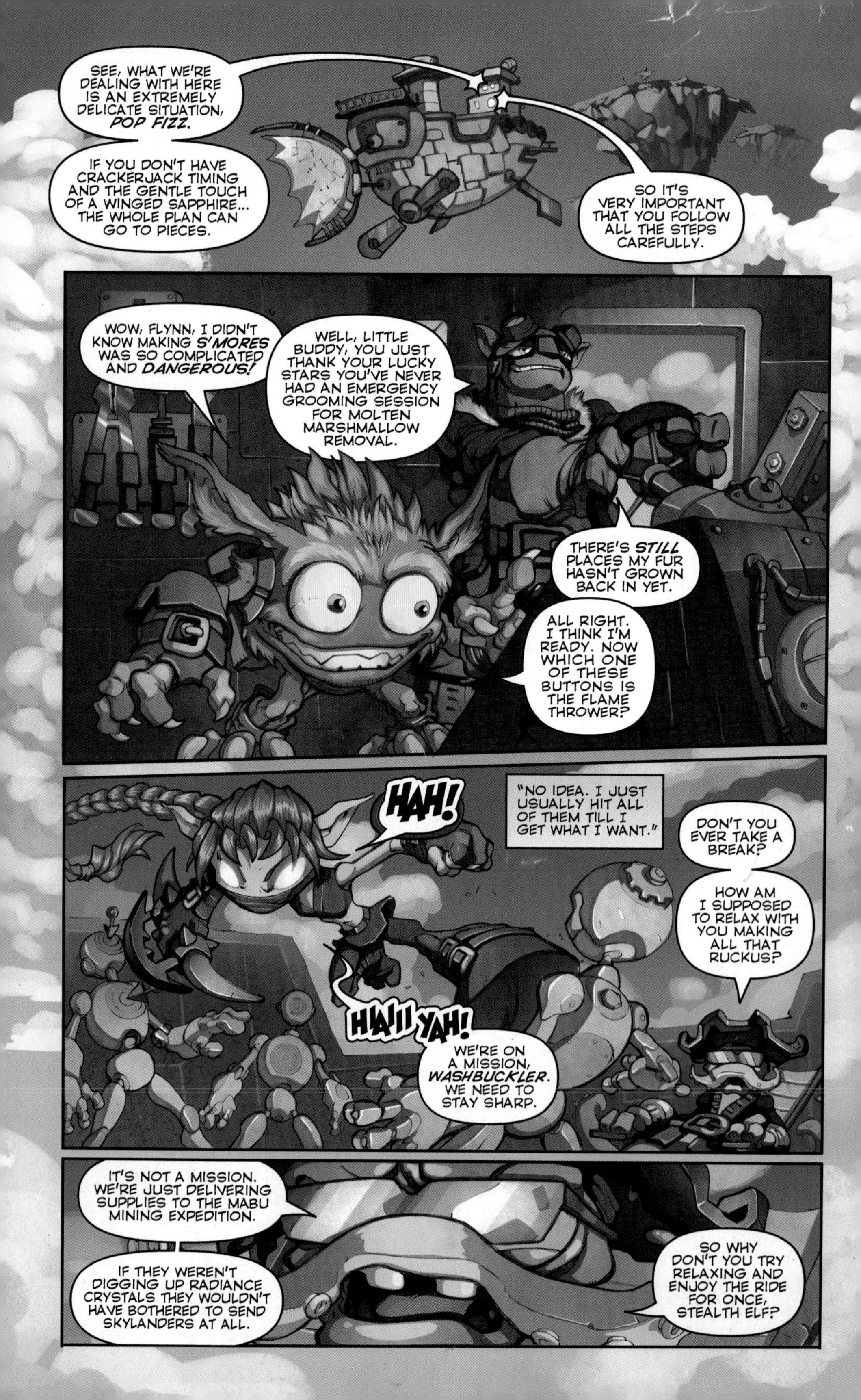
SEE, WHAT WE'RE DEALING WITH HERE IS AN EXTREMELY DELICATE SITUATION, POP FIZZ.
IF YOU DON'T HAVE CRACKERJACK TIMING AND THE GENTLE TOUCH OF A WINGED SAPPHIRE... THE WHOLE PLAN CAN GO TO PIECES.
SO IT'S VERY IMPORTANT THAT YOU FOLLOW ALL THE STEPS CAREFULLY.
WOW, FLYNN, I DIDN'T KNOW MAKING S'MORES WAS SO COMPLICATED AND DANGEROUS!
WELL, LITTLE BUDDY, YOU JUST THANK YOUR LUCKY STARS YOU'VE NEVER HAD AN EMERGENCY GROOMING SESSION FOR MOLTEN MARSHMALLOW REMOVAL.
THERE'S STILL PLACES MY FUR HASN'T GROWN BACK IN YET.
ALL RIGHT. I THINK I'M READY. NOW WHICH ONE OF THESE BUTTONS IS THE FLAME THROWER?
HAH!
"NO IDEA. I JUST USUALLY HIT ALL OF THEM TILL I GET WHAT I WANT."
DON'T YOU EVER TAKE A BREAK?
HOW AM I SUPPOSED TO RELAX WITH YOU MAKING ALL THAT RUCKUS?
HAIII YAH!
WE'RE ON A MISSION, WASHBUCKLER. WE NEED TO STAY SHARP.
IT'S NOT A MISSION. WE'RE JUST DELIVERING SUPPLIES TO THE MABU MINING EXPEDITION.
IF THEY WEREN'T DIGGING UP RADIANCE CRYSTALS THEY WOULDN'T HAVE BOTHERED TO SEND SKYLANDERS AT ALL.
SO WHY DON'T YOU TRY RELAXING AND ENJOY THE RIDE FOR ONCE, STEALTH ELF?

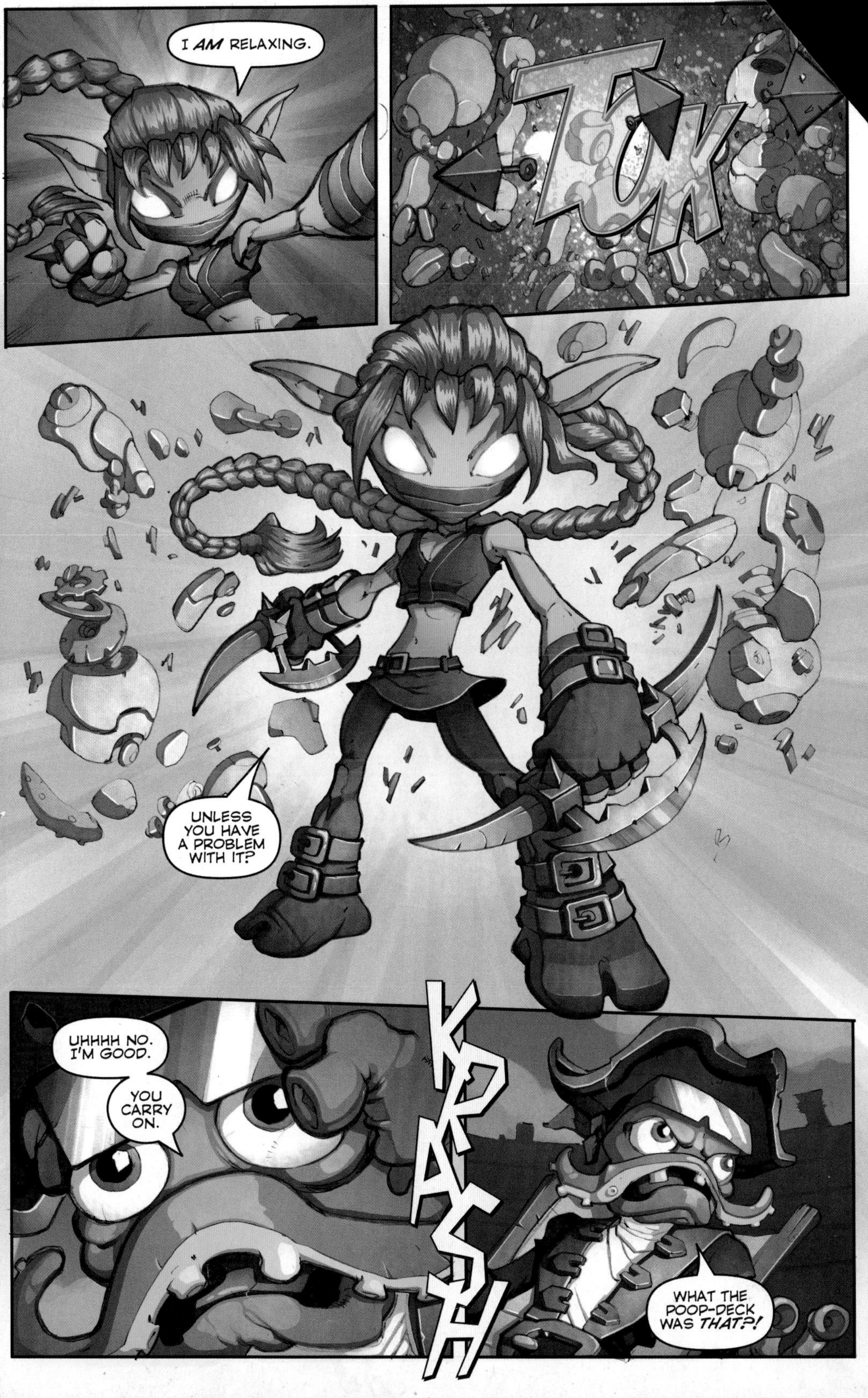
I AM RELAXING.
TOK
UNLESS YOU HAVE A PROBLEM WITH IT?
UHHHH NO. I'M GOOD.
YOU CARRY ON.
KRAKASH
WHAT THE POOP-DECK WAS THAT?!

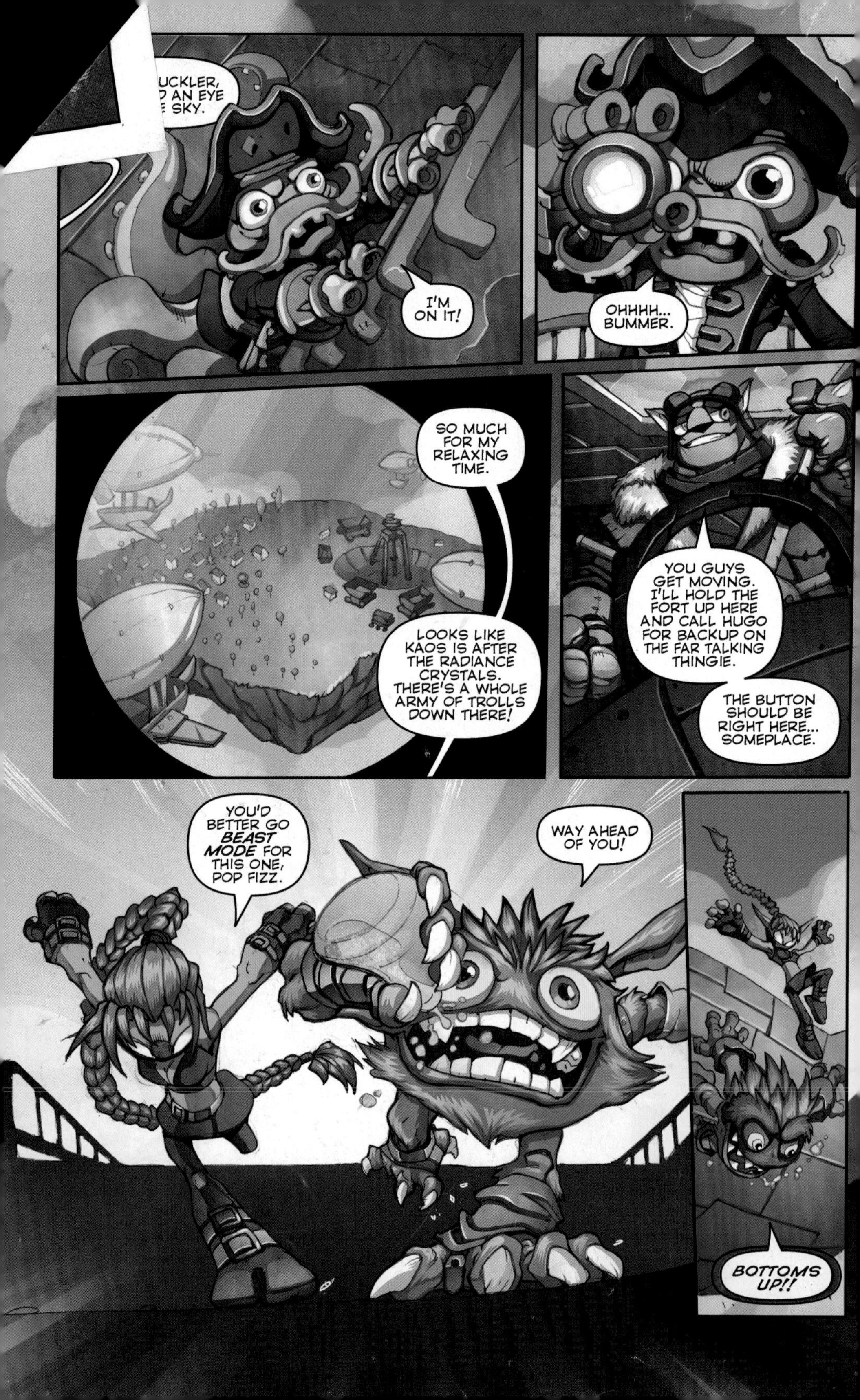
UCKLER, D AN EYE E SKY.
I'M ON IT!
OHHHH... BUMMER.
SO MUCH FOR MY RELAXING TIME.
LOOKS LIKE KAOS IS AFTER THE RADIANCE CRYSTALS. THERE'S A WHOLE ARMY OF TROLLS DOWN THERE!
YOU GUYS GET MOVING. I'LL HOLD THE FORT UP HERE AND CALL HUGO FOR BACKUP ON THE FAR TALKING THINGIE.
THE BUTTON SHOULD BE RIGHT HERE... SOMEPLACE.
YOU'D BETTER GO BEAST MODE FOR THIS ONE, POP FIZZ.
WAY AHEAD OF YOU!
BOTTOMS UP!!

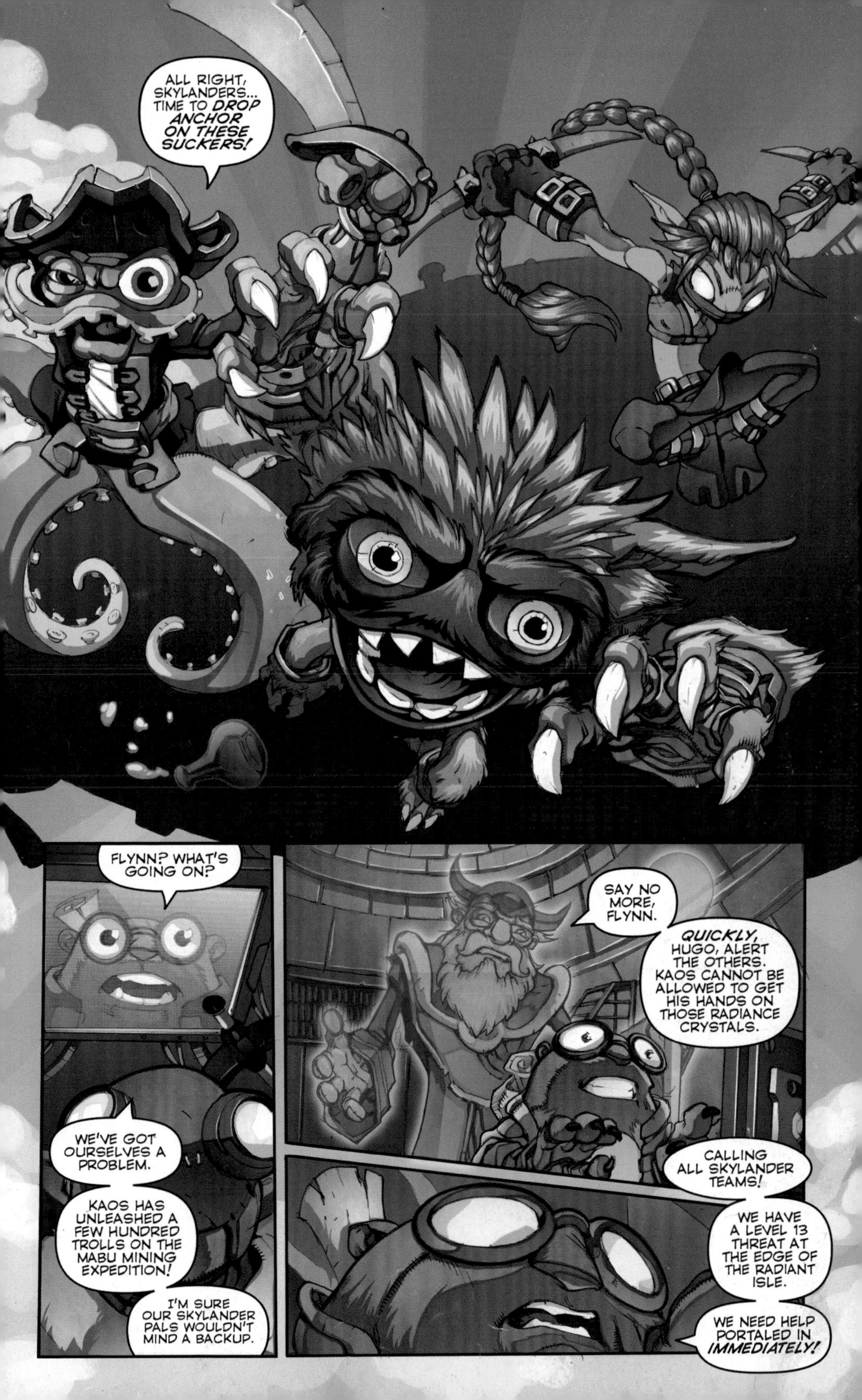
ALL RIGHT, SKYLANDERS... TIME TO *DROP ANCHOR ON THESE SUCKERS!*
FLYNN? WHAT'S GOING ON?
WE'VE GOT OURSELVES A PROBLEM.
KAOS HAS UNLEASHED A FEW HUNDRED TROLLS ON THE MABU MINING EXPEDITION!
I'M SURE OUR SKYLANDER PALS WOULDN'T MIND A BACKUP.
SAY NO MORE, FLYNN.
QUICKLY, HUGO, ALERT THE OTHERS. KAOS CANNOT BE ALLOWED TO GET HIS HANDS ON THOSE RADIANCE CRYSTALS.
CALLING ALL SKYLANDER TEAMS!
WE HAVE A LEVEL 13 THREAT AT THE EDGE OF THE RADIANT ISLE.
WE NEED HELP PORTALED IN *IMMEDIATELY!*

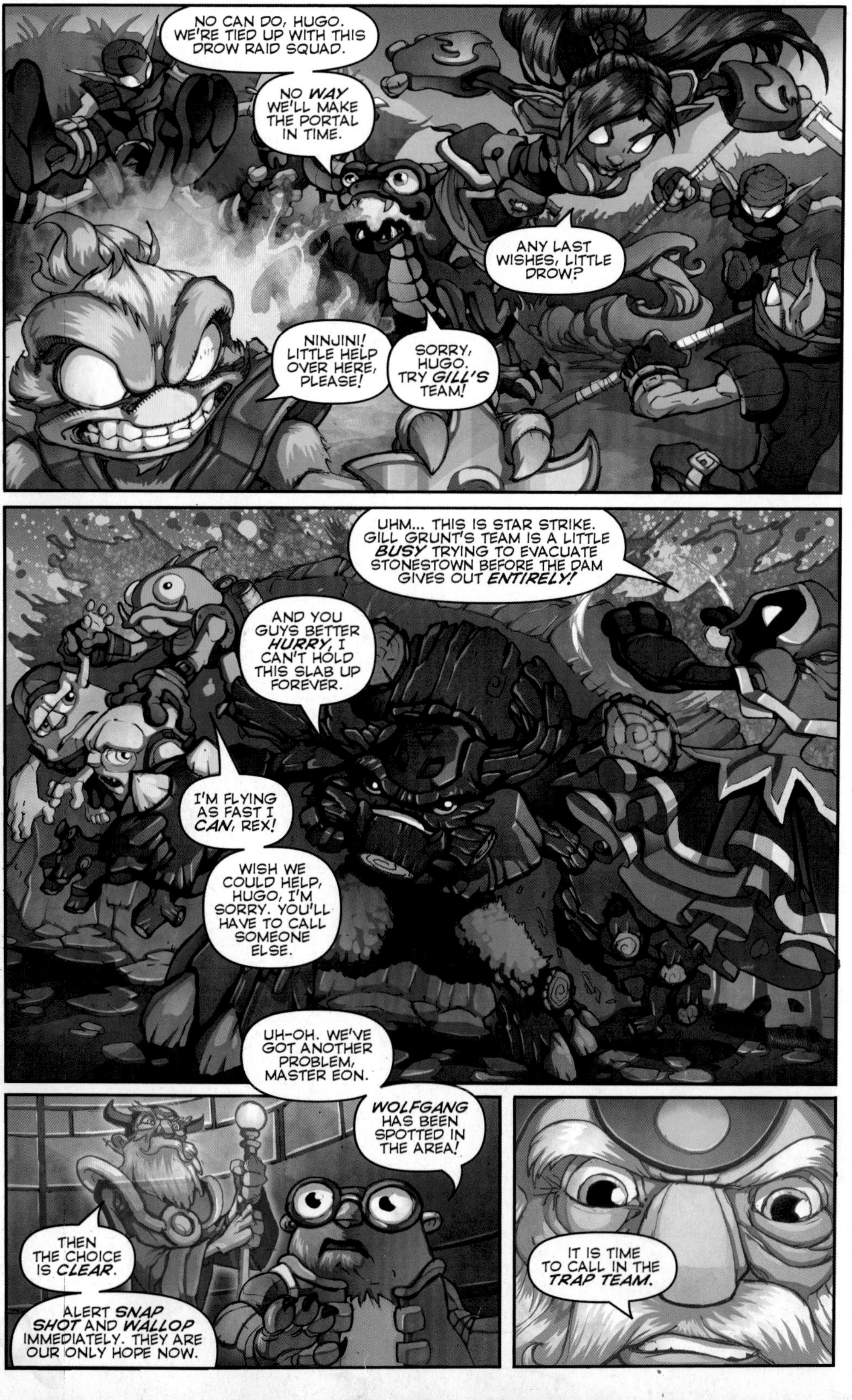
NO CAN DO, HUGO. WE'RE TIED UP WITH THIS DROW RAID SQUAD.
NO WAY WE'LL MAKE THE PORTAL IN TIME.
ANY LAST WISHES, LITTLE DROW?
NINJINI! LITTLE HELP OVER HERE, PLEASE!
SORRY, HUGO. TRY GILL'S TEAM!
UHM... THIS IS STAR STRIKE. GILL GRUNT'S TEAM IS A LITTLE BUSY TRYING TO EVACUATE STONESTOWN BEFORE THE DAM GIVES OUT ENTIRELY!
AND YOU GUYS BETTER HURRY, I CAN'T HOLD THIS SLAB UP FOREVER.
I'M FLYING AS FAST I CAN, REX!
WISH WE COULD HELP, HUGO, I'M SORRY. YOU'LL HAVE TO CALL SOMEONE ELSE.
UH-OH. WE'VE GOT ANOTHER PROBLEM, MASTER EON.
WOLFGANG HAS BEEN SPOTTED IN THE AREA!
THEN THE CHOICE IS CLEAR.
ALERT SNAP SHOT AND WALLOP IMMEDIATELY. THEY ARE OUR ONLY HOPE NOW.
IT IS TIME TO CALL IN THE TRAP TEAM.

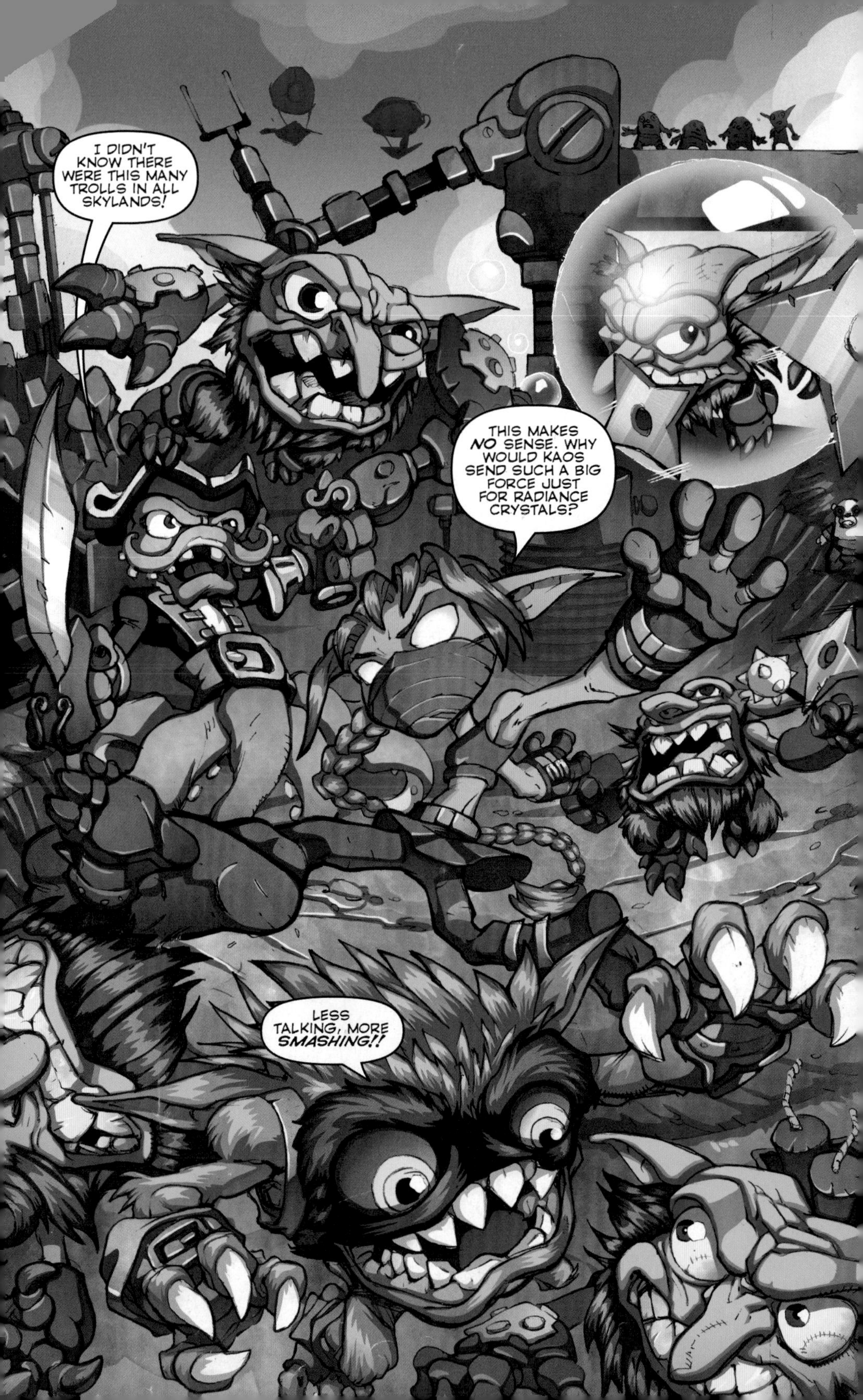
I DIDN'T KNOW THERE WERE THIS MANY TROLLS IN ALL SKYLANDS!
THIS MAKES *NO* SENSE. WHY WOULD KAOS SEND SUCH A BIG FORCE JUST FOR RADIANCE CRYSTALS?
LESS TALKING, MORE *SMASHING*!!

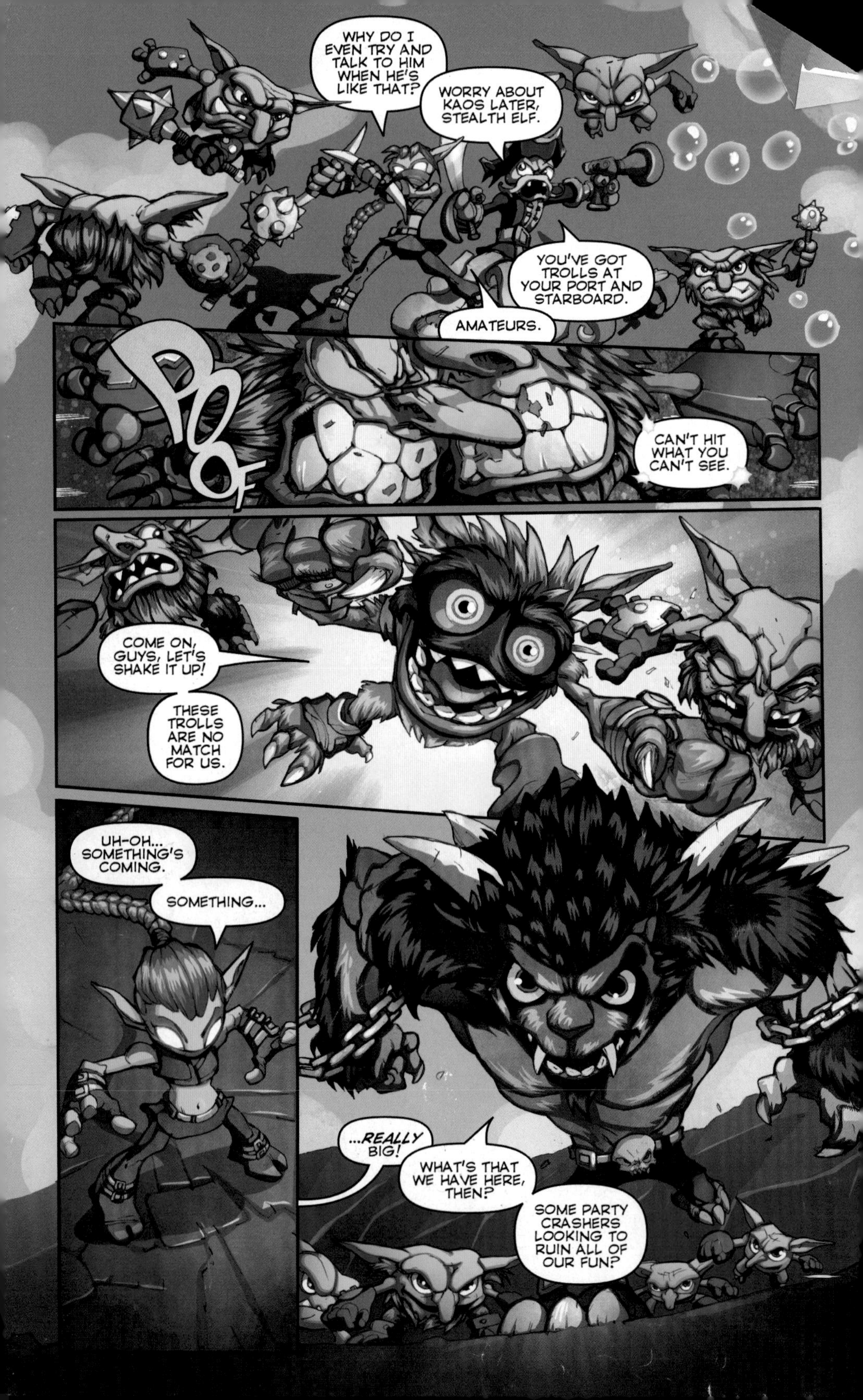
WHY DO I EVEN TRY AND TALK TO HIM WHEN HE'S LIKE THAT?
WORRY ABOUT KAOS LATER, STEALTH ELF.
YOU'VE GOT TROLLS AT YOUR PORT AND STARBOARD.
AMATEURS.
POOF
CAN'T HIT WHAT YOU CAN'T SEE.
COME ON, GUYS, LET'S SHAKE IT UP!
THESE TROLLS ARE NO MATCH FOR US.
UH-OH... SOMETHING'S COMING.
SOMETHING...
...REALLY BIG!
WHAT'S THAT WE HAVE HERE, THEN?
SOME PARTY CRASHERS LOOKING TO RUIN ALL OF OUR FUN?

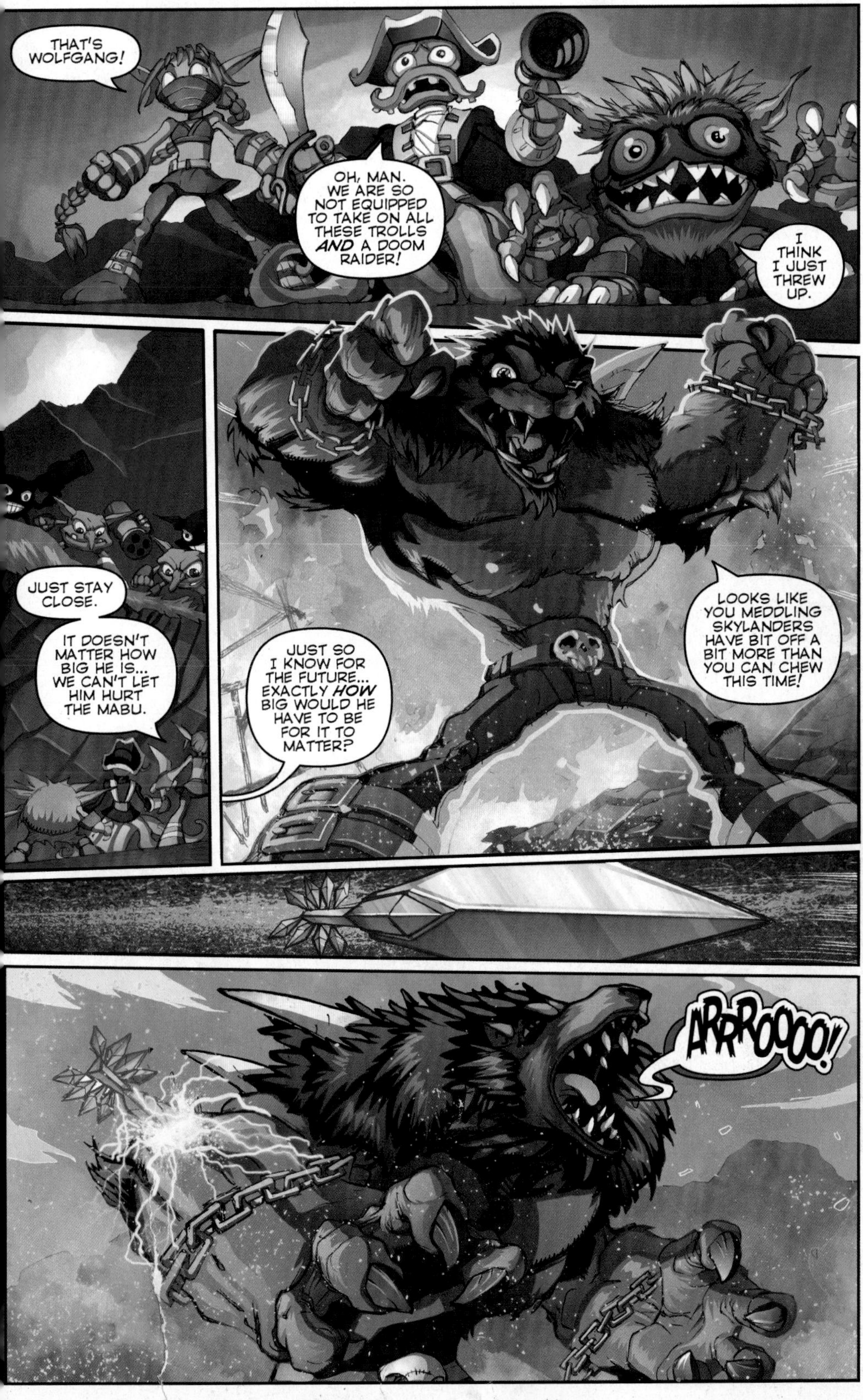
THAT'S WOLFGANG!
OH, MAN. WE ARE SO NOT EQUIPPED TO TAKE ON ALL THESE TROLLS *AND* A DOOM RAIDER!
I THINK I JUST THREW UP.
JUST STAY CLOSE.
IT DOESN'T MATTER HOW BIG HE IS... WE CAN'T LET HIM HURT THE MABU.
JUST SO I KNOW FOR THE FUTURE... EXACTLY *HOW* BIG WOULD HE HAVE TO BE FOR IT TO MATTER?
LOOKS LIKE YOU MEDDLING SKYLANDERS HAVE BIT OFF A BIT MORE THAN YOU CAN CHEW THIS TIME!
ARRROOOO!

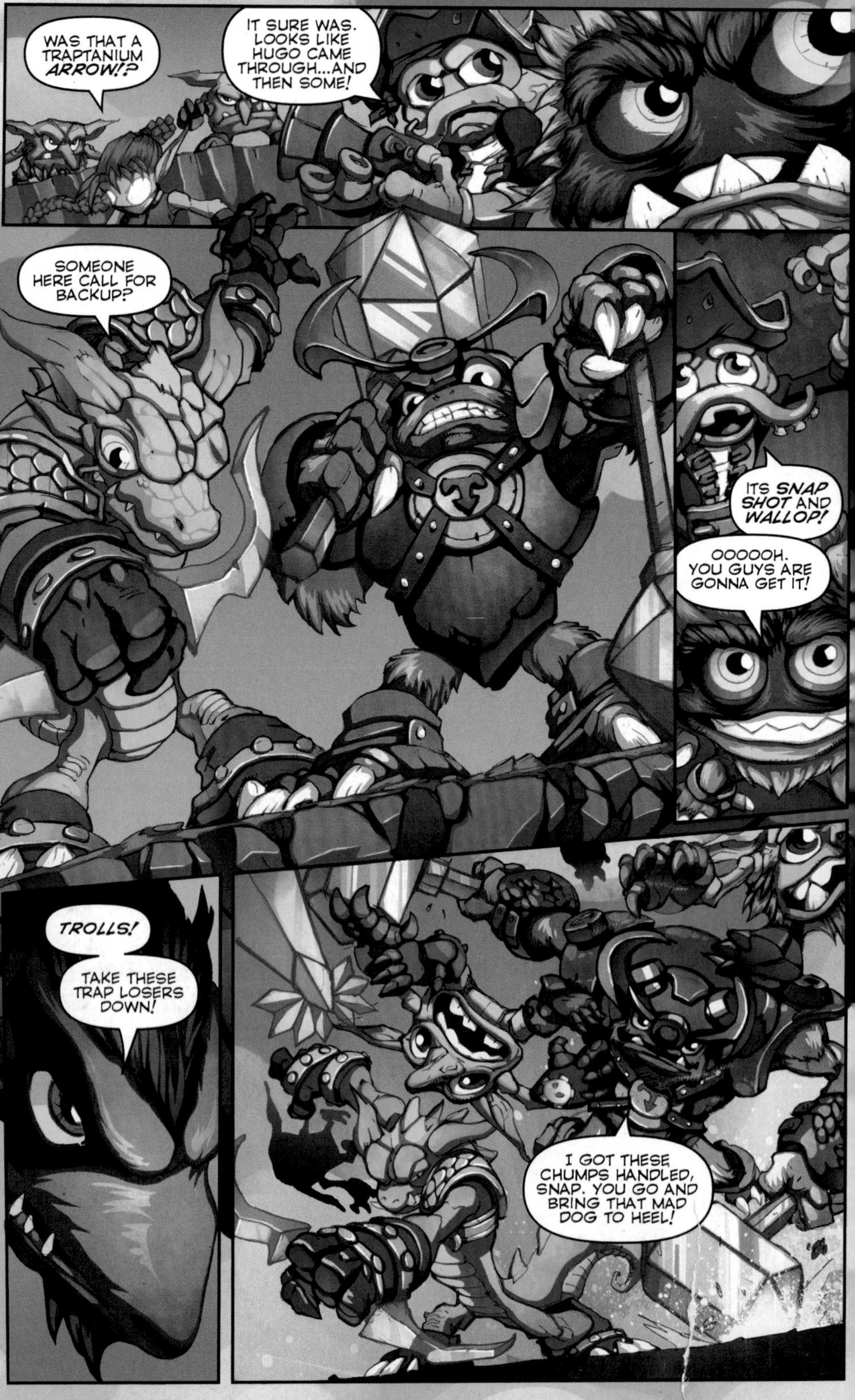
WAS THAT A TRAPTANIUM ARROW!?
IT SURE WAS. LOOKS LIKE HUGO CAME THROUGH...AND THEN SOME!
SOMEONE HERE CALL FOR BACKUP?
ITS SNAP SHOT AND WALLOP!
OOOOOH. YOU GUYS ARE GONNA GET IT!
TROLLS!
TAKE THESE TRAP LOSERS DOWN!
I GOT THESE CHUMPS HANDLED, SNAP. YOU GO AND BRING THAT MAD DOG TO HEEL!

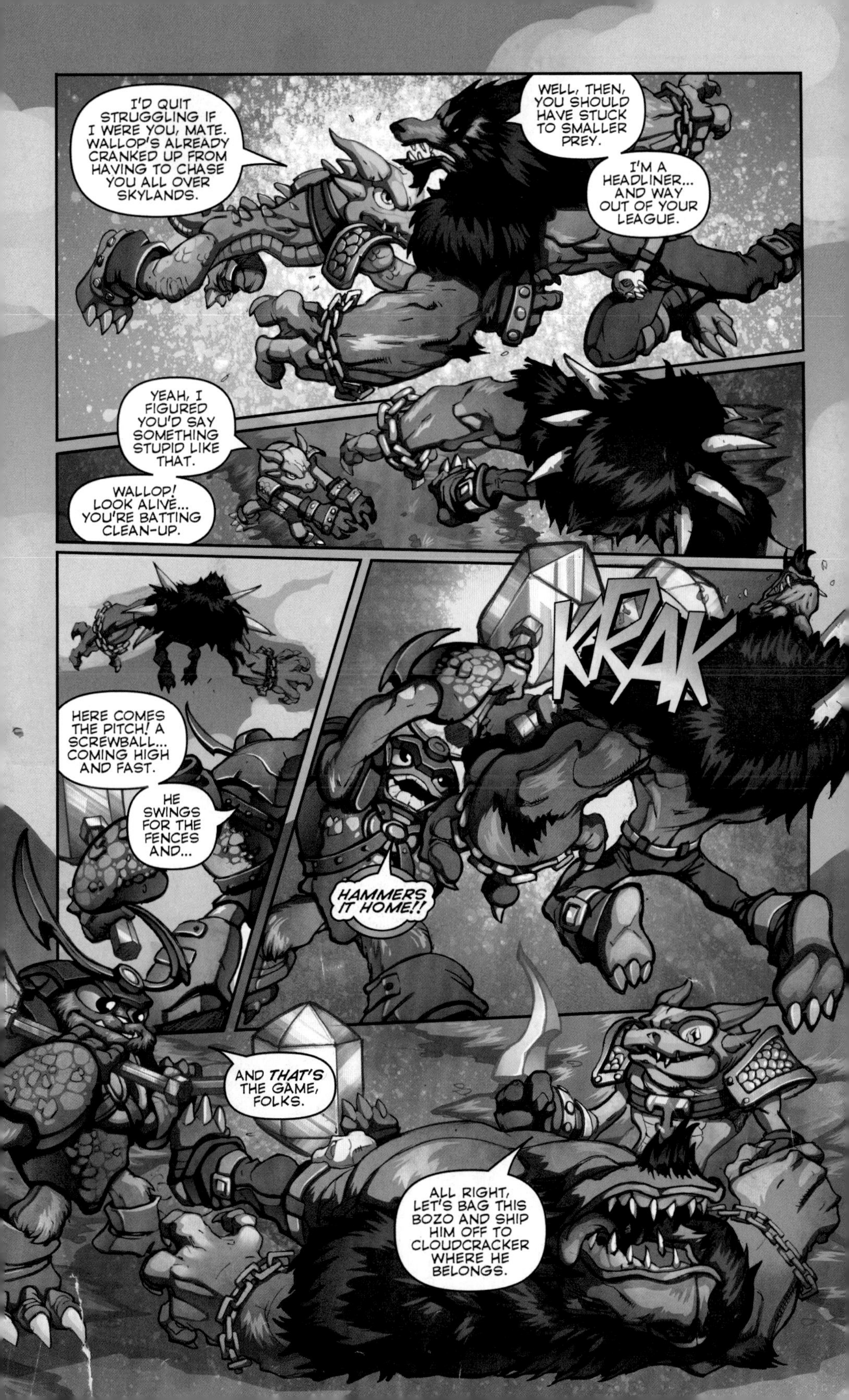
I'D QUIT STRUGGLING IF I WERE YOU, MATE. WALLOP'S ALREADY CRANKED UP FROM HAVING TO CHASE YOU ALL OVER SKYLANDS.
WELL, THEN, YOU SHOULD HAVE STUCK TO SMALLER PREY.
I'M A HEADLINER... AND WAY OUT OF YOUR LEAGUE.
YEAH, I FIGURED YOU'D SAY SOMETHING STUPID LIKE THAT.
WALLOP! LOOK ALIVE... YOU'RE BATTING CLEAN-UP.
HERE COMES THE PITCH! A SCREWBALL... COMING HIGH AND FAST.
HE SWINGS FOR THE FENCES AND...
KRAK
HAMMERS IT HOME!!
AND THAT'S THE GAME, FOLKS.
ALL RIGHT, LET'S BAG THIS BOZO AND SHIP HIM OFF TO CLOUDCRACKER WHERE HE BELONGS.

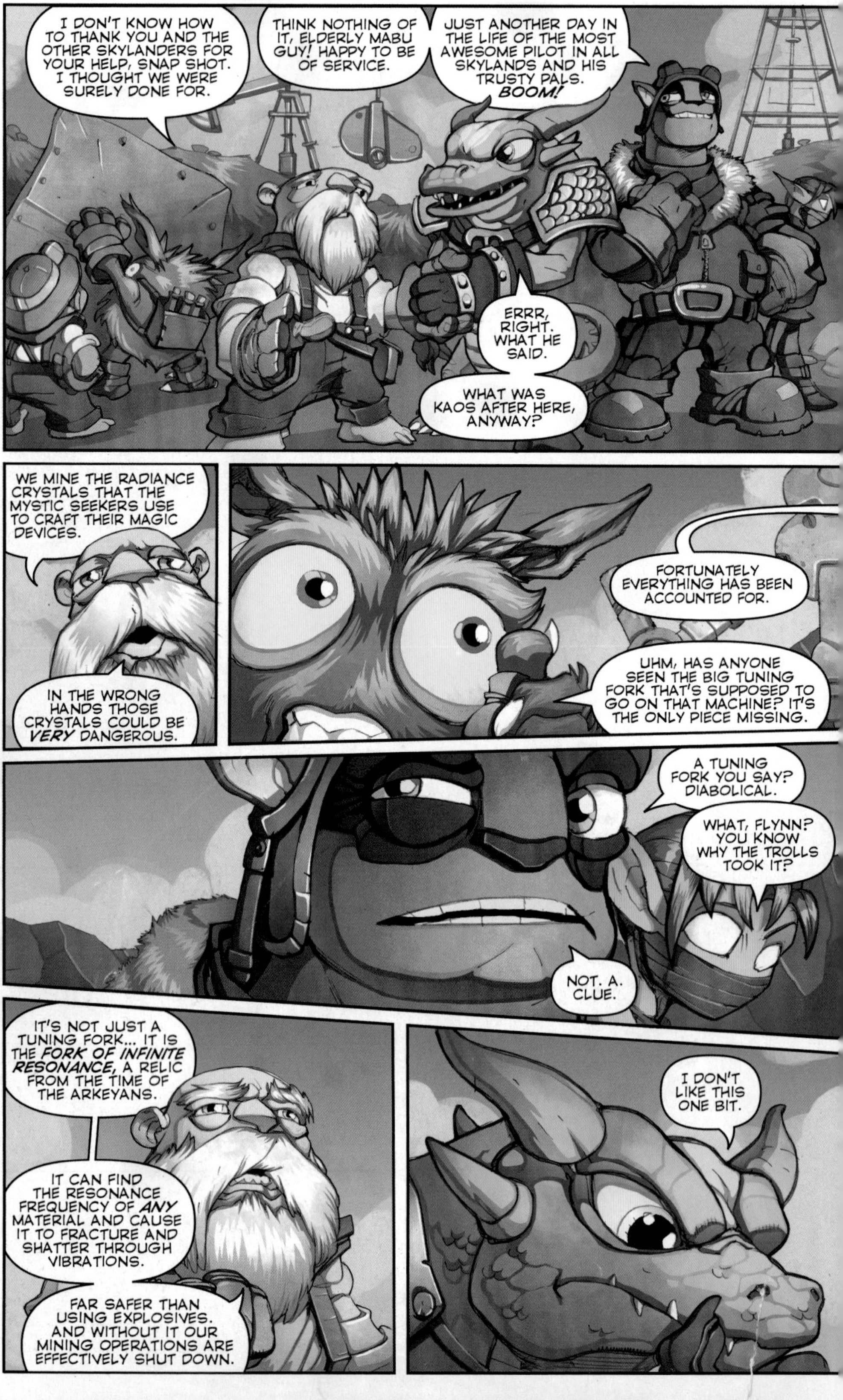
I DON'T KNOW HOW TO THANK YOU AND THE OTHER SKYLANDERS FOR YOUR HELP, SNAP SHOT. I THOUGHT WE WERE SURELY DONE FOR.
THINK NOTHING OF IT, ELDERLY MABU GUY! HAPPY TO BE OF SERVICE.
JUST ANOTHER DAY IN THE LIFE OF THE MOST AWESOME PILOT IN ALL SKYLANDS AND HIS TRUSTY PALS. *BOOM!*
ERRR, RIGHT. WHAT HE SAID.
WHAT WAS KAOS AFTER HERE, ANYWAY?
WE MINE THE RADIANCE CRYSTALS THAT THE MYSTIC SEEKERS USE TO CRAFT THEIR MAGIC DEVICES.
IN THE WRONG HANDS THOSE CRYSTALS COULD BE *VERY* DANGEROUS.
FORTUNATELY EVERYTHING HAS BEEN ACCOUNTED FOR.
UHM, HAS ANYONE SEEN THE BIG TUNING FORK THAT'S SUPPOSED TO GO ON THAT MACHINE? IT'S THE ONLY PIECE MISSING.
A TUNING FORK YOU SAY? DIABOLICAL.
WHAT, FLYNN? YOU KNOW WHY THE TROLLS TOOK IT?
NOT. A. CLUE.
IT'S NOT JUST A TUNING FORK... IT IS THE *FORK OF INFINITE RESONANCE,* A RELIC FROM THE TIME OF THE ARKEYANS.
IT CAN FIND THE RESONANCE FREQUENCY OF *ANY* MATERIAL AND CAUSE IT TO FRACTURE AND SHATTER THROUGH VIBRATIONS.
FAR SAFER THAN USING EXPLOSIVES. AND WITHOUT IT OUR MINING OPERATIONS ARE EFFECTIVELY SHUT DOWN.
I DON'T LIKE THIS ONE BIT.

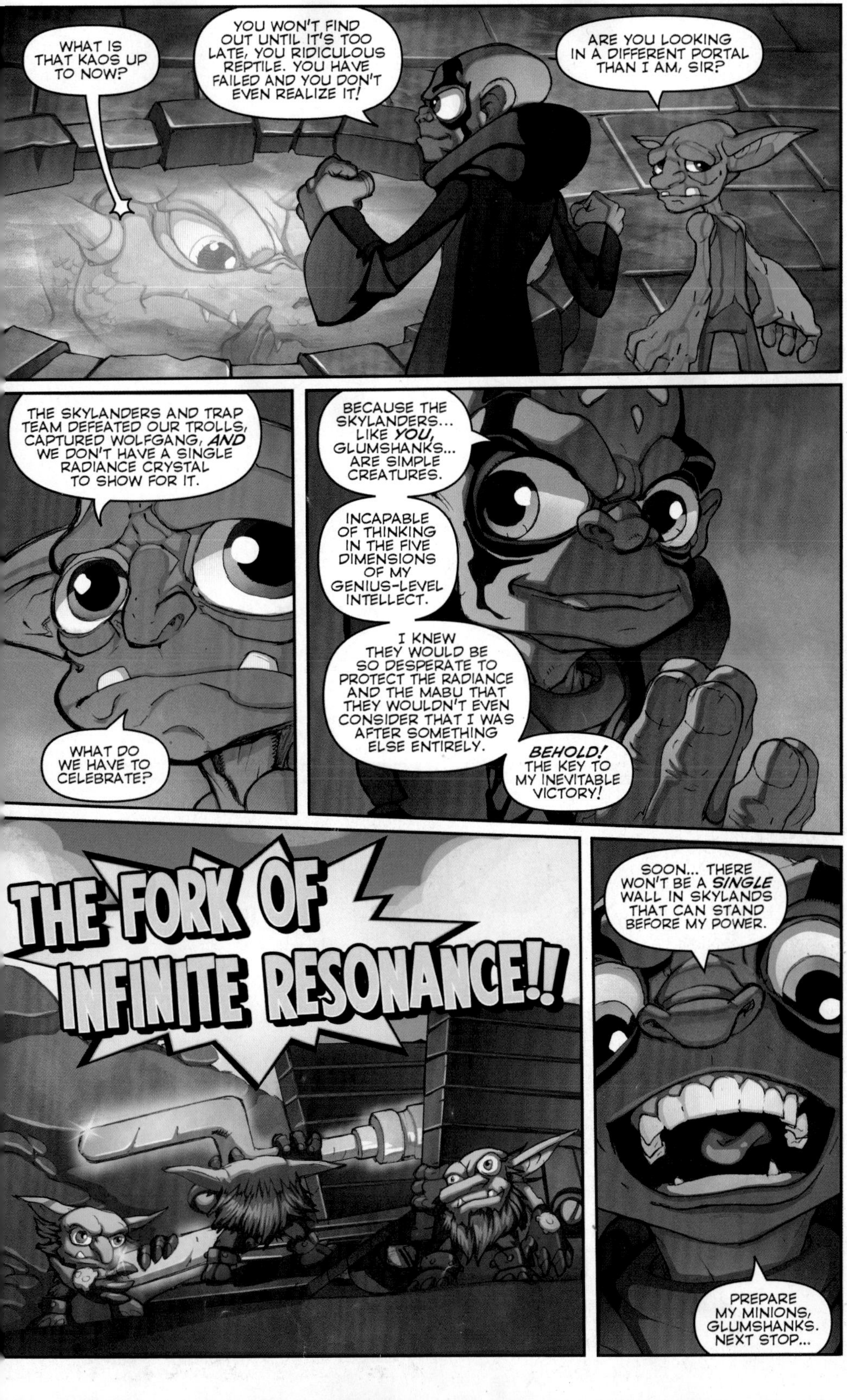
WHAT IS THAT KAOS UP TO NOW?
YOU WON'T FIND OUT UNTIL IT'S TOO LATE, YOU RIDICULOUS REPTILE. YOU HAVE FAILED AND YOU DON'T EVEN REALIZE IT!
ARE YOU LOOKING IN A DIFFERENT PORTAL THAN I AM, SIR?
THE SKYLANDERS AND TRAP TEAM DEFEATED OUR TROLLS, CAPTURED WOLFGANG, *AND* WE DON'T HAVE A SINGLE RADIANCE CRYSTAL TO SHOW FOR IT.
WHAT DO WE HAVE TO CELEBRATE?
BECAUSE THE SKYLANDERS... LIKE *YOU*, GLUMSHANKS... ARE SIMPLE CREATURES.
INCAPABLE OF THINKING IN THE FIVE DIMENSIONS OF MY GENIUS-LEVEL INTELLECT.
I KNEW THEY WOULD BE SO DESPERATE TO PROTECT THE RADIANCE AND THE MABU THAT THEY WOULDN'T EVEN CONSIDER THAT I WAS AFTER SOMETHING ELSE ENTIRELY.
BEHOLD! THE KEY TO MY INEVITABLE VICTORY!
THE FORK OF INFINITE RESONANCE!!
SOON... THERE WON'T BE A *SINGLE* WALL IN SKYLANDS THAT CAN STAND BEFORE MY POWER.
PREPARE MY MINIONS, GLUMSHANKS. NEXT STOP...

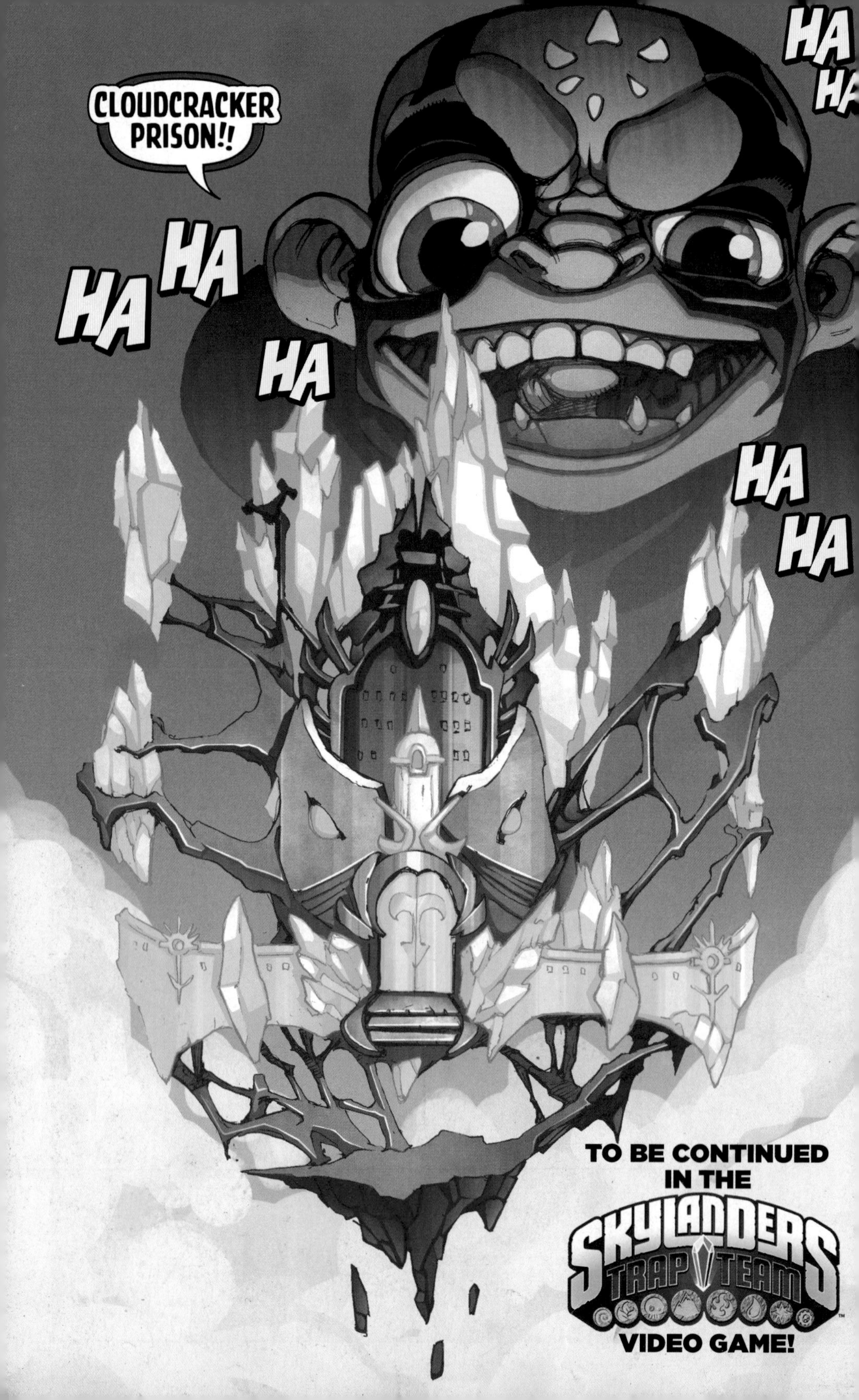
CLOUDCRACKER PRISON!!
HA
HA
HA
HA
HA
HA
TO BE CONTINUED IN THE
SKYLANDERS TRAP TEAM
VIDEO GAME!

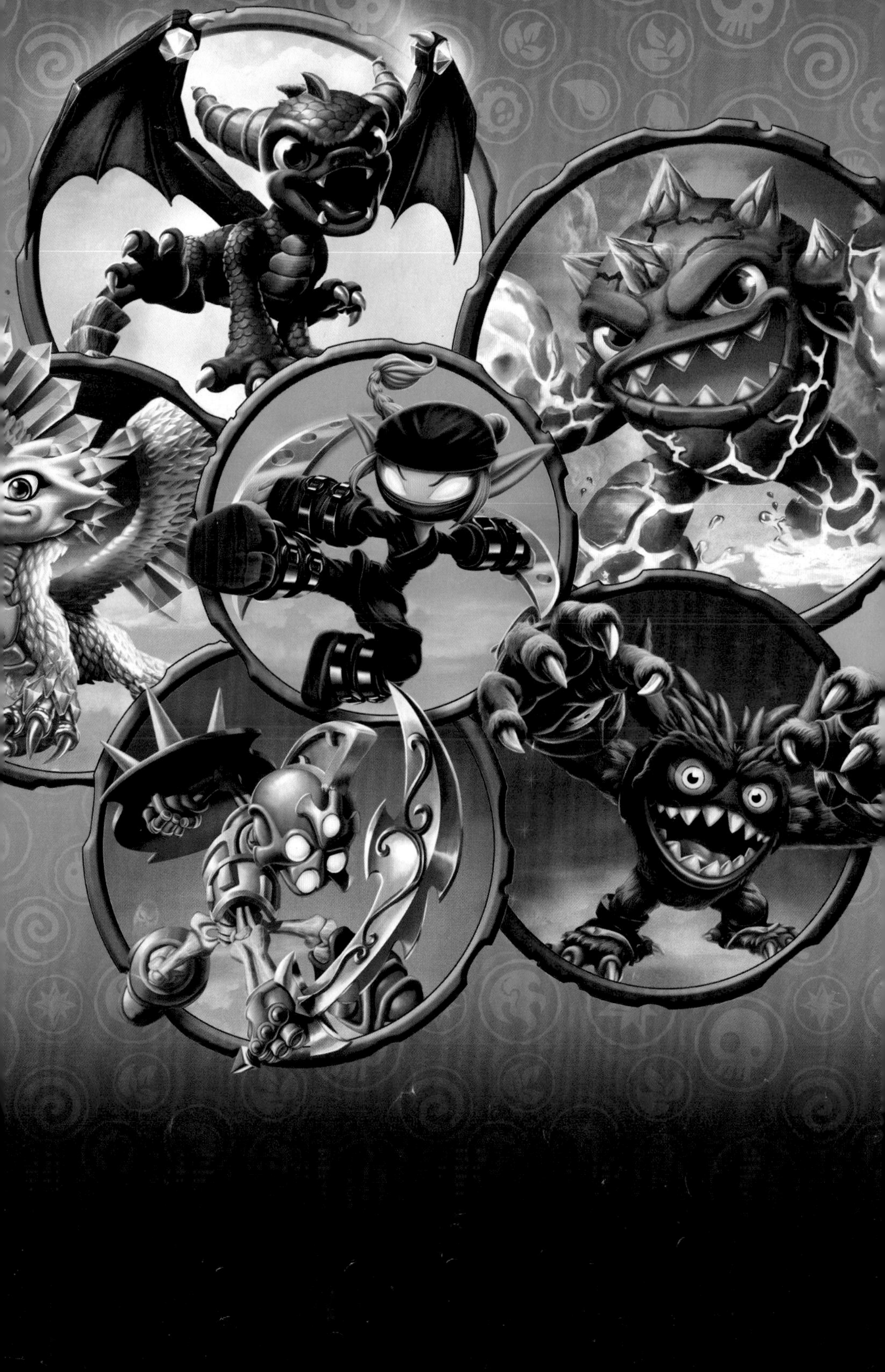

FOOD FIGHT

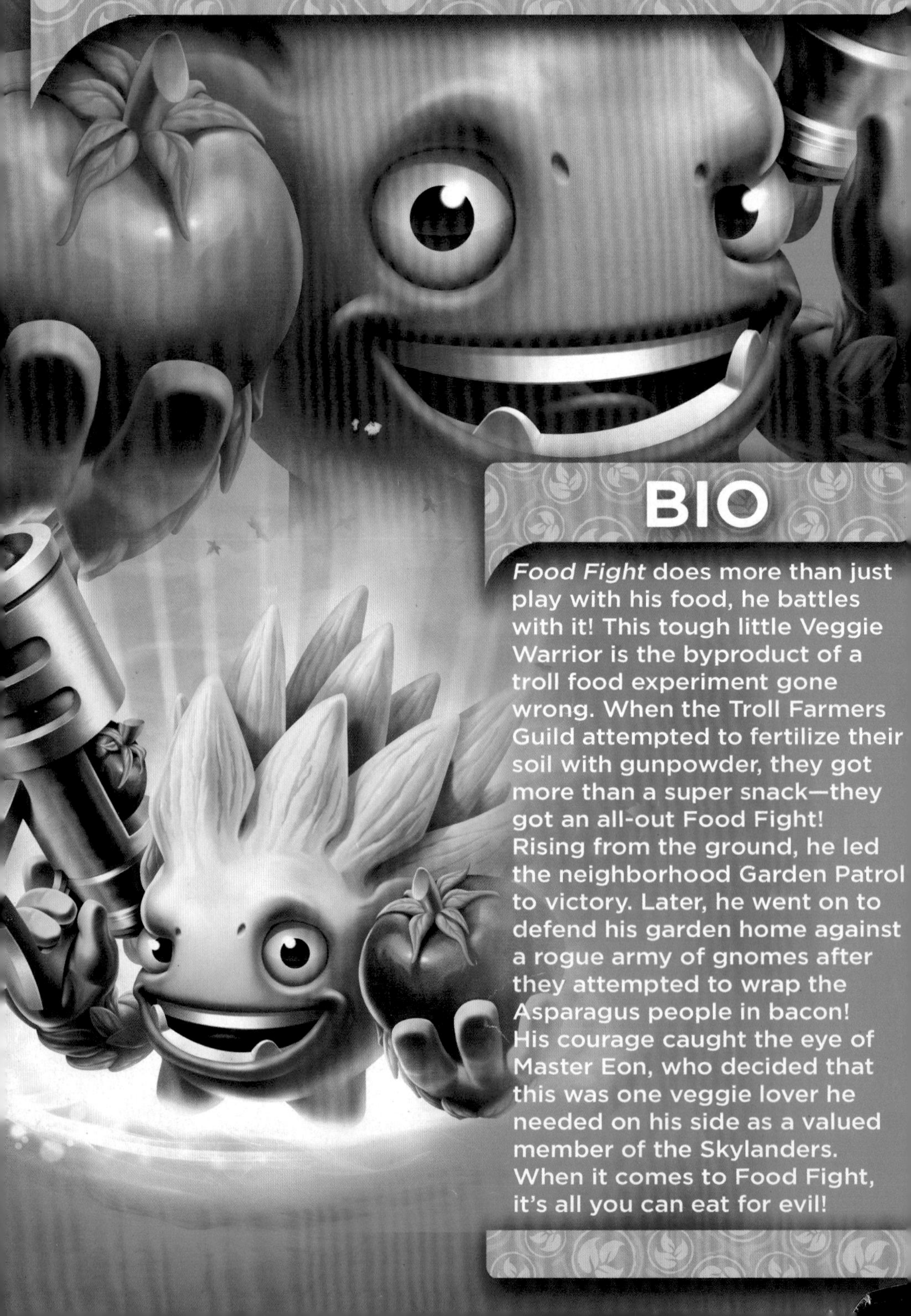

BIO

Food Fight does more than just play with his food, he battles with it! This tough little Veggie Warrior is the byproduct of a troll food experiment gone wrong. When the Troll Farmers Guild attempted to fertilize their soil with gunpowder, they got more than a super snack—they got an all-out Food Fight! Rising from the ground, he led the neighborhood Garden Patrol to victory. Later, he went on to defend his garden home against a rogue army of gnomes after they attempted to wrap the Asparagus people in bacon! His courage caught the eye of Master Eon, who decided that this was one veggie lover he needed on his side as a valued member of the Skylanders. When it comes to Food Fight, it's all you can eat for evil!

WILDFIRE

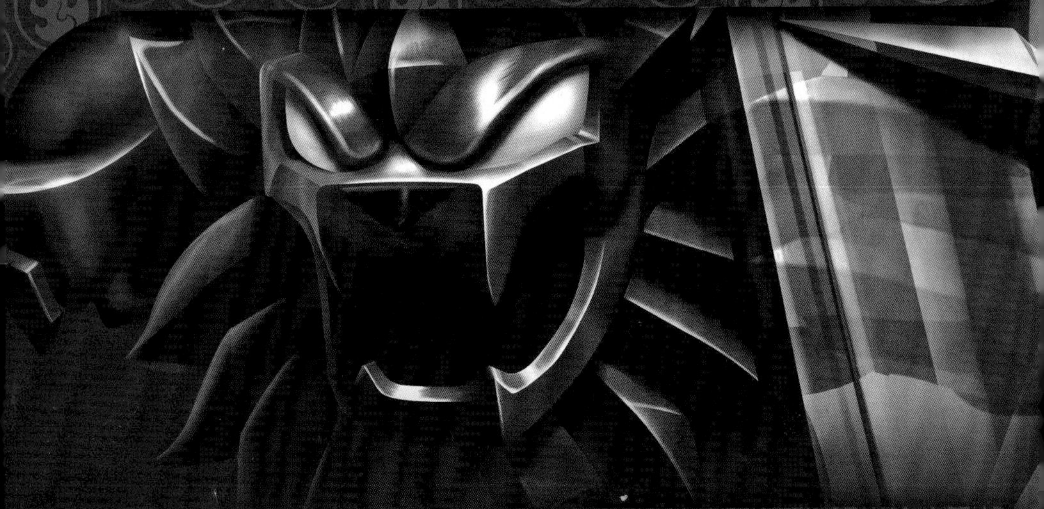

BIO

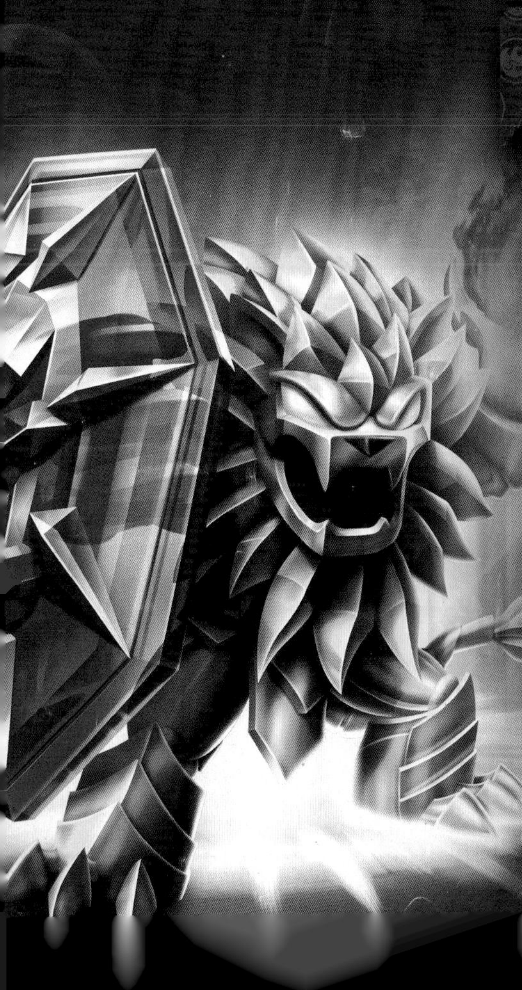

Wildfire was once a young lion of the Fire Claw Clan, about to enter into the Rite of Infernos—a test of survival in the treacherous fire plains. However, because he was made of gold, he was treated as an outcast and not allowed to participate. But this didn't stop him. That night, Wildfire secretly followed the path of the other lions, carrying only his father's enchanted shield. Soon he found them cornered by a giant flame scorpion. Using the shield, he protected the group from the beast's enormous stinging tail, giving them time to safely escape. And though Wildfire was injured in the fight, his father's shield magically changed him—magnifying the strength that was already in his heart—making him the mightiest of his clan. Now part of the Trap Team, Wildfire uses his enormous Traptanium-bonded shield to defend any and all who need it!

SNAP SHOT

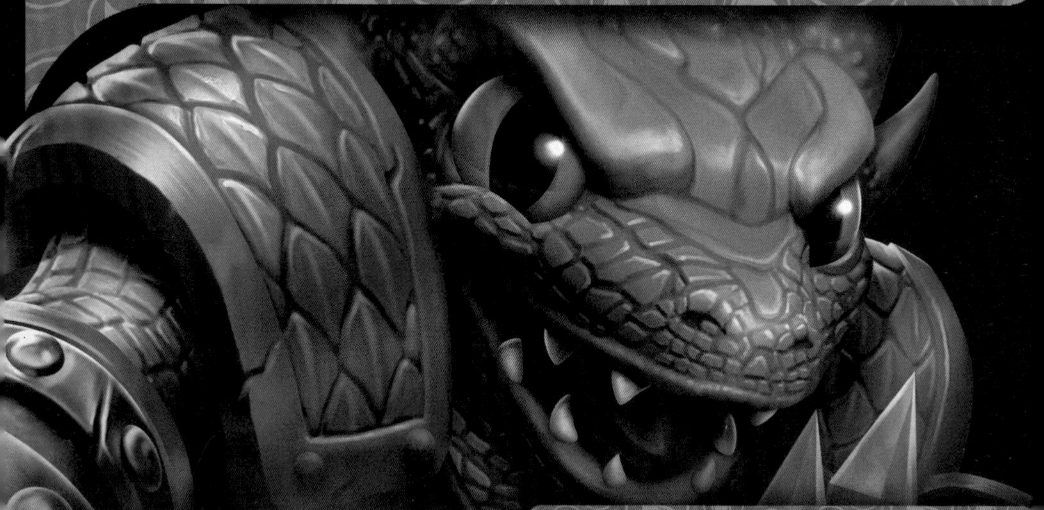

BIO

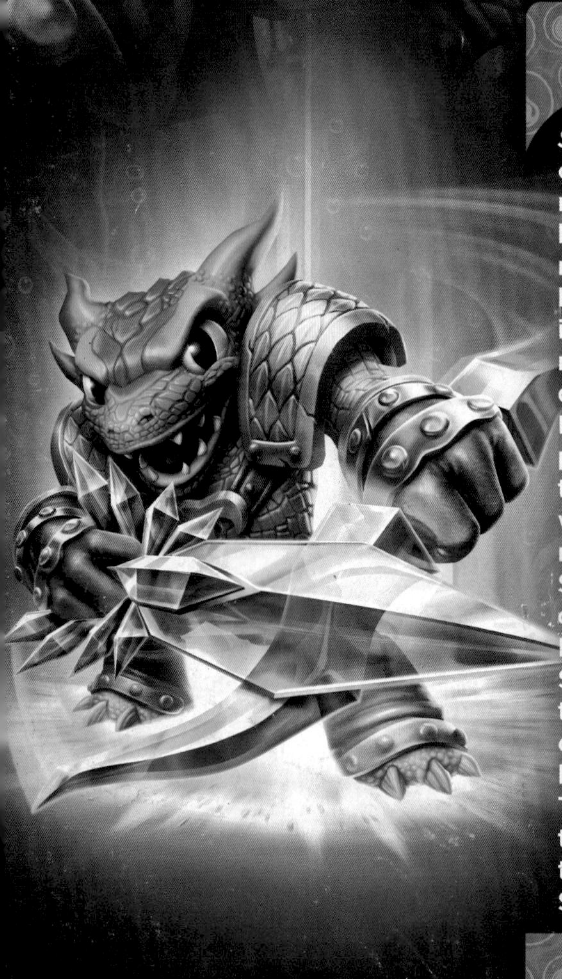

Snap Shot came from a long line of Crocagators that lived in the remote Swamplands, where he hunted chompies for sport. After rounding up every evil critter in his homeland, Snap Shot ventured out into the world to learn new techniques that he could use to track down more challenging monsters. He journeyed far and wide, perfecting his archery skills with the Elves and his hunting skills with the wolves. Soon he was the most revered monster hunter in Skylands—a reputation that caught the attention of Master Eon. It then wasn't long before Snap Shot became the leader of the Trap Masters, a fearless team of Skylanders that mastered legendary weapons made of pure Traptanium. It was this elite team that tracked down and captured the most notorious villains Skylands had ever known!

WALLOP

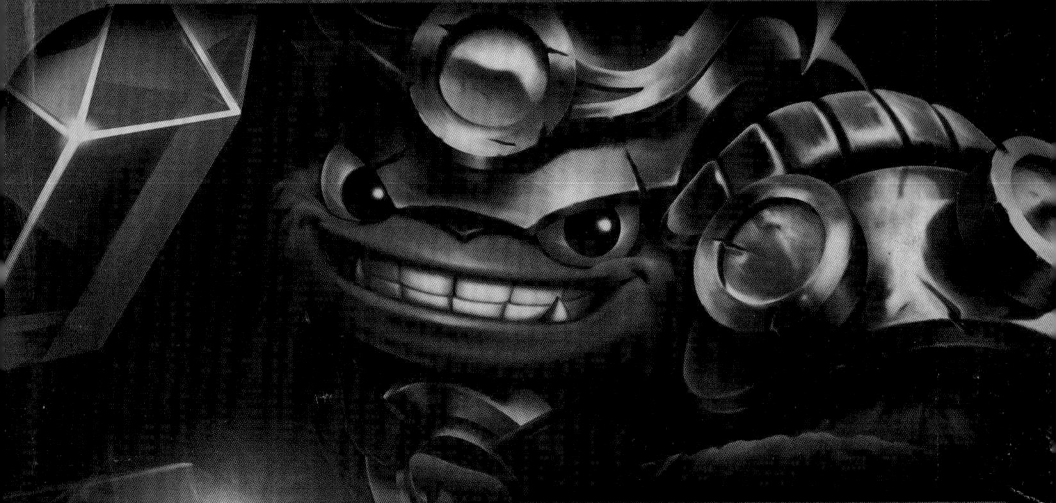

BIO

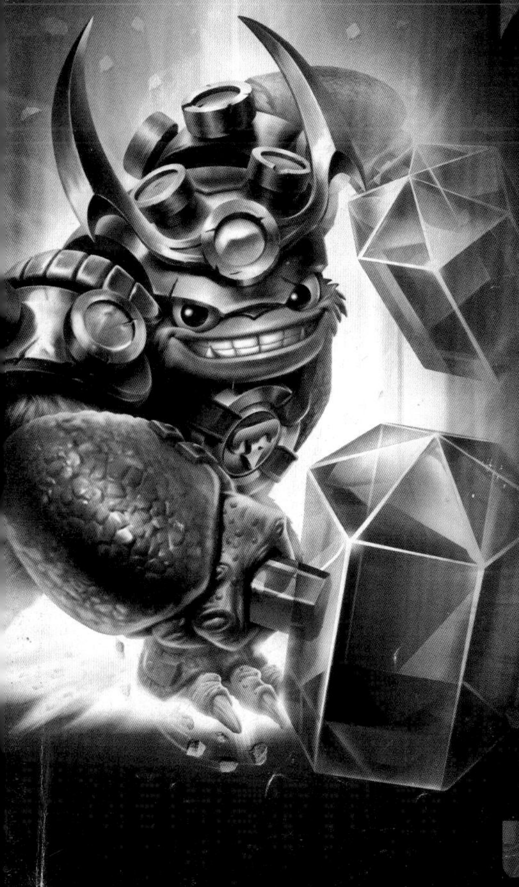

For generations, *Wallop's* people used the volcanic lava pits of Mount Scorch to forge the most awesome weapons in all of Skylands. And Wallop was the finest apprentice any of the masters had ever seen. Using hammers in both of his mighty hands, he could tirelessly pound and shape the incredibly hot metal into the sharpest swords or the hardest axes. But on the day he was to demonstrate his skills to the masters of his craft, a fierce fire viper awoke from his deep sleep in the belly of the volcano. The huge snake erupted forth, attacking Wallop's village. But by bravely charging the beast with his two massive hammers, Wallop was able to bring down the creature and save his village. Now with his Traptanium-infused hammers, he fights with the Skylanders to protect the lands from any evil that rises to attack!

SKYLANDERS

FIND MORE
SKYLANDERS™ COMICS